The Second Chance
Home for Girls

The Second Chance Home for Girls

HEATHER OSTMAN

OPEN HAND PRESS
NEW YORK   DANBURY
www.openhandpress.com

For Magnolia

Acknowledgements

This book has been a labor of love, as they say, and the love and support of numerous people helped an idea manifest onto the page. I wish to thank my family, especially my husband Ralph and our children, as well as my parents, for their always-support and unwavering belief in me.

I especially want to thank Robyn Schlesinger, Elise Martucci, and Xánath Caraza for reading multiple drafts and for sharing their wisdom and guidance as I revised. I have deep thank-you's for Kristyn Östman, Katy Binder, and Sara Tweedy, who talked out many different aspects of this book with me.

Last, I will say "thank you" to Max Rodriguez for seeing this book from beginning to end, but even as I write that, I know "thank you" is not quite enough to express my eternal gratitude.

The Second Chance
Home for Girls

Table of Contents

I

Death

As soon as Lorilee walked in, I saw them girls eye-balling her, sniffing her over like dogs. I knew they was up to something. You know how girls are. Always plotting and sneaking. These girls were no different, even though Sally-anne believed that every one of them could be reformed. They all nodded their heads in Group, chanted their affirmations at vespers, and swore up and down that they'd seen the Light and they'd never ever, ever, want another drop of booze or snort or shoot nothing into those young, precious bodies.

But you know how girls are. Bunch of liars. And these were a bunch of hoodlums when it came right down to it. Didn't matter that some had things and some didn't. So it was up to me. I had to be the one to keep an eye on them. See what kind of mischief they was fixin' to do. By the time spring started to dawn, their boredom had gotten the best of them, out-riding their homesickness, 'specially since most of them had kicked in the fall or winter—some nearly the summer before. These girls sweated it out in their detoxes, but they was just too fucked up to go home yet. That's when we'd get them. They run the risk, Sallyanne always said, of

1

relapse. Of returning to the old ways. People, places, things, she said, called them back and they was weak. Sometimes Sallyanne could just only see the bright side. They was weak, but the Lord was good, she'd say. But I knew better. I could see what was in these girls. They was restless, empty, and just plain old mean. Sometimes I thought just a good, swift kick in the ass would set them straight.

At Second Chance, we kept a tight ship. Up early, chores, church, Group, and recovery meetings. Girls had to go to them—in-house meetings, so nobody'd leave the premises. Help 'em step to recovery, all 12 steps. But we never kept the girls long enough to hit numero twelve-o. The money usually ran out before we got there, so we'd have to ship them off to the state. Then there was school. They had to do that. State of Texas mandated. But they never left for their lessons neither. We drug a trailer out back and set up schooltime. We gave them school all year round: there weren't no sense of time at Second Chance, one day bleeding into the next. Everybody's stayed in they own grade and they got two hours a week of learning with Miss AnnaMae, who drove allaway here from Euless. Not sure where Sallyanne found her, not sure she was a real teacher, with her big hairdo and housedresses, but the girls loved her. I ain't even sure what she taught them every week. Some of them seemed nearly retarded or hadn't been in a school in years. And shit, I knew at least two of them girls could barely read.

But they wasn't here for the reading and what-have-you. These girls needed to straighten their shit out.

Nobody comes here by accident, Sallyanne used to say.

I should know. One day I'm heading to jail for dealing crank, next thing I know I am living here in one of the

2

backrooms, cooking and cleaning and watching. Sometimes a few girls got homesickness something fierce or them wounds from the past just broke open and the memories wouldn't stop bleeding out. That's when Sallyanne sent them to me in the kitchen and I put them to work, which is probably the only cure they all needed— no group therapy, no program, no hugs nor affirmations and whatnot. Just work. But they always slowed me down. Not one of them had known a day of work in her life.

Of course, sometimes the girls brung major attitudes with them from the streets, or the old anger flared up sometimes like they were living with they's mamas and daddies. When the leftover defiance come out and some she-devil thought she was going to get one over on Sallyanne or ole Starlene, thought she was smarter than she really was, we disciplined her out at the back fence, made her kneel for a few hours on that old gravel out there, till them knees started getting all bloody and pulpy-like. But if some heifer was real bad and ain't nothing was going to break her, we slept her out in the doghouse by the back fence—right near where she'd been kneeling. Sallyanne insisted on chaining them to the doghouse, so they cain't run away. If she's gonna act like an animal, we're gonna treat her like one, Sallyanne would say about some she-devil getting what was coming to her. And then she'd say, It's in the Lord's hands now. And while I ain't never been sure what she meant by that, it sounded like if some heifer lived or died out there, it weren't her problem, so I'd always breathe easier-like when I saw them girls dragging some other girl's ass back in the house the morning after. All scrunched up-like in that old shitty doghouse, a girl never walked straight right away. And between you and me, girls never came back the same from an

3

overnight out in that shit house. But that ain't neither here nor there.

But for the Grace of God, there I go. That's what I say now. But for the Grace of God. Because one day—one of them godawful hellish, hot spring days, the kind only Texas knows—in comes Salvation, wearing a navy jacket- and-shorts set, with little white socks turned over at the ankle, like she was going to private school and not just out of rehab and here, with the rest of them little bitches, at the Second Chance Home for Girls. They were like the cats and Lorilee was their ball of yarn. Well. At first it seemed that way. Then, I don't know, nobody was sure who was the cat and who was the yarn. Things got mighty confusing once that girl showed up. Maybe it was just her coming made the number of girls go up from twelve to thirteen, and y'all know what thirteen means: that's some bad luck right there. That girl done showed up in that picture suit and ain't nothing was ever the same again.

Some Salvation.

Lorilee comes in that first day like it's some kind of cake walk. The girls were scrubbing windowsills with toothbrushes that morning. The blond one who looked like a cheerleader wiped the sweat from her eyes. She was the queen, even though she had a wrinkly old lady face from all that crystal meth. She done wiped the sweat from her forehead, and I swear if I didn't see them eyes narrow at Lorilee. Her eyes did all the talking. Girls across the room in their nasty sweatpants and too-small tank tops communicating like with no sound. We had a couple of Indian girls back then. Magda was one of them and she was always trying to pass as Mexicana, but she weren't fooling ole Starlene: I could see what she was in her face bones. Ain't nobody foolin' me.

You know what they say: you can sober up a horse thief, but then you still got a horse thief—don't make no difference if it's a Mexican, Indian, or American one. A horse thief is a horse thief. And an Indian is an Indian. Still Magda and them other Indian girls moved and talked like the rest of them vile bitches. Moving around Lorilee without moving. Not a hello or a howdy, nothing, and then all them girls got back to scrubbing.

That was the first sign. Them little she-devils didn't never just work. A simple job like sweeping the Group room took like two hours longer than it would take a normal human being. Just so lazy. So that's how I knew something was up. Something just wasn't right.

Nobody did the usual bullying stuff. Like no pushing Lorilee when they thought nobody's looking. Nobody stole her stuff. The days went by and Sallyanne gave me one of her Christian looks, nodding and saying, See? The Lord *is* Good. Her eyes rolling around the Group room, while some stray was sharing, dropping a brick, we used to call it, like when someone tells a deep dark secret that never was told before. This one was talking about her teacher molesting her, and the tears was just pouring down her face and I like couldn't hear everything she was saying, but it don't really matter: it's always the same story. They all wind up here, round the circle on them folding chairs, from Lord knows where, telling their stories, crying, and then the meanness swallowing them up as soon as they out the room.

Lorilee didn't fool me neither. She comes into the kitchen when I'm making pancakes and puts on an apron. Sallyanne put her on kitchen duty. I don't say nothing, so she sits and starts to talk. I'm fixin' to make a soup later, so I hand her some carrots, and when she reaches for the peeler,

I seen the track marks on the insides of her arms. She ain't wearing that picture suit no more. She looks like one of the other girls, more or less, except her sandy hair's all done up different, like her head's ready to go to the prom.

She wants to know if I got any kids and so I tell her I have a girl. I do not tell her about my boy.

"She's thirteen now and lives with her Grammy and Pop-pop."

"Yeah?" she says. "How come?"

"Sugar," I say. "Ain't you figured out where you are?"

Lorilee looks at me all blank. Her big pan face shining like the moon.

"They got custody after I got arrested the last time. Me and my husband used to cook up crank in the kitchen, in like big garbage cans."

Empty moon face. Shit, sometimes they seem so young. But I knew better. I seen the tracks.

"Life in the fast lane," I say to her. "You know, like the song says?" Again, blank. "The freeway? No? OK. So anyway. My husband, he was screwing my cousin and using all my shit and one day I just hit like rock bottom. Couldn't take it anymore. Gimme that spatula over there, Sugar."

Lorilee reaches and hands it to me, never leaving her stool. She don't say nothing, so I keep going. "I was living the junkie's life, like Sallyanne says, living fast and getting nowhere. And my little girl, she woke me up one day wanting breakfast and she came like real close to my face and said, 'Mama, why you got so many scabs on your mouth?' and I was like, she's fucking right. I need to turn my life around."

"That's what you said?"

"What?"

"You're going to burn those." Miss Smartypants Heroin Tracks points to the pancakes I'm cooking. "Is that what you said?"

"No. I probably said something like, Shut up, you little shit. Because that's the kind of person I'd become. But for the Grace of God, there go I."

"What?"

"What, Sug?"

"What does that mean?"

"It means I got lucky and turned my life around. And so can you, Sugar."

"Where is your husband now?" She puts the peeler down, sharp side up, and steps next to me and takes the spatula from my hand. I hear the griddle hiss.

"Gone," I say after a time and I start stirring the batter some more.

"Gone where?"

"Gone-gone, Nosey."

"He's dead?" She flips the pancakes onto the plate next to the stove.

"Yes. Where you learn to cook like that?"

Lorilee acts like she don't hear my question. "I guess we all get lucky sometimes."

Somehow it feels like this girl knows what I done. But that just ain't possible. Don't nobody know. For all anybody knows, that man had a mighty unfortunate accident—almost inevitable-like, since he was high all the time, twenty-four seven—y'all know what I mean. But Lorilee's looking at me, waiting-like, as if she knows what I done. What I *had* to do. So I don't know what to say because my throat gets tight and I am afraid if I say another word I will be not be able to breathe at all.

"When did it happen?" She takes the ladle from the counter, the batter all over the place, and dips in the bowl I'm stirring. "When did you get sober?" This question brings me back. I breathe.

"Last year." I hold up my blue recovery chip around my neck. "I've done a 360."

"180, you mean."

"Don't make a damn bit a difference how many," I say and I take the ladle from her.

Miss Heroin Moonface gives me a funny look. And I could see why them girls didn't like her.

It took weeks until the other girls started including Lorilee in their stupid games, bored calves that they were. But it still wasn't right. Something just didn't feel right. One day they was all drinking Big Red and no sooner than the girls started to laugh—who the fuck knows what they were laughing about, I couldn't hear shit from the kitchen—then Lorilee, who was trying not to laugh, started pouring out red fizzy pop from her mouth. Well, the other girls took to laughing even harder and soon just about every one of them had Big Red dripping down on their t-shirts, which they would have to wash themselves and good luck getting that dye out. They all looked like they was bleeding from their mouths. And just for like a second I got the shivers.

Animals, I thought. Not young calves but vipers. Because I knew that they were only leading Lorilee on. Leading her on to the inevitable end. Building the trust. Making her come to them like a lonely bird. The end closer than it seemed.

"What's that supposed to mean?" Lorilee wore her navy blue shorts, like she was going to prep school, and a white blouse, tidier than anything I'd ever had. Her finger on my good arm.

"That's my Paul Booth." I touched the tattoo with my other hand and got flour over the ventricle of the Devil's heart.

"That supposed to mean something?"

"That, my girl. That is art."

"You mean it is *illustration*."

"The Devil ain't no illusion."

Lorilee snorted. I shoved her pokey hand away from me so I could finish making the bread for the devils who lived right under that roof.

"I ain't afraid of the Devil. Now *that* is an illusion." She rubbed flour from the pile on the counter into her palms and picked up a ball of dough. Puffs of white made blooms on her sleeves. But she didn't seem to see them or care if she did. She just kneaded that dough as if she were folding Time itself.

Next day in Group them girls got something going on. I could see it. Nobody's talking at first. As usual, they're waiting until someone gets up the nerve to talk about their lives, their hurts, their ain't-nobody-loved me stories. Their bullshit, is what I say. I sit on the steps that lead up to the dining room so I can watch, like I got the high seats at the circus. I sit with my elbows on my knees bent and open like a man on the commode. This is better than afternoon TV. Everyday I'm perched on the stairs and no one cares that I'm watching them spill their guts. Then the Cheerleader straightens up and calls on Lorilee to share. She says it in this like mean-girl voice, as if she's outin' Lorilee or something.

Lorilee looks around and then looks at me, and I know she don't want to but the Truth will set you free, so

I'm nodding go ahead, even though I know these girls are up to no good. And I don't know. Maybe I feel some meanness coming on too. I just feel like I want to see it, like seeing an animal get hurt, like getting hit and drug by cars on a highway. I want to see her bleed out, spill the hurt out onto the road, where she can't act like she don't feel nothing.

Sallyanne, who, bless her heart, is so fucking oblivious, says, "Go on, child. Tell us your Big Secret. Share your burden."

Lorilee looks around. She's a junkie through and through, calculating like, looking for the way out, but she knows right away there ain't no way out of this one. I'm not sure, but I think I seen her crack the tiniest smile at me. Then she starts.

"Well, there ain't much to tell. I have a four-year- old son. I had him when I was 13. Unmarried, yes, I know. But that's how it was." She ends as if there is nothing more to say, but of course them girls can't let it go—not like any of them are so pure or don't have some kids of they own or even had abortions, more than one.

"*What* was how it was?" Magda says.

Lorilee looks at Magda like she's seeing her for the first time. She smiles again, kind of funny-like, and Magda forgets her question, drops it, goes dumb.

That ratty faced girl from Colorado then breaks in, "Who was the father? You still with him?" This little bitch— her name's Crystal—has frizzy black hair pulled into a puffy ball at the top of her head. Her coffee skin tells me everything I need to know. She looks at the Cheerleader and when she gets her approval, she slides back against her folding chair.

"Ah, nobody. Just some guy." Lorilee was together— I'll give you that. She didn't give an inch, but all these girls, they're just junkies, too, junkies in a weigh station, waiting to roll out and hit the road again. They could smell bullshit a mile away and they're tenacious as they come.

"Tell the truth now, Sugar," I say from my perch. I make sure my voice is all sweet and drippy, and I get my own nod from Sallyanne, who looks like she was fixin' to say it herself. And for like one second, I mean it. This girl needs to tell her story, as we say in the Program. Lighten that load. Share the burden of your godforsaken existence.

Lorilee looks right at me. That look nearly gives me the chills again, except it is so fucking hot again today. Then she sighs heavy-like and says, "Aw-right. He is my brother's son." She don't slouch or say it low. She says it like she was saying the sun is settin' in the western sky.

Don't nobody speak up now—this one is hard to top. Carrying your brother's son is definitely up there in the range of the Very Mighty Fucked Up. But the girls are scheming. A small girl with a beak for a face and with a few side teeth missing looks over at the Cheerleader, who, for a second looks confused before her eyes flatten into slits. But her face decides it for the girls: there's blood in the water. They'd been waiting for this day.

I'm sitting straight up now. This is even better than all the afternoon soaps together.

Before any of the girls start in, Lorilee goes on like she's at a tea party or something. "He's a good boy. Minds himself. Loves playing cars."

And then I can see him. Like my own son, lining up his cars on the floor. My boy who ain't never coming back. I see him, mine, his small head with all the hairs gone, on the hospital pillow. I cain't even hold him that long because they brung me back to jail. My boy. I start clapping my hands, even with my shit arm the way it is, when Lorilee is finished talking. The girls look at me, traitor that I am, but then they start clapping too. Lorilee has dropped her brick and I don't even realize it at first but I am so very proud of her.

"We love you, Lorilee," Sallyanne says, because she really thinks the girls do too.

"Thanks, y'all. Mighty good of you to say." Lorilee nods her head and then stands up and starts walking. That's right. She done up and walks. She stopped on the other side of the Group circle and leans over to that spooky nobody girl Summer, that girl who's always got her head in a notebook or some other such book, not talking to nobody, and she says: "Why don't you come help me in the kitchen." Like the kitchen is now her place.

Summer's eyes get real big and she don't say nothing, because Lorilee ain't waiting for her answer. She keeps walking.

Nobody ever done that. We all sit and wait for Sallyanne to say something like, Jesus loves you and died for your sins, including this one, and all that other shit she says about Truth and righteousness and redemption. And then usually some other girl would get up her courage and start talking about a sleazy uncle molesting her or her mother burning her with hot oil, but Lorilee just dumped her crazy-ass story and sidestepped the whole freak show. She squeezed my shoulder and stepped past me on the stairs up on the way to the main floor and said, "I'll see you at supper."

She was already chopping radishes when I got to the kitchen, the apron over her pressed shorts and her sleeves rolled up.

"That was mighty brave of you today," I say. And when she says nothing, I go on, "I'm real proud of you." And I mean it. *I am* proud of her. I didn't know she was that fucked up, and like here she's been talking to me like I'm her mother. And then it hits me. Lord. God *does* work in mysterious ways.

"It's all right now," I say. "I'm here." I put my hand over her hand.

She looks at me all close-like. "What happened to your arm?"

I know they all see it, but ain't nobody but Lorilee's going to ask me about it. They all know I don't want to talk about it. But today it's all right. Today, I'm OK. I say, "It got broke and done set wrong."

"Who broke it?" How this girl knows it is a who, I don't know.

"My husband. We were fighting. He done it."

Lorilee looks at me. She's just waiting. She knows there's more.

"I was using then. You know. So I never went to the hospital." I wait. Her eyes are watching my face. They see miles and miles inside me, over the hills and valleys of my private hurts. "He didn't let me go. And it never got set. You cain't really see where the bone pieces don't match up, but a little you can."

"Then he died?"

"Yes," I say. "Then he was dead."

"He probably deserved it." She runs her fingers up my arm, up until she feels the knot where the bone joined on its own. Her fingers circle the lump. And I feel like I am going to cry. Jesus H. Christ, I think, what is happening to me? She traces the knot of bone under the skin, over and over, and I feel like I am going to fall. Tears of eternity feel like they're going to push right through me. But then I remember this is about *her brick*. This girl needs *me*. This is my time to be of service, like they say in the Program. Stop being so selfish, Starlene, I tell myself.

"It's all right," I say to her. "Everything's all right." Then she starts to shake a little and I grab onto her. I hold her real tight. She is my sheep, my lamb. Lamb of God, you take away the sins of the world, have mercy on us. "Mama's here," I say real quiet-like, because now I know how good God is.

"You wanna tell me about your boy?" I want to hear more. "Tell me what he's like." I stroke her hair.

Lorilee pulls away. She don't say nothing at first. She's still looking at me and it feels a little like we're at the zoo and I'm the one in the cage, but then she says, "He's like real sweet."

I will tell you: I listened for every word, ready to swallow each one like speed, dying for the next hit.

Lorilee's shoulders start shaking harder and I'm holding her tighter, but they move violent-like and now I'm holding on as if she's a young colt trying to break free. "I've got you, Sugar. Come on, tell me."

But she don't say nothing. She roars and her head comes back and I ain't sure if she's laughing or crying.

Now I watch her, different-like. I see the other girls still stay away from her mostly, but I keep a close eye on them, too.

In Group, I'm up on my perch and some other girl is talking. Telling about how she used to lick carpet fibers to get out the last of the coke she dropped on the floor. Now that's a junkie for you. All them girls are listening— half of them feeling sorry and shit, the other half licking their chops, tasting the fibers, tongues already going numb.

Lorilee, she ain't doing neither. I see her and she's watching me. That's all right. I nod and she winks at me across the room.

Later on, Sallyanne is making up the new schedule in the office, and she assigns me another girl. "Break her in," she says.

"Can I have Lorilee in the kitchen?" I ask.

Sallyanne looks at me queer-like but finally she says aw- right.

"Come here, let me show you how." In the kitchen, I am teaching Lorilee how to make pie crust.

Her fingers pinch at the dough, following what mine do around the edge of the pan. Her hands move easy-like, so I'm not sure I'm teaching her something new.

"What's your boy doing now?" I keep my voice steady. I ain't wanting to scare her off or nothing.

"My boy?" Her eyes on the dough. "Oh, you know."

"He's with family?" I know she don't want to talk, but I can't stop asking. The more she speaks, the closer it comes.

"Yeah. Something like that." She closes the circle around the pan. "Here. That good?"

"That looks real good, Sug."

Finally she lifts her eyes from the pan and looks at me, and I swear if I don't see light, like a glow. I look around the kitchen for something else to make her do, to make her stay with me for just a little longer, but then that mopey girl Summer comes in to work, and Lorilee is helping her, out of my reach now.

Next day I put the little cars on the counter so Lorilee can see them when she comes in the kitchen. I kept them after my son done passed. They was in a box next to my bed in the back room. I lined them up one next to the other like he used to do.

At first she don't see them. But then she does. "What are those for?" she asks me.

"For your boy. I want him to have them. He'll get good use out of them."

She walks past me and pulls an apron over her head. She grabs a knife and starts chopping celery.

"Don't be shy. Take 'em."

"I'm not being shy."

"What?"

"I was lying." She don't miss a chop. "It's not true."

"What ain't true?"

"I don't have no boy." The knife flat on the counter now. "Come on. That is fucking crazy: my brother's child. I don't even have a brother. I thought you knew."

For a few seconds it felt like the air got too thin to breathe again. And I don't know why—I mean, how could this happen—but it felt like I lost my own boy again, like I was in that jail cell and the miles just stretched and stretched all over again and I couldn't hold him. Because I cain't. Because no matter what I do I cain't touch him. He ain't never going to know how sorry I am. The vein opens and I cain't stem the hurt. This is my burden, my cross to bear. It will always be my fault.

My breath came back and I stared at her. No'm, she weren't like them other girls—they was animals, vipers. But Lorilee. She was Something Else.

And that is when I knew it is up to me to stop the Devil. He is a wily one—taking the form of a teenage junkie. But this is my role in this life. I now knew that I had to keep an eye on things for the Lord. I finally understood what I was chosen for—it didn't seem like it all them years before, but now I knew. I'd done it once. I would do His bidding again. I nod my head so she don't know I know her Real Secret. "I'm going to help you with the salad," I say and I take out my own chopping knife. I move slow, like a big cat, like the kind you see on *Animal Kingdom.*

That night I wait until them girls were all asleep. I should have known that Lorilee don't sleep normal. She don't do nothing like these heifers do. I creep into her room, her with three other girls who wheeze and breathe heavy in their sleep, their lungs already a holy disaster from all the shit they've smoked. And she's awake, looking out the window.

She is standing in the dark, with her hands down, like she's holding hands with night in one and day in the other. She smiles at me, straight and tall, as if she was waiting for me all along, and then turns back. I come to the window next to her and I can feel the chopping knife press against my leg with each step. The stars speckle the night and we both can see for miles. Through her I see the beginning and the end of the pasture out the back. I see the past and future all in the field, mixing up what is now, and I can't think right. It's night—dark, like—but I swear the room feels too bright. I close my eyes, and she says, you know who I am. And I say, I surely do. And she says I have known you for eternity and I say I know I know I know. But it is all too much. One of them girls coughs some nasty thing up in her sleep. I think Lorilee says, Lay it down, Sugar, but it feels like it's me saying it. I blink and the spell is broken and my eyes adjust to the darkness.

Lorilee turns to me, one last smile. She sees me and I cain't do it.

Second Chance Girls

As soon as Lorilee walked into the room—more like waltzed—we knew we'd have to do something. She walked in and we were cleaning, like we always were, scrubbing the floors like we worked there and not like the broken, pathetic junkies we actually were, inmates living one day at a time, trying to recover, trying to work those Twelve Steps, one step at a time, at Second Chance. She glides in and she had Miss Sallyanne fawning over her something fierce, like she wasn't just a girl, just a junkie, just a drug addict like the rest of us, but something Special. She walked in and the house bowed inward, got smaller-like. And so did we.

We went back to work. Back to scrubbing and sweeping and brushing. We were cleaning out the meeting room. Lorilee didn't know it yet, but she was going to spend one full miserable hour in there every day. And each day would bleed into the next, but Group would be the days' anchor. All life centered around one shitty hour listening to some shitty girl telling her shitty story. We were all used to it, we all lived in the stories—true and false ones—because they belonged to all of us. One insufferable, eternal hour bent time itself into that rectangle-shaped room and breathed life back into our own suffering. The white walls blank and waiting to absorb the stories. We didn't have T.V. in the house, so that room was the entertainment, the drama, the pain, the loss, the lives we used to have, only as close enough as the words themselves.

Otherwise we were just waiting, all the time. We thought we were waiting for the past to leave us alone and waiting for our lives to begin, when we could leave this god-forsaken place and go back to where we came from. And then Lorilee came and we knew what we'd been really waiting for.

So we played along. We took turns. Miss Sallyanne didn't even have to call on us in Group anymore. We knew the order: Newest first—if only because we'd heard each other's stories over and over already. The new girl would step into line, and we'd start the order all over. We didn't get new girls all the time—there were thirteen of us now with Lorilee. We'd all cycle out eventually, but it didn't feel like that then. Our time at Second Chance overlapped and dovetailed and blended and before you knew it, you'd been there for seven, eight months, then even a year. A year! But most of us cycled out and cycled back later. We should have known then there was no escape from eternity. Some of the girls came back to Second Chance after they'd been discharged. And they'd tell us that we had no idea how good we had it, them coming back way thinner than when they'd left. They'd come back and shout the recovery program slogans—"Get clean now!"; "It works if you work it!" "But for the grace of God, there go I!" "Be in the now!"—like any of that crap made sense.

The program's words took the place of their own, displacing normal conversation. They became the model citizens. The true believers. They would enlist themselves as the enforcers and the snitches. Miss Sallyanne didn't have to work too hard—she had her officers already under the roof, clinging to affirmations ("I am a *good* person today!" "God loves me, and so do I!"), organizing the chores, and leading the prayers, belting out the *Our Father* like it was a passport to Heaven and they were cutting the line to get in. They'd seen where they could go, where we all could go—out there, in rehab, in jail— and they were like, Uh uh, we are not going back. So we'd absorb them again, back into the *We* who were thirteen, who were waiting, waiting, waiting to breathe again. Breathing out only during Group, when the stories took hold of us and we saw ourselves on those white walls, where the music and the beach and the sun and the boys— oh God, the boys—were. We saw them and us, and we could tip toe past the black eyes, the hangovers, the O.D.s, and see past to the fast cars, bikinis, and some other time when things were not like this, when we didn't care that we couldn't feel the ground and didn't need to know where the center was. We could see the good times, times almost none of us had ever had, because they lived out there, with everything else, past those white walls, somewhere, nowhere near here, where the cattle grazed at the pasture behind our house. And only God knew who owned the ranch over there—its pastures so vast that we never actually saw people—but they might have been the same people living those good times we imagined, for all we knew, living the elusive dreams we'd never live. We never saw the rancher, his hands, his kin, his truck, nothing—his pastures as colossal as our despair, as we had to remind ourselves daily to draw breath under the weight of that Texas sky.

When we weren't living in other girls' stories during Group, romantic daydreams about boys we'd never see again distracted us. Never mind that half of these boys we knew out there were grown men who initiated us into new worlds, seducing us with ancient dreams of who we would never be. Never mind that many of those man-boys had been the instruments of force and the seeds of our despair, the causes of broken bones and unforgiving bruises, of virginity stolen and other violences we still can't name.

So we'd also imagine the neighborhood boys—if you could call where Second Chance was a neighborhood. Besides the cattle ranch behind the property, across the road a green pasture opened the northern sky, punctuated only with a tall, single white silo that stretched well up to the heavens above. Our only real hope for boys centered on an occasional ride-by on a motor bike, a dusty boy who lived up the road. Who we *thought* lived up the road. For all we knew, he could've been riding his motor bike to see his girl. But no, no, there weren't other girls up this way, none worth visiting—of that we reassured ourselves, especially when all other hope failed, which it did regularly. That dusty boy, who had blond hair if you asked some and dark hair if you asked some others, tore by Second Chance at different times of day, different days of the week, unpredictable enough to let us all draw a life for that boy, that *heartthrob*, who sped past the plain, sad house we never left.

Of course, there wasn't any reason for him to slow or (oh Jesus) stop in front of the Second Chance Home for Girls. You'd never notice the house if you didn't know that thirteen wayward, beaten-down, ex-drugging, ex-slutting teenage girls lived there. There wasn't any sign out front—thank God. You wouldn't know the sadness those outer walls held or the longing that scratched at its windows. Oh, you might have known that two of the girls tried to run away once, but the deputy sheriff was Miss Sallyanne's cousin, and no way, no news of runaways would make it beyond the flat acre surrounding Second Chance. You might have thought you'd seen a pregnant girl walking around and then been wondering about her baby when you didn't hear any cries, but she and her baby girl disappeared to Some Other Place—one of those places Miss Sallyanne invited survivors from to Second Chance to warn us, to keep us from wanting to leave.

But Miss Sallyanne didn't have to work too hard to keep us there, her enforcers notwithstanding. As much as we dreamed of leaving, the terror of what waited outside kept us up at night or penetrated our dreams over and over until we were too weak to fight back and woke up. Oh, we talked big talk about running away sometimes and all the things we'd do—Get high! Get drunk! Get laid!— but we weren't going anywhere. Our nightmares kept us tight under the roof of the Second Chance Home for Girls. They kept us cleaning, scrubbing, scraping, and sweeping that place, trying to exfoliate the wounds and scars of what once was. Our nightmares made us willing to submit to Miss Sallyanne's Jesus and planted in us aspirant good girls where a self used to be, long before despair poured through the cracks of who we once were.

So that boy on the motor bike saw us shiny and new; we imagined him showing off for each and every one of us, in our new obedience. We imagined he saw all thirteen of us, one girl at a time, and knew she was something special, something to slow down for, something, maybe, to pull over for and ask how-do. He could see our tan skin, brown skin, pale skin, and maybe one day tell us how beautiful we were; he could touch our blond hair, brown hair, black hair, and tell us how shiny it was, but that was after he looked into our blue eyes, hazel eyes, brown eyes, and saw eternity in them, saw the vast space of our longing and didn't look away from it but said how he could get lost in our longing, how we were the best girls in the world, and how he was going to get a good job—a job!—and a car and how with the job and a car he was going to go to college and marry us and take care of us and we would be happy. And no, there wouldn't be any kids in that scenario, not for a long time, not for any time; nearly everybody here knew the burden of needy children, our own or our mamas'. No way. Thank you very much.

We were going to be loved—and not in the Jesus way, like Miss Sallyanne hammered into our soft, broken heads day after day. We were going to be loved by a beneficent boy on a motor bike, goddamnit. Loved until the end of Time itself, till the rivers ran red with blood. This boy, who sped past the house, never stopping, never noticing the plain brown house where despair breathed through the walls and terror wracked our dreams, held all of our hope, and stole away with it every day he rode past to some unknown place, probably right down the road, but still some place we were too afraid to imagine, let alone venture down the road to look for.

But unless we were doing outdoor-work, and really, our work was all on the inside, Miss Sallyanne said, both literally and figuratively, that boy never would have seen us. He sped past the dull house, with its two ash trees and yellow grass, a house like any other house on that road, in that town, in the state of Texas, hemmed in by a ranch fence and somebody's confused good intentions. And the truth is, even if he had stopped, if his motor bike had gotten a flat tire and he had to change it outside of the empty front yard of the Second Chance Home for Girls, and he saw any one of us thirteen peering out at him or—oh my word—even talked to one of us, he'd have known right away that sorrow lived there. Angular and plain, the house had darkened over time, its paneling weathered from the elements and contrasting the pristine blue sky that surrounded it. The home— if you could even call it that—stood lonely on an acre of random land carved from a sprawling ranch that belonged to someone else.

A wooden ranch fence ran the perimeter of the property, only interrupted by the gravel driveway that linked the house to a dirt road stretching west to east. The fence hemmed us in, an emblem of our shame, and then, when Miss Sallyanne saw the Devil in us, an instrument of our discipline—but we are getting ahead of ourselves. On someone else's property, there might have been a porch out front, so the people inside could come out and stare at the wonder of the Texan landscape, shielded from the relentless sun, but not at Second Chance: the house stood as a forgotten idea, porches, shutters, and other details never added, abandoned as if the sadness the place would contain had already become unbearable and it was better for the builder to cut his losses and walk away from the project before finishing it.

An addition, some afterthought, clung to the western side of the house. Miss Sallyanne's office and another bedroom took up space there, but the other girls slept in what would have been a family's ordinary bedrooms, with bunk beds crammed in every which way to sleep four and five girls to each room. But no family had ever lived here, and maybe because misery itself had a pre-destined home there, somebody thought to sell it to Miss Sallyanne and her family—her brother Tad and her father, the Reverend, whom we came to know and dread later—as they peddled recovery and Jesus to us girls not quite ready to return to the chaos of our former lives—or, more likely, not quite ready to return to families who did not want us in the first place. So any normal human being would have known that the drain in the universe was somewhere in the middle of that house, in the center of the Group room. And he, some boy on a bike, or anyone else, would have high-tailed it out of there, speeding or running, leaving his bike behind if he had to, to escape the suffering that lived in that house like a disease.

Sadness and boredom governed our days. And when we weren't in Group, Miss Sallyanne would have us chirp the false notes of optimism: we sang affirmations of selves we would never be, like the prom dresses we would never wear. So it wasn't ever odd to hear spontaneous announcements during the day, during ordinary activities—these spur-of-the-moment claims that Miss Sallyanne liked to hear:

"I'm Crystal, and I'm OK today," a girl might sing out during dinner clean-up.

"We love you, Crystal!" we'd chirp back.

Or another girl would look up during Group, interrupting some other girl who was sharing her story and say, "I am Terri and I do not use drugs no more." To which we'd all sing back, even the interrupted girl who was sharing her burden, "We love you, Terri!"

Magda would chime in sometimes, but it never rang quite right, almost like her face froze around the words, as she'd affirm, "I'm Magda and I belong!" Her dark face knew what her brain refused: that no matter what she claimed, no matter how many affirmations she shouted, her bloodlines tied her to a land some of our ancestors sought to rape and steal, to a people ours sought to eliminate. Of course, we didn't know that then, but we felt it. Her blood ran through ours, a graphite-colored river, blood of the oppressors, blood of the oppressed, each coopting the other. There is no release from the slaughter, passed unrecognized from generation to generation. So when Magda shouted out her affirmation, clinging to the teenage hope that words might make it so, we absorbed the difference and shouted back that we loved her, somewhere inside knowing that if Lorilee hadn't come along, we might've tried to run her off or kill her instead.

Of course we didn't love anybody really, but we thought so sometimes. We thought if we made our claims—"I'm Laura, and I respect my body and so do others"—that might stave off the inevitable futures that were waiting for us when we were discharged from Second Chance. We thought that if we said so, it would be so, that the currents of time and fate would shift in the streams of our lives, and the pain and loss we knew out there would not be waiting for us when we got out. We thought that because we said so, those who waited outside, beyond the fortress of the house—those we might not have even known yet—would get the message and leave us alone, free to be free, on our own terms, in ways we were never allowed at Second Chance.

We never said it out loud, but we all knew artificial affirmations bore no protection out there. Discharge was nothing if not terrifying—the return to "home" did not promise freedom, and none of us were ever ready. The false words did not steel our nerves for what awaited us back where we came from. Thankfully, there was no forward in Second Chance, even though Miss Sallyanne— bless her heart—told us we were making progress and changing all the time. There was only circular motion, moving around the same days over and over, in and out of those white walls, scrubbing the floors, the windows, the bathrooms, the kitchen, as if the suds would clean out the suffering that had paralyzed our hearts.

If you asked Miss Sallyanne, she would tell you that we were cleaning our way to Salvation, scrubbing the sin from our lives and finding our Special Purpose. She loved us, she would say, but the sin was endless. So when we scrubbed dishes, flatware, glasses, floor tiles, window sills, bathroom fixtures (a personal favorite of Miss Sallyanne's for expediting

Salvation), doorjambs, light bulbs, gravel, grout, our hands raw and cracked, she saw the blood of Christ. When we felt dizzy from cleaning chemical fumes, she felt the Holy Spirit. When one girl passed out from the hot sun while washing Miss Sallyanne's car at noon on a July day last summer, Miss Sallyanne saw Ascension—a rare phenomenon that was reversed with consciousness.

Work did not come easily to any of us, we could admit, so when we fell short, which happened often, we'd be sent out to the back fence, out to kneel in the sun or the rain (and if you've ever seen Texas Rain you know it is not for the light hearted) or the wind, on the gravel poured on the space right beside the fence. We'd hold on with fingers interlinked with the barbed wire keeping in the cattle on the other side, where the ranch land reached the boundary of Second Chance's property, as the sharp gravel pierced the skin stretched over our knees. The fence was some distance from the house, of course, and it would have seemed easy to either let go of the metal or sit cross-legged, but Miss Sallyanne posted her secondary and tertiary eyes to the back of the property: Starlene or one of her momentary favorites, her temporary sentinels, would be watching for fatigue, ready to tell on the weak of spirit, who'd already stumbled miserably on the Road to Salvation. And then Hell would begin, because there was a doghouse—for the old mangy dog that had adopted us—and that was where you'd stay overnight, chained up until you got it right or until you'd nearly died pleading with the sun, the moon, and the heavens for mercy or at the very least for Miss Sallyanne to remember that you were still out there so she could check to see that in fact you were visibly back on the Road and on the way to your Special Purpose here on earth.

So when Lorilee walked in, already wearing freedom like she stitched it herself, already not needing meaningless affirmations or Group or tears, we knew we had found our Special Purpose. She walked in as if she were free, and we knew we were going to knock it from her to Kingdom Come. Forget Magda and the bloody lust and greed of our ancestors. We knew that the reason for living we'd been missing had just walked into Second Chance Home for Girls. The once destroyed would become Destroyer.

Swords

April 4, 1986

Hello. I'm here. I took this notebook from the school trailer. I took it and I am going to keep it. I am going to write in it, because if I don't, I think I might disappear. I don't have much to say yet. I don't know. I don't think I do. I might.

I will. They say the pen is mightier than the sword. And I'm going to need something to keep me together. I'm going to need like many swords in this place. So this is my sword. My pen is my many mighty swords. Ha ha ha.

April 5, 1986

I saw those girls whispering out back. They were in the backyard, in the smoking area. I'm not even sure why we call it that, because everyone smokes everywhere here, even girls who never smoked cigarettes before are smoking now. We smoke and we talk. There isn't anything else to do (and I'm not counting cleaning, even though, holy shit, we clean constantly. But we talk during that too!). All we do is talk, talk, talk. But we're not really talking. We make sounds, but they don't sound like anything I can hear.

And I could barely hear what they were saying just now in the back. I'm pretty sure it was about that new girl Lorilee. Her name sounds regular, but she isn't like any girl I know. Not like any girl here, anyway. She looks like us in the face and all—like she probably should be in high school somewhere out in the real world, but she dresses like she is better than everyone. She acts like that, too, like she doesn't need to be here, like she doesn't care if we talk to her or not. Sometimes I catch her looking at me, like she's studying me, as if I'm some kind of experiment in bio lab. She doesn't know I see her. But I don't know. Sometimes she might. Either way, I don't talk to her. I barely talk to anyone here. I'm just glad I'm not the newest girl anymore. I'm the last one to come to this shithole, and that was months ago. Lorilee came and now we are thirteen—she changed *that* at least.

Lorilee is weird, but so are these other girls. I don't know girls like these girls. We weren't like this back home. These girls look like pictures of girls I've seen. Kimberly looks like a cheerleader, but she is like a middle-aged cheerleader. Maybe all that crystal meth she did made her look so old. I bet her insides are like a senior citizen's. In another life, she'd be the queen. She acts like she is in charge. All these girls look at her and want her to like them. She walks around as if in her real life, she wouldn't have hung out with any of us, like she was made to be carrying two pompoms and bouncing into the arms of strong, too-good looking men made out of glass and steel. She doesn't have to act all stuck up, though. The girls here would give in to her on looks alone. I would, too, between you and me. I'd kill to have a body and hair like her, and not my wavy hair that you can't do anything with and my skinniness (please God, some tits! Ha ha ha!).

She looks older than all of us, but somebody said she's in eleventh grade.

Was in eleventh grade, I mean. Nobody's going to school now, not real school, anyway. We're all in fake-school, a joke in a trailer that somebody dragged out back and shoved between the house and the ranch fence. Miss AnnaMae is our teacher. The girls call her Teach. That feels stupid to me, but it's simple and Miss AnnaMae, if she is anything, she is a simple lady who wears housecoats like my grandma. I'm not sure how she gets her hair so piled high, but the big curls must be set with orange juice cans at night. She reminds me of something I feel like I used to know, with her blue eye shadow and pancake makeup on her big round face. The other girls love her. I guess she's all right. There's nothing to not like: Teach smiles at us, her mouth as wide as her face, but it's almost like she is empty, like her face is a house that no one lives in. Everything is always fine, everything is always good, and I want to say to her sometimes: did you see Terri when she came back after her first discharge, with her arm in a sling and a black eye? I don't think it's all good for her! There's a girl here missing teeth because somebody knocked them out. And, did you notice that the rest of us haven't seen our families or been home in months and months? Hello!? Anybody home??? Ha ha ha! But she's so happy and empty I don't think any of it gets through. She probably wouldn't stop smiling for all the world. Maybe that's why she lets us all grade our own work.

Yes, that's what I said, we grade our own school work. We get workbooks and we fill them out and then we check our answers with the answers in the back and write down how many we got wrong. In pencil. I'm no star student, but even I

know that letting a bunch of junkies grade their own work—
or even normal girls at a normal high school—is letting
them all give themselves A's and unlearning any little bit of
smarts they once had. Though for some of them, that isn't
that much, I know. (I keep trying to help Carla Bobby learn
how to read, but I don't know, she just keeps mixing up the
letters and sees them backwards. It's like she has some kind
of special super power that she can't use in normal life. I'm
starting to think I need a new system to try and teach her.)

Now it's starting to bug me. What *were* those girls whispering about? I hope it wasn't me! God almighty. They better
not think I'm actually friends with Lorilee. I swear, when she
walked out of Group the other day, I nearly died. I thought
she saw me—I was trying not to laugh out loud—that shit
about her brother's son— please! And then next thing, she's
starting to walk out of Group and then she looks at me and
says, Are you coming? Like somehow we are friends. That's
all I fucking need—these other girls thinking I'm friends
with the Freak. I really hope that's not what they're whispering about out back, that we're like best friends and all.

I mean, sometimes I wish I was more in with those girls. But
I don't know. I'm not sure I can take Kimberly. The queen.
Kimberly has that long golden blond hair, the kind that
Farrah Fawcett has, but Kimberly's is even better: longer,
blonder. She looks tired but it helps that she is gorgeous.
Your basic cheerleader nightmare. She's got the perky thing
too, always cheering people on—but it's all fake. She's one
of those real mean types. Smiles to your face, but you never
really know what is underneath. She looks like she walked
out of a Whitesnake video. She's perfectly thin—not too tit-
sy. And she's got these like perfect sky-blue eyes. They are so

pretty, so damn pretty, but when you look at her, they seem almost flat. Oh God. I'm talking about Kimberly again. Ugh! I guess she scares me a little. But even though she acts like she belongs on a Whitesnake video and is just waiting her time out here, she is like us. Stranded here. Alone, really, but with all of us loners. It's like we're all holding our breath, waiting for when we can leave and just breathe easy.

Well, not everyone seems like she wants to leave. That creepy girl Crystal seems like she's right at home at this place. She's one of my roommates. She also looks like twice her age, with frizzy gray-black hair that's all broken at the ends. She keeps it in a puffy pig-tail. I almost thought she was somebody's mother, because she looks so damn old too, but she's in high school. She wears her hair like that so she looks like an old crank addict pretending to be a kindergartener. To make it worse, she smokes those long 100s cigarettes. Who does that? Only senior citizens smoke those things! She carries the soft pack in her hands with the lighter tucked under the plastic, and she wears these hand-me-down shirts with little flowers. All she needs is a housecoat and a shopping cart to put empty cans in. She doesn't fool me, though. She thinks she's sly and she looks pretty dopey, but she's the first one to tell on you if you cut corners on doing your chores that day. She'll out you in Group, raise her hand and tell right in front of everyone, then settle back in her chair, waiting for the piranhas to attack.

They all seem a little like that. You can't trust anybody around here. I was trying to teach Carla Bobby her words the other day, and she reaches out and grabs the heart charm on my necklace from Tommy and starts telling me how nice it was, and I don't know, but there was something in the way she was saying it that made me think she was looking it over for later, if you know what I mean, asking if I wore it at night and where I kept it when I wasn't wearing it. Geez. She's not even slick about wanting to steal it!

Maryanne's not sneaky. She isn't like your typical junkie. More like a house pet lost in the woods. I get the feeling though she's been used up and not known it. She's kind of pretty and has a huge rack (I wish I had a chest like that!!!), and I just can imagine how many guys got her high just to fool around with her. She seems kind of innocent enough to go along with it—or dumb enough (ha ha ha!). Maryanne just kind of goes along with whatever. She's usually smiling, like she's at summer camp or something. She does her chores (OK, not very well, but who cares? It's not like they're paying us to work!), she goes to Group, and she does what she is told. One time in Group, she talked about her boyfriend cheating on her, and I don't know, even that she kind of smiled through. It was hard to know if it was really bothering her. She'll smile and then yell out an affirmation. Her latest has been, I'm Maryanne and I'm a good girl! Miss Sallyanne seems to like that one about being a good girl, because she smiles this huge smile and shines those black pencil-point eyes at her every time. It's kind of creepy, if you ask me.

The other girls are a lot less cheery. Terri cries all the time. Or really, she just looks like it. Her eyes are always a little puffy and her nose kind of red. She smokes constantly. Lights one cig with the end of another. She seems kind of in love with Kimberly, because she's always following her around, though she's not saying that much.

Shit. I have to go. Chores bell is ringing!

April 6, 1986

I hate this place.

They made me kneel by the fence today. Miss Sallyanne didn't like how I cleaned the bathroom. Fucking rained on me all afternoon. My knees are killing me.

April 7, 1986

I want to go home. I hate this place.

April 8, 1986

I hate the people who live here. I really hate the people who run this place. I wish they would all die.

I hate this place.

Tommy Tommy Tommy. Where are you? I want to go home.

April 9, 1986

During chores, I was goofing off, like laughing, with Carla Bobby. We were on floor duty—mopping the common rooms. We were pretending to be rock stars with our mops. We were singing into them. She picked hers up like a guitar and accidentally knocked over one of the buckets of soapy water. It spilled everywhere. It spilled everywhere and Crystal was walking by—wasn't even working like she was supposed to be—and she freaked out and told on us. *Told on us.* Carla Bobby was crying so hard that she couldn't talk, and they thought I knocked it over. I don't know. I am stupid. I didn't say anything. I just stood there. Starlene started going off on us, calling us dumb heifers and sinners, and then she marches me only out back and tells me to kneel at the fence, on the gravel, like I didn't learn anything the other day, she said. She said one more time and I'd be sleeping in the real doghouse.

Jesus!!!! This place!

The sun wasn't bad, but I guess she forgot about me. I was out there for hours. It felt like day and night changed places while I kneeled there. I couldn't feel my knees anymore and then the top part of my legs started shaking. I had to hold onto the fence and lean on it.

It seemed like no one remembered me until after dinner. When Terri, that sneaky bitch, must have told someone I was still out there.

I have sunburn on my hands and arms. There's like little bubbles under the skin in some places.

It is night now. Night and late into it. My whole body aches but it feels like somebody else's body. I am so so so tired but I can't sleep. I can see the doghouse from my bunk bed, out the window. I see where I was. I see nothing before and nothing ahead. There is nothing but now.

I fucking hate this place.

April 10, 1986

Maryanne's mom sent her a record player. A record player! Like the little girl kind, with a top that comes down when you're not using it. I am soooooo glad she is one of my room-mates and oh my god that she loves Zebra! She plays "Tell Me What You Want" over and over and over. It's awesome!

Maryanne even lets me play it when she's doing something else. I listen to her Zebra record, but also the other ones: Led Zep, she's got, and Pink Floyd, too. Truth time: I hate Floyd.

But Tommy loved *Animals*. I just listen now because of him. I lie on the floor, with my arms under my head and I look up at the white ceiling fan in our room but I don't really see it. I see him. Tommy comes back to me. If I don't focus my eyes I can see him and me and we're on the beach again, drinking beer, and I know he likes my two-piece and he knows so do the other guys. But they all know he's a fighter—he'll take a swing at anyone, if he has to—and we're all like having a good time, our time, and nobody wants to ruin that.

When you going give me some of that?

Some of what? I'm just pretending that I don't know what he means.

Tommy tries to swat my butt, but I roll away from him on the blanket, out of reach, but not too far.

He's got a cigarette between his lips and he's looking down at the chords of the guitar he has across his legs, bare under the cutoff line of his old jeans. His long hair pours forward over the guitar. He is burning, I see. His shoulders and his knees are pink. His skin will be red later and I will rub aloe on him and tell him, I told you should've used lotion out there, like I'm his mom—or his wife. And he will fall asleep from all of the sun and I will watch him breathing until it's time to go home, not because I'm afraid he'll be late (OK, a little I am afraid he'll be late) and not because I'm not tired too, but because when I remember him now I realize how little time we had for the good times, and if I could go back, man, I would never have wasted time sleeping or spending a minute away from him. I'd have stayed awake for the whole thing, so I'd have more to remember him with now. But out there on the beach, he's only about his guitar. He's trying to be careful not to get sand in the opening but even more careful to listen. He's listening listening listening, hearing something I am sure I can't hear, so I just wait until he sees me again.

And then he does.

He finishes some tune he's working on and looks over at me. He's smiling now and the cigarette is still balanced between his lips so his smile is crooked.

Fuckin' hot, he says, and I hope he's talking about me, but maybe it's the sun, which is now on the early legs of dusk. I have to go home soon, make an appearance, so it's believable that I was at my job at Walmart. I don't want to leave. He is the sun. When his light shines on me, I am like a little more than I usually am.

Thank you, I say. I know.

Get over here. Tommy puts the guitar down gently in the case, but he's never really not aware of it, never losing consciousness of it, even when he jumps up to chase me into the ocean. I am laughing and I'm running. He is laughing, too, and I make sure I land in his arms.

The ocean is rising. The waves come harder and faster. Evening is coming. The end of a dream. That's it. Like a dream. I almost can't remember.

P.S. I still fucking hate this place.

April 11, 1986

The only time I can write is at night. Most nights, the moon shines right into our room in little lines of white through the blinds. Our room faces south, so I can see over the backyard well past the ranch behind us (A ranch! I know! With cattle and cowboys! OK—I haven't seen actual cowboys yet, but they must be there! The cattle is!). Otherwise, on cloudy nights it's like impossible. But tonight it's all right. I hear Crystal sawing wood over there in her sleep. She snores like an old man. I thought maybe she was awake for a minute, because she stopped and it seemed like she was just listening in the darkness, waiting to hear a noise she thought she heard before. Then the saw started again. I can see her nightly restlessness because I'm on the top bunk across from hers. The one underneath hers is Maryanne's. Lorilee (weird, new girl) is in the bunk under mine. I can't see her, but it feels like I can feel her—if that makes any sense. I don't think Lorilee sleeps much—once or twice I've seen her get up and walk around in the dark (creepy!). I just pretend to sleep. Keep one eye open. One time she turned toward my bunk. I shut both eyes right fast, and I swear if I didn't feel her breath on my face then. Damn near peed myself. She might've done that to all three of us—not that these other two would've noticed. Especially Maryanne. She just sleeps like nothing's wrong. Maryanne might as well be at boarding school, the way she sleeps.

Boarding school without the school. Definitely with the boredom . . . (Ha! Get it???)

We four are in the back. Our room is part of an extension that has white paneling. The windows are on two sides and the room juts out into the backyard. There are some extra rooms on this side of the house, like Miss Sallyanne's office. We know when she's in there because she blasts country music (yuck). On really good nights you can see clear for a few miles it seems like, out past the ranch, all the way to a highway, which is really far, but, man, you can see the cars whizzing by, flying by, going to all of their places. And then there's the stars. Holy shit. I'll say this about Texas, which is in every other way a fucking shithole, the sky is the most incredible thing you will ever see. It's kind of like heaven bent a little closer to earth just to be nearer to Texas.

Ha! I guess I don't really know about that. If there is a heaven, the angels are probably like, what the fuck is wrong with this dried-up state that has like one tree per square mile? But it maybe is worth the look. Maybe the angels see me here. Maybe they will let me go back home to North Carolina soon. Maybe they're the reason I got lucky and got this bunk that lets me see out at night and nobody can see me writing up here. Yeah, right.

Thank God I can write. I hide this notebook inside my pillow case, downside (of course!). Because as soon as anyone knows I'm writing a diary, it's over. Eyes will start snooping through my pages, pouring like water into all of my crevices. There is no fucking privacy here. Even when we get dressed, Miss Sallyanne or Starlene (holy shit! What is wrong with that woman!!?!) just walks in here like they're our mama and don't need to knock. I wouldn't keep anything on top of my dresser (yes, I do get one— one really skinny one), and I wear my necklace to bed. You think I don't see Crystal looking over what I wear, too—she's just like Carla Bobby. Can't keep her fingers to herself. She likes my silver and when she went to look at the heart charm, I stepped back before her dirty finger nails came anywhere near it. Oh hell no, I thought. This is the only thing I have from Tommy. I'm not letting it get defiled by Ole Dirty Fingernails, and I'm definitely never taking it off—I wasn't going to anyway, but definitely not so that Miss Dirty-Fingers can lift it when I'm asleep. Not that I have to worry. I never really sleep here.

I'm just doing my time here. Trying to stay off the radar until I can be sent home. I don't start trouble with anybody. For all they know, I really believe all that Jesus- will-save-you crap. But I'm just saying Yes until I get to go back home. I will lay low here and everything will be all right.

As long as that Lorilee stays away from me.

April 12, 1986

It was Terri's turn in Group today. She's that ratty-looking girl—I heard she was eighteen but got left back so many times that she's still in high school, like in the tenth grade! Anyway, Terri volunteered before she got called on by Miss Sallyanne. (I was sweating until I heard Terri's name called, because I'm pretty sure I'm due a turn.) She starts telling this story that is off-the-wall crazy. And if she wasn't like so creepy looking, with her stringy black hair and pebble eyes, it might have been cool. But Terri's story wasn't a good story. She's crying through the whole thing, telling us she was living with some bikers in a cabin in Colorado somewhere and everybody was doing coke. All kinds of it. And she'd hooked up with some guy. Some old guy, no doubt, but she didn't say that. His ole lady was still hanging around.

So one day the ole lady started to pick a fight, she was all: why are you hanging around my man and go back to your mama. Terri said she ignored her. But then the ole lady slapped her in the middle of the Big Room, what they called it. They got into a thing right there, but then the ole lady backed off when she got a bloody nose, saying she didn't want to have to kill the girl right there, like she was warning Terri.

But Terri said it was probably like she was afraid of getting her ass kicked too—Terri was fucking her ole man and then was going to beat her up too. So the woman backed off. And Terri thought just maybe she should go home, but the coke was so good—and free! (I totally get THAT!) The very next day, she's balling the woman's man again. (Ugh! I can just imagine how gross that must've been. Those bikers are so revolting with their leather and denim. I would *never* fuck one.)

Well, after a couple of those kinds of run-ins, with the ole lady backing off from kicking her ass, or at least saying so, nothing happens for a while. So Terri is like, cool, I'm golden now. I won. Except that one day she snorts some bad coke. Like real bad and she winds up in the hospital. And who winds up visiting her? Nobody. She's near dying and nobody comes for days. After about a week, somebody tracked down Terri's mother over in New Mexico to say come get her. Her mom gets her and drops her here. Doesn't want anything to do with her. No wonder that girl is such a sneaking bitch. Nobody loves her. Maybe that's why she can't stop crying.

But for the grace of God, there I go. That's what Miss Sally-anne said after the story. I have no idea what she means.

Anyway. After she finishes her sad-sack story, all the girls were saying Amen and then saying, We love you, Terri.

But I don't know. I mean, I was saying it too. I was even clapping this time, which is totally ridiculous—I don't why we're clapping for complete failure, but there you go. When in Rome... ha, ha, ha!

She told the story like she came to Second Chance for safety, like now she's got some real second chance, which made

Miss Sallyanne start beaming all over the place. But I heard it under her words: she's here because nobody wants her. Not even a bunch of low-life bikers. Not even the asshole who was fucking her. That's kind of pathetic. This place, this fucking house, is where, like they say, the elephants come to die. There's nothing going on here. No boys. No parties. No school (not that shitty trailer out back where we do work and grade it ourselves. What a joke! Who thought that one up?!?!). OK, we can smoke cigarettes. There's that. I bet as much as Miss Sallyanne wanted to get rid of smoking, she just can't keep the tidal wave back on that one. We'd all freak out, rebel, if we couldn't smoke. Even her soldiers who patrol us would mutiny, if they couldn't light up.

Miss Sallyanne tells us she loves us, that she's like a mom. Like a super mom—but with no kids of her own. Just us. She's another one who looks older too, but someone told me she's like only 34. 34! Jesus of Mercy! Those pills she'd been popping must have aged her by decades. Also, the way she's dressing doesn't help. I'm no fashion plate, but I know that the next step after Hushpuppies is death. And if that isn't a sure sign, then it's the pageboy hairdo. *Holy* Jesus of Mercy. But I don't like to get too critical-like of Miss Sallyanne. She's got those old pock marks all over her cheeks, and I know what it's like to have your skin breaking out. It's so not funny. She must've had zits real bad. So there's that. We all got something, I guess. But that doesn't excuse the bad fashion and the Jesus crap. Or anything else—like that fucking dog-house bullshit. If I ever get chained up in that, I will freak out. Some of the girls were talking about it the other day, like about when a girl stays out there all night, she never comes back the same. Scary.

But I don't want to get too depressed now. I'm not going to get in trouble anymore. I'm going to be like really good. No doghouse for me.

(Someone just came down the hall, so I hid my notebook. Whoever it was, she never came in.)

What does Miss Sallyanne think? That we can just come here after living our lives out there and do nothing? That's it's OK living here, going to Group, doing fake school, cleaning a house that isn't ours? Who the fuck are we cleaning it for?

It's not who, she says. It's what. For your sins. You girls are sinners. The worst of the worst. This is your last chance, she says.

One time after she said that, I said, I thought it was our second chance, ha ha ha!

And she said, What'd you say? I could tell she didn't think it was funny so I didn't repeat it, but her voice got all knife-sharp and she kept it going. Did you say something, girl?

Before I know it, Kimberly's repeating what I'd said. Then, next thing, I'm out back, kneeling on the motherfucking ground in my underwear by the fence. The fucking fence again. Fuck me!

I'll tell you something else. Some of these girls want to die here—they are never going to leave. They don't care how much they have to clean or how long they have to kneel at the fence. But that is not OK with me. And I am leaving as soon as I can. I am going to do everything Miss Sallyanne says and get discharged, so they can never send me back here. I am leaving this fucking place and I am going home.

Second Chance Girls

Lorilee wound up in the south room. Maryanne, Crystal, and Summer were already in that room, and now they were four with Lorilee. So we knew right away that Lorilee didn't sleep like nobody else—all three of them were talking about it. Within two weeks, we'd find out she'd be up pacing the house, with the moon nudging her out of bed. What was weird—one of the weird things, that is—was she wasn't ever tired the next day, when we knew she'd been up all hours. One of us always noticed her on our stumbly way to the bathroom in the middle of the night or just her restlessness alone kept us up. Depended on the moon, we thought. We weren't the only ones who noticed. Miss Sallyanne noticed too and said something in Group about wandering the house at night. Before Lorilee got there, all of us slept the Sleep of the Dead to postpone the dawn. None of us were roaming and wandering around. There wasn't anything to see outside at night when the moon was full and pouring over the pastures behind the house. But Lorilee would be at the windows facing south, staring out there at something, communicating—like with something nobody else could see. Before you knew it, a couple of us started getting up after a while, made suddenly too restless to stay in the folds of sleep. We'd wander to our own windows and stare sometimes at the darkness, trying to see what Lorilee could see.

Another weird thing was Tad noticed her, like *really* noticed her. He'd come to check on Miss Sallyanne and the house every week. His main job was looking after the old house, where the boys still lived, and God Almighty knew where that was. Some of us had been there when it was co-ed, before everything changed, but nobody could remember exactly where it was. Now he drove out here once a week or so to check on us and bring paperwork and supplies to Miss Sallyanne. The house had become a new part of our collective mythical past, the precursor to our imminent salvation. God and Tad and Sallyanne all knew where the old house was—where all the boys still were, but weren't telling us. Not that we had a car or a sense of direction or any way to get there—and for some of us not even a desire. For some girls, the Second Chance House for Girls was more like a relief, a big sigh letting go of having to pretend to like boys and their stupidity. Not for the rest of us, though. Most of us missed boys and the way they'd make us feel—the good ways, that is. And Tad was their counselor, and our only connection to those sweet boys.

So when Tad showed up the day after Lorilee came, we knew something was up. We knew we were right to ignore her but not ignore her all the way. To keep her in our peripheral view, just in case. Because he walked in and he saw her. His jet black eyes saw the past, present, and future all at once. He saw her and couldn't stop staring at her. We all witnessed it. But when he took off his cowboy hat and opened his mouth to say howdy, after Miss Sallyanne prompted him—we were all in the common room hanging out after dinner one night—the words sounded foreign and strange and formal, like an impromptu Pentecost, language as new to him as Lorilee was.

Tad put his Stetson back on his head and seemed small—a toothpick of a man with a large olive-shaped head. He *was* a small man, but we all thought he was the Sexiest Man Alive, like the contests in the tabloids. When he wasn't around, we played at organizing contests where he was the winner, the only winner always, because he was the only man who ever talked to us and because we didn't know Don Johnson, who sometimes showed up as a runner-up. He wasn't the only man who came to Second Chance, but he had the very special status of being the only one who could sit in on Group with us. Over in the boys' home, he had been around boys all day and still walked like a boy and dressed like a boy—with his old Levi's and rancher's shirts tucked in—and that was enough for all of us to be in love with him, voting him in day after day, winning out over the likes of John Travolta, Val Kilmer, and David Cassidy (who was old news, but still a favorite anyway).

Tad walked like he came in on a horse: bow legged and tilted, but the only things he'd probably ridden are Harley Davidsons and big women. He and Miss Sallyanne were family, we all knew that, but once Crystal said she saw them alone, when they thought no one was looking, and he swatted Miss Sallyanne's ass. Crystal said she thought Miss Sallyanne was going to swing at him, but instead, she just giggled like an ole girl.

That story alone made us all look at Tad a little differently, but we secretly hoped he looked at each of us differently too, and not the *we* all of us were together.

So the day Tad first met Lorilee, he raised his Stetson and then put it back on his head. We couldn't see his eyes, but we knew he was still staring at Lorilee, who'd already gone back to wiping down the dining tables. We knew something just wasn't the same anymore. She acted like she didn't see him, like he wasn't worth her time and attention, and that was enough to harden our uneven contempt.

Tad's visits were a little like drop-ins from Santa Claus. Once a week, he'd come by and work for a day. He'd sit in Group like he belonged there, and we just assumed he did, even though we'd be forever adjusting to the presence of a man in the room, a sort of manly, but soft man, whose expressions made no distinctions between our tragedies. They all earned his sympathies. Nothing got us more worked up than to have his sad jet- black eyes hold us in our sorrows.

When Maryanne dropped her brick in Group, that time she started talking about when her daddy left, Tad's big black eyes seemed to round out and cry with Maryanne. We all saw how he gazed at her, wrapped her in robes of sympathy. We didn't even feel jealous—we were held in those robes too. Wrapped up safe and tight, we knew that Tad had us all, that he could absorb the hurts, the sads, the disappointments—and there were so very many of them. The gift was his attention, once a week, his unwavering, empathic, deep attention, given to one, given to all.

What he did the other six days a week we could only imagine. He was the male counterpart to Miss Sallyanne in that other mysterious house for boys. None of us were even from this part of Texas, so it wasn't like anybody knew how to get to the other house. It could be right next door for all we knew—because next door was at least another mile or so away. Who knew where the boys were? Tad did, and for all our staring and longing, he was a skinny, bow-legged, bragging, grown-up boy and not some anonymous fantasy on a motorbike. He was a real, live man who knew us.

We were all surprised when we heard the roaring muffler of Tad's motorcycle the next day: its scratchy crawl up the gravel driveway that led to the house, the motor's roar getting louder and louder until the engine suddenly cut and dropped us into nothingness. Well. Almost all of us were surprised. Lorilee, we could swear, when we talked about it later, seemed to be *expecting* him.

"Howdy." He comes around the corner of the house that next day, smiling like the first rays of the morning sun. We are just sitting on the back patio, smoking after dinner. Of course, Lorilee is with us—she smokes too, but it doesn't seem like she always did. She probably does it to pass the time. The sheer boredom of being here makes her smoke like the rest of us—makes her almost as human as the rest of us. His eyes pass over and through us. We don't know who he's looking for until he sees her. It isn't hard: she's sitting a little to the left, off from the rest of us, with us and not with us, which is where she's always at and where we want her to be.

He sees her and says nothing at first. He sees her and then Lorilee turns to look toward the pasture in the back. All we see is her hair down her back, over her blouse (A blouse! Have you ever?), tucked into the back of her dark green shorts.

"Howdy," Tad says only to her. He's close now, in the middle of us, and totally not seeing us. Nobody's talking anymore. Just listening. Not that he'd know. He stands there for like an eternity, but it's probably only a few seconds, except she's not saying anything, and walks inside. We are staring at Lorilee's back, trying to will her to turn around, but she won't. Tad glances around at us and opens his mouth but no words come out. He sees us but sees nothing, then disappears into the house. The backdoor slams, reverberating with our nothingness, and we can hear the heels of his boots on the linoleum tiles inside.

"Let's play a game!" Kimberly's tinny voice interrupts the quiet. Her perkiness usually redirects us, makes us forget. But we can't forget what we just saw.

The games we play outside are like the games we play in Group: Truth or Dare, Secrets and Revelations.

These games reveal what is underneath, and, no, they are not therapeutic, though Miss Sallyanne thinks so and says as much. They are more of the same. Nobody here knows privacy. Nobody here has ever known privacy. There is a world out there, where we come from, probing and poking and pushing us. We have endured the initiations of our powerlessness. Nearly every girl here has a rape story of some kind, though that is not what we all call it. We swim in euphemisms and nuances, not naming the unnamable, but still knowing. We all know the signs, and we all know the expectations for what we must be: open, receptive, good. Regardless of the violence we have known, we will always seem fine, containable. We all know the drill—like every other girl across the country, those who are free (or at least think they are) and those who are like us, here, or in a place like this. We learned it long before we ever got to Second Chance.

We are going to play Revelations, and we are not going to talk about what we just saw.

Lorilee comes back out—alone.

She sits with us in a circle. In this game, we close our eyes and tell a secret when our name is called. It's a game with no winner and no end, because we all bear countless secrets, infinite shames. Kimberly calls out a name:

"Crystal!"

Crystal knows what to do. "When I was twelve, I lost my virginity."

We start out light, acceptable. Easy revelations. We keep our eyes closed.

"Carla Bobby!"

"I wish I were a boy." Carla Bobby's voice is quiet.

"Tell a real secret," somebody snickers.

"Terri."

The house dog gets into the middle of the circle. His damp smell alerts us.

"That mutt better not touch me."

"Git!" somebody says. "That mangy dog just licked my leg!" Our eyes flutter open, and Cassie (a boy dog—go figure) is trying to lick Terri's face. "Git!" She pushes the dog away, and his fat, swollen ticks roll from under his matted fur. No one really knows where this dog came from. He is ours, as much as he is anyone's. He has chosen us to hang around. We are sure Starlene feeds him every night, giving him leftovers when she thinks no one is looking. He sleeps somewhere on the property, not in the doghouse (even he can't bear it), but no one knows where—and no one wants to go looking.

"OK, y'all." Kimberly tosses her perfect hair to the left. "That shit dog is gone. Close them eyes!"

We do as she tells us. Of course. We always do. We who listened to no one, never, not our mamas, and not our daddies, not our teachers or our preachers, but we listen to Kimberly.

She resumes the calling of names: "Carmen."

"I have had sex with someone for coke."

More snickers—nobody's impressed. We've all done that.

What is the point of this game? We couldn't say. We play it every week, spontaneously, repeating the same secrets and new ones, real ones and fake ones. The game is not different from Group. Only there, our eyes are open. Here we tell our secrets first, we volunteer, before they are ripped out of us in Group, forced to confess the secret shames, the acts—done and done to us—before Miss Sallyanne calls us out as cowards and liars in the name of the Lord and tells us He loves us but we still are going to Hell.

None of us really believe any of that shit, but we kind of do. Salvation, Miss Sallyanne tells us, is what we're here for.

In Group, we try to convince her of our worthiness. We say program things like:

"Nobody's here by accident."

"But for the Grace of God, there go I."

"We're going to get this deal."

"Work the program, you're worth it, so work it!"

And other such nonsense.

We say, "God grant me the serenity to accept the things I cannot change, courage to change the things I can, and the wisdom to know the difference."

We say this prayer morning, noon, and night.

We say it during affirmations and during vespers.

But not even one of us knows what serenity is.

Nobody's even heard the word before now. Summer told us it means like being calm.

Right.

And, really, nobody knows what any of that other shit means either, but we say it all, we smile it, and Miss Sallyanne smiles back. And we are nowhere closer to leaving.

Kimberly has taken over the Revelations game, calling with the fervor of an auctioneer. Our eyes are still closed. The Texan sun is bearing down on us; there is no shelter out on the cement patio behind the house.

"Lorilee!" Kimberly doesn't even hide the triumph in her voice. Lorilee has never played. She is so new, that she doesn't seem to know it is what we do until one of us told her: if you're sitting at the circle, you must spill the beans.

Silence speaks back.

"LORILEE. Girl. It's your turn."

Our eyes flutter open again.

Lorilee isn't here again. There is a gap in the circle where she was. The backdoor swings open and Tad stops midstride and stares at our circle. He stares as if he's never seen us before, like we are from outer space.

His black eyes are like points, searching us for something but not finding it, he storms to his bike. He swings a bow-leg over its seat and slams down on the clutch. The bike thunders and we can't hear anything. We are obliterated by his rage, his not seeing us has changed us forever.

Not Kimberly.

"Where the fuck is that girl?" She says it like a promise. We nod our heads, not as an answer to her question, but an affirmation of the promise she has not spoken.

Swords

April 13, 1986

Every day here feels like forever. Like I've been here forever. Every day I have this feeling of déjà vu, and not because we do the same things over and over: morning prayer, affirmations, school, Group, clean up, vespers. It's the same over and over, one thing as dumb as the other. We sit outside smoking in between. Sheesh, I never smoked as much as now, but that's all there is to do in the in-between. Someone else is always on the pay phone. I never get a turn. Not that I have anyone to call. My mom is still not talking to me.

But forget her!

My town doesn't have farms with cattle and livestock and barns, but the rest of North Carolina does. We have sidewalks and parks, and you can hear the sirens from the fire house when they go off. But here it's quiet all the time. The ranch behind us stretches all the way to the ribbon of the highway well far off. The quiet feels like it will make me deaf sometimes, even when there is noise in the house. The quiet is all around us, even though I see cars and trucks and such racing up and down the highway. I wish I were in one of them. Take me anywhere, I'd say. Take me somewhere else. Take me home.

But I'm here, where time doesn't move straight anymore. Where it's like I've always been but didn't know it.

April 14, nighttime

Out back the sky holds zillions of its stars just like a dome over the fields. It is hot as hell tonight, so we have the windows open and the breeze doesn't help much. The cattle have gone somewhere else, though I can smell their smells through the open window. Not sure how come it's so hot, but of course it is. It gets hot back home this time of year, too, but not like this. Hot as Hell. I knew I recognized this place (ha ha ha!).

I don't know what is going on, but it seems like everyone else does. I have this feeling like I missed a day at school—no, more like a week—and I don't know what the homework was. This girl Lorilee got here and she's like too proud for all of us. That's what the other girls say. Like she thinks she's better than us. For someone who's too good but really too bad for us, the girls sure can't stop talking about her. But sometimes they get really quiet, or they stop talking when I get near. And if I didn't know better (I don't), I'd think they were talking about me. But . . . there's something in the way they look at Lorilee. They can't stop talking about her. They stare at her, eyeballing, ogling-like, taking her apart limb by limb. They feel like a force that moves under the earth, something you can't see, but it's raging, murderous-like. A whole looking to ravage its own parts. I don't know girls like this. I don't want to know girls like them. But I really don't want to be on the out with girls like them.

These girls aren't the only ones who seem different. Starlene is too. I don't know what happened but she acts like she's seen a ghost. No. Wait. It's more like she *is* a ghost, like in between worlds or something, floating from one place to the next, not making any noise, except for maybe that bum arm bumping into things once in a while. That woman was always kind of weird, but now I just stay way clear of her. I'm not the only one. Everyone hates, I mean, HATES, having cooking duty, because it's like being with the walking dead in there. Not sure what happened to make her quiet and so lurky. She's always watching us. But I swear, and I'm only telling you this, I think it was something that that Lorilee did. I don't know why, but that's what I think. Maybe she's like a witch or a wizard-woman or something. I just don't know. But since she came, nothing has felt right.

P.S. I cut bangs into the front of my hair. Not sure I like it. Makes my face look square now. I bet Tommy would hate it if he saw it.

April 15, 1986

Tax Day! Ha ha ha! Like any of us are paying taxes—like any of us even ever had a job. Freeloaders are what we are! We wait for care packages, hoping, hoping. (I don't get shit, by the way, but I am always hoping for something!) Kimberly gets something just about every week from some guy. He sends her chocolates, hair clips, concert t- shirts, and little love notes. So cute! I wish I had a boyfriend like that. But she is one of those kinds of girls: she is just gorgeous. The whole world waits for a girl like that. They wait to be allowed to brush her hair, put lipstick on her pout. We all live and die for a girl like that (even if we don't like girls—you know what I mean!). She barely talks to me. It's like I am almost invisible to her and her clique-y roommates. Better that way, I guess.

They kind of ignore me sometimes, but I have news for all of them: We are all here together! Nobody's getting out any time soon. Lorilee just filled the last bed, numero thirteen-o, and nobody's getting in and nobody's getting out.

P.S. Tommy was never romantic. I knew he loved me, but he didn't have to tell me in all the Valentine-kind of ways. He gave me this necklace with the charm after our 1-year anniversary, and that was cool. He was like, this is for you.

April 16, 2016

I heard a secret. A big secret. Why am I so afraid to write it? I don't know. Sometimes it feels like I can't write. Because if I do, I won't stop and the words will eat me alive. The words will keep coming and coming until—oh, I don't know. I don't know why I feel afraid sometimes. Good news is I've got this awesome hiding place. Still. It doesn't totally feel safe. I wish I could write in a secret code.

OK, here goes: some of the girls were talking the other day about leaving. You know, running. I'm not going to mention any names here, but a couple girls were talking some big talk about running away—that's not good, though. That gets you chained up in the real doghouse overnight. I wouldn't even bullshit like that—because that's what those girls are doing: just talking, I bet. None of them really seem to want to leave. Well. These girls did sound serious.

Not me. I am just happy riding out my time these days so that I can get sent back home proper and NEVER COME BACK TO THIS MOTHERFUCKING PLACE.

I heard that sometimes girls—and boys from the other place, when boys and girls were together before this house was made—had been caught running and then got sent to worse places. Places where they didn't think twice about hitting you or putting you in solitary confinement. Solitary confinement! Could you imagine? OK, so even though that sounds a little like it'd make you crazy, I kinda like the idea: think of all the writing I could do!!!!!!!

OK, back to reality.

I am not running anywhere. I am going to just stay here and wait until I can leave right.

I am Summer and I am an Addict, and I am OK with that today.

I am Summer and I am an Addict, and I am OK with that today.

I am Summer and I am an Addict, and I am OK with that today.

I am Summer and I am an Addict, and I am OK with that today.

I am Summer and I am an Addict, and I am OK with that today.

I am Summer and I am an Addict, and I am OK with that today.

I am Summer and I am an Addict, and I am OK with that today.

I am Summer and I am an Addict, and I am OK with that today.

I am Summer and I am an Addict, and I am OK with that today.

I am Summer and I am an Addict, and I am OK with that today.

It's not sinking in yet. But maybe it will soon, if I write it and say it enough.

April 17, 1986

Wouldn't Miss Sallyanne just LOVE to send us away? The other day, I guess to scare us or freak us out, she had us all come into the Group room, not for Group but to watch a movie. A movie! Yes, we all were totally psyched, except, of course, it was a movie about these shitty treatment centers that beat the inmates. Inmates! Yes, that's what they called the kids.

So Miss Sallyanne like calls us all into the Group room and wheels a TV into the front of it. First of all: what the fuck! Where's she been hiding this old box?! We could be watching *Who's the Boss*? Or *Family Ties*! Holy shit! We could've been watching *Dynasty* all this time!!!! But that's probably where the damned TV has been: stuffed away in her office, where's she is salivating over Steven and Krystle and Sammy Jo.

Jesus Christ, I hate this place sometimes.

Anyway. We all come on into the Group room, and set up to watch this documentary thing. And they showed the kids— who kind of looked like us, the girls, anyway— getting put into headlocks and then yelled at. The counselors were like really mean, big ugly people who screamed in front of a room full of kids telling them to shut the fuck up and act like grown ups.

Then the solitary confinement room came up. And they showed kids who came out of it. They were like not right. The people doing the movie interviewed one of them, and you'd a thought he'd had his fingernails ripped out. He was all shaking and not looking at the camera.

Frankly, I think it was all bullshit. I mean, what fucking country is this? You can't just lock kids up like that. Don't they have parents? Don't their schools notice they are gone? Doesn't anyone notice that they are gone?

Did anyone notice I am gone? Did my friends notice?

Miss Sallyanne must think we are all a bunch of idiots, because she stands up in front of us and she says, See?

We're like, See what? But nobody actually says anything.

I start feeling around in my pocket for my cigs. I'm going to make a bee-line right out the back door as soon as Miss Sallyanne says we're done.

See how bad it can be? she says. Y'all got it made here at Second Chance. Y'all are allaways respected and keered for. She looks over at Starlene, who's like haunting the stairs again, but then Starlene vacates fast.

I'm sure I wasn't the only person who started to think about the fence and the doghouse. If that's being cared for, then kill me now and get it over with.

When nobody talks, Miss Sallyanne keeps going: Y'all are going to get this deal. Don't nobody needs to go to Scared Straight or some such place as on that movie. She points to the TV like it's the box's fault these kids are getting the shit beat out of them.

Nobody's talking now. I mean, nobody. Not even Lorilee, who always has something smart to say.

OK, girls. I know y'all are scared. I'm not sending anyone there, but there by the Grace of God, go I. Miss Sallyanne's eyes move around the room from right to left, making sure each of us is about to piss her pants, scared to death. I love you girls, she says.

Holy shit. That woman is terrifying. She's waiting for us to say something.

Finally we all sing, Love you, Miss Sallyanne.

She breathes out, heavy-like, and it's all I can do not to push her out of the way to get a smoke. I'm hot. The sweat's dripping down my back and that fucking room feels way too small again. I don't think I'm getting sent to one of those shit places, but just in case, I'm going to keep a bag packed, I think. I am going to be ready to run. Nobody is going to send me away again. I need to get home.

When I sit here in the dark on my bunk—I wait up sometimes until everybody's asleep (which isn't easy these days, since somebody's always wandering around, thank you very much, Lorilee)—I can see the Little Dipper (I think) and the other constellations out the window. They are like hieroglyphics. I have no idea what they are saying, but they are telling me something. I wish I knew what.

I had to put my notebook away before.

I saw Lorilee walking around here. At first she didn't see me, and I saw her walk to the edge of the yard, right up to the doghouse, right by the wire reinforcement that borders the cattle fence on the south end of the property. The fence is our punishment. It's kind of worse than the doghouse—at least in that, you're cramped but you're covered up. Out at the fence, the elements tear at you. Somehow somebody's only out there when there's an electrical storm or a hail storm or when the sun is so hot it's peeling paint off the shakes of the house. There is no protection from anything. If you're sent out there to kneel and hold onto its metal, you know you are one step short of being sent away—and not sent home. Not the good sent-away. Like this but so much worse. Nobody ever went out there just to look. We could all see just fine from the back patio. Nobody had to get up closer to the fence just to see the same ranch land or stare at the highway way yonder. But not Lorilee. She walked right over to it and wrapped her hands around the wire, and I swear she must have hurt herself, there are little barbs around the whole thing. But she held on tight. Didn't seem to matter. Then that mangy dog came right up to her, but she ignored him. Cassie wouldn't leave her, that poor thing. Just came up right next to her and stared out at the field.

But then she turned around quick, and I swear she looked right at me, saw me through the window, it seemed. I shoved my notebook away and rolled over on my bed, like I was still sleeping. Lorilee walked up fast to the house and like lightning she's standing next to my bunk and asked me what I was doing.

I know you're awake, she said. Open your eyes.

I said nothing.

Come on, she said. You're always awake.

And I just didn't know what to say, so I said, not this time. Then she made a noise that sort of sounded like a humph and threw herself on her own bunk.

What am *I* doing, she wants to know! I should be asking *her* the same thing! She's the one outside in the night! Geez!

Second Chance Girls

We all knew that Lorilee was different, strange-like. We didn't need Summer going on and on about it, but we were curious. We had to admit. So when Summer started in this morning, while we were all bent over those books Teach brings in, the ones with the answers in the back, we didn't stop her. We could copy answers as good as anybody. Hell, that's the only way some of us would get through school. Some of us really needed help, though. Even copying wasn't that easy for them. Some girls couldn't read right. Like Crystal and Carla Bobby. Well, Crystal couldn't read at all. That girl was dumb as a stump. Ain't no cure for stupid, we all knew that. But she was a nice enough girl. And Carla Bobby read backward- like. Summer usually had to read something to her and she told the answer for her to copy it down. When we were feeling especially mean, one of us would volunteer instead of Summer and would copy her answer down wrong, but she never said if Teach failed the assignment—because Carla Bobby knew she couldn't even tell if the answers are right or not. Teach might not have known too, because she didn't say anything either way. She'd just smile and say the

Lord will provide. Well, he didn't always provide the answers! That's for sure.

Today, Summer can't keep it in. She bursts out saying that she's seen Lorilee outside at night. Outside— like down by the fence.

"The fence?" somebody says, but just mentioning it makes us all tense up a little.

"Yeah, back there." Summer's face is flushed. She's been holding this in all morning, waiting to tell us when a staff member isn't hovering. Teach doesn't count. She's on Planet Jesus and doesn't hear shit from down here on Earth. Summer looks around the school trailer. Lorilee isn't in here—and nobody knows where she is. "She was standing out there last night, looking up at the moon or something. Holding onto the fence."

At first, it doesn't sound like much, until it dawns on us: what the hell is Lorilee doing outside at night? What is she looking at? Summer watched her the whole time. Summer, who can't ever sleep, saw Lorilee get up. She says she knew she wasn't sleeping since that first night because her breath is not regular like the other girls.

"What?" Carla Bobby says. "How long you been watching her?"

"You're like a spy!" Magda says. She says it like it's a brilliant remark or something. We all roll our eyes. Some girls are just hopeless. But it's not lost on the rest of us that Summer's probably spying on all of us, too.

Kimberly takes over—we're all around the big table now in the trailer. Teach has wandered off somewhere. She is simple as simple goes. It must be easy when all you have to think about is Jesus.

"What'd she do?" Kimberly says. We all look at Summer. "Well?"

"Well." Summer's voice lowers and pulls us all closer to her. "Lorilee went to the back fence and stood there staring."

"Staring at what?" Crystal says. She can't read good, but she sure is direct otherwise.

Kimberly cracks her gum. "Yeah. Staring at what? Nothing's out there."

"I didn't say there was something there. I just said I saw her. She was standing, holding onto the fence." Summer is about to stop talking and end the fun, but we are bored, bored, bored, just dying for something to do, something to talk about. Copying answers out of a textbook just doesn't do it. We keep her at it.

"Go on," Terri interrupts. Gets us back in focus.

Kimberly gives Crystal a look. "Yeah, keep going," shesays to Summer.

"Well, that's it," Summer says.

"What's it?"

"Lorilee." Summer gets real quiet. "She just stood there. Looking."

"That's it?" "That's what I said. But that's a lot. "That's what I said. But that's a lot. I've never seen any of out there."

"Yeah. That's weird." Kimberly confirms the report. "That's like totally odd."

The word "odd" hangs in the air in front of us. We knew Lorilee wasn't right. And now we have some evidence, although nobody's sure what it proves. Somehow the fact of *her* sleeplessness gets us mad. The mystery of what makes her do anything gets us madder, but nobody knows why.

"Let's make her go next in Group," Kimberly says. "It's her turn anyway. Bet that odd cat's got some more odd bricks to drop."

We start laughing and Lorilee walks into the trailer and Kimberly shuts up, we all shut up. Lorilee sits down at the other end. And we don't know where she's been, but it feels like she knows we've been talking about her. Like she heard the word "odd" and it was her cue to come in.

But in Group later that day, Lorilee just sits there. Miss Sallyanne calls for someone to start us off. Everyone gets quiet. Kimberly gives Crystal the Go look.

"How about Lorilee?" Crystal sits up. She looks at Kimberly for the approval.

Lorilee's gaze falls on Crystal, and something in it-makes Crystal say, "Well, only if she wants. I think she went not that long ago."

We can't believe what just happened. We had Lorilee in place, Kimberly set it up. And Crystal let her go.

"I ain't ready," Lorilee crosses her arms and smirks at Kimberly.

"She ain't ready, girls. It takes time," Miss Sallyanne says. "All in God's time, Lorilee, all in God's time. She's already dropped a major brick, y'all. We know she's got more, but it takes time. It takes time to heal the wounds of our past sin." Miss Sallyanne has the final word. Nobody can believe the special treatment. What earns Lorilee a pass, we all want to know.

Magda begins to say, "But—."

Miss Sallyanne cuts her off. There is no way to argue with her. There is no arguing, ever. "Terri?" she chirps instead. "How about you? How's your spiritual condition today, honey?"

Later after vespers, we're all outside having the last smoke of the day, and Kimberly says, "Like I said, that girl is like totally odd."

We all know who she means. "Yeah," we say. "Totally."

Kimberly flips her hair to remind us of what we already know: she is a queen. She is the desired. "Y'all," she says.

"I have an idea. Want to play a game?" "What kind of game?" someone asks.

Kimberly just smiles.

II

Birth

My story ain't much, y'all. But here goes. I'm Starlene and I'm an alcoholic and addict. Can y'all hear me OK?

I know all y'all know this story. I'm a garden- variety addict, as they say. And the easiest way to say it is that I was once lost but now am found. But for the Grace of God, there I go. And tonight I've come to tell you my story: what it was like, what happened, and what it's like today, because that's what we do in the Program.

Before now, before I came to believe, I was all strung out. High sailing with Zephyr's breath, flying like a kite. You know what I mean. Up all night. Shaky-like. Can't sleep for days.

Going to work—going most days, then some days. Then not going out at all. Public assistance next. Grinding my teeth. You know how the story goes.

I didn't grow up that way. We were working people. I was a good girl. I was the fourth child of seven. Like the middle-middle child. Not really nowhere—if you get what I mean. And there was good reason not to be anywhere. My daddy—you know the type—was quick to raise his hand and wasn't saying sorry if he hit the wrong kid. And my mama wasn't about to interrupt and correct him, because she knew she'd get it too. Rather them than her, was her motto, I expect. But that's OK. I'm OK with that today. I have forgiven her. She done the best she could with what she had. But for the Grace of God.

And we ain't had much. You know: hand-me- downs, government cheese. We were out all day long until it was dark, and then some—and you know what that's like in west Texas. Mmhm. I see some heads nodding out there. Y'all know. West Texas. I don't got to say much else, I can see.

For a while we did family things but then my daddy done left and never came back and those family things— you know, things like Easter, Christmas—started to stop. Birthdays were first. My mama kept to herself, not coming out of her room for days. And it was just a matter of time until I was hanging with the wrong crowd. Running, running. I met my husband that way. We was high school sweethearts, even though after a while we wasn't never in high school. And then we wasn't like sweethearts anymore, if you get me. But me and Roderick, we done so much together. But people, places, things. They all will bring me back if I ain't careful, watchful-like. That's what I do now: I watch. I see.

Me and Roderick got into some crazy-ass fights. I was just so mad, madder than a wet hen all-a time. I started them fights with him, criticizing him, provoking him-like, whining about not having enough—this was when after we got married. I was about eighteen, and like, I don't know what I thought—maybe being married, a married woman and all, would change everything. I'd be out of that godforsaken house, away from all my brothers and sisters and my mama who never left her room. But out of the fire into the frying pan, they say. Roderick was just as heavy handed as my daddy been. And those fights, well—I'm not saying I didn't deserve it sometimes—but I've got a few mended bones now—some aches and pains to remind me that I can never go back there. But ole Starlene. She's still alive. And I ain't never letting nobody treat me like their punching bag. Never again.

But for the Grace of God, is what I say now.

Me and Roderick started dealing to make some cash. It was his idea. And I—stupid cow that I was—went along with it. With everything he said. I mean, it was hard not to. He'd get all mean and in my face if I didn't, telling me I was nothing, telling me he liked my sister better, telling me he'd beat the living daylights out of me. My arm is still not right, never set right from one of those nights.

Sorry. I done forgot myself again.

Anyway. After a while we wasn't just dealing. We were cooking it ourselves. When we was in school, it was just small shit, the usual stuff: weed, downs, acid, that kinda thing. But once we were married and we were in the bars legal and all, we started making connections. And those connections led to other connections. Next thing you know, I've got a full-on operation running outta my kitchen. I got people coming in and out all hours of the night. The kinds of people who don't blink when they see you with a big ole black eye or yer arm in a sling. They don't give a shit. Hell, I didn't give a shit. Roderick, he was sometimes screwing some of them girls that come in there. Some of them as young as the girls back at Second Chance, giving them drugs for ass.

I didn't care. We had some money, but it was coming in and then leaving just as fast. Life in the fast lane, it was.

The kids, half the time I didn't know who was watching them. My mama has my little girl now, she and her new husband have her, and that little girl ain't really little no more. Then my son. Well. He ain't never seen me sober. Never going to, neither. He departed this earth before I could be the mother I'm supposed to be. God rest his soul. God bless his loving heart. My boy-angel.

I'm all right. Thank you. I only need one tissue.

Thank you. Where was I?

And one day—Roderick was already in the can for drug charges. Jail time started. Roderick was getting picked up more. He was getting sloppy. Honestly, I liked it best when he was gone, locked up-like. For one thing, I didn't have to worry about somebody pounding me for small shit. He wasn't around to break my other arm, you know? But for another, I started running things on my own. I got good at the operation when he wasn't there hollering and worrying me. I could think straight and keep numbers in my head.

I started thinking I might be even better without the drugs. I definitely was better without my man around. But I could really make some cash if I weren't consuming so much of the product. So then I was trying to detox on my own. But y'all know how that goes. Nothin' doin'. In fact, the harder I tried to stop, the harder I was sucking on that pipe, the harder I was jamming that needle into my veins. I hadn't no good veins left in my arm—I could only do the one arm too, because the other one didn't bend no more. So I had to find other places.

Then one day, the Light shined on me. I didn't think that then, but I got my second chance. I hit that bottom. Just when I couldn't imagine it getting any worse, things then did. Roderick got out of the can, and I'm getting black eyes again. Missing teeth. My little girl couldn't look at me. I was a fright to see. A disgusting mess, is what I was. Them kids wouldn't even want to visit me after a while. Just revolting-like. So I started to really try. Now I wanted to get clean. But you know how things go. You cain't just quit. When you're a full-blown addict, it's like trying to use willpower to stop yer diarrhea. Willpower just won't work.

It takes an act of G.O.D. An accident. Yes. The hands of God reached in and there was an accident. Roderick done died. He felled off a bridge one night, hit by a car and done shoved off. Ain't nobody seen that car. But for the grace of God, there I go, I say now. Justice done have her way.

Still. I hit bottom. After the accident, they came around the house, and they found them drugs. They seen my kitchen. They knew what was up and it was over for me.

I woke up in jail, detoxing there. Shaking hard. Holy Jesus. Holy Mother of God. You ain't known the shakes until you're coming off H. Like shaking so hard the mattress feels like concrete.

So many things happened then, but it's all a haze. I remember, I remember...hell, it's all a haze. Sorry folks.

That's just how bad I was. I just simply don't remember the details none.

But I'm grateful today for what happened, like they say here in the program rooms. I am grateful today for all that shit led me here today. Almost all. I have come to the river and I have had a cool drink. I had had enough! Yessir-ree. Ain't nobody going to take my sobriety away from me today.

So that was what it was like, and that is how it happened. More or less, folks. More or less. You know what I mean. But for the Grace of God, there I go.

When I got to Second Chance, I had nothing. Nothing. No money. No looks. No hope. Yeah, and OK, my kid was with my mama and pop-pop. Oh my little girl. She was the one who led me to my bottom. She was the one who looked me in the eye and told me I was nothing but a sack of bones with nasty ole scabs on my mouth, a waste of a human being, a weak failure of a mother. A mother in jail! Even she couldn't look at me none when I was at the bottom. My son—he was already gone by then.

OK. Where was I?

So I came empty handed and empty hearted, as they say. I had nothing. A sorrier sight there never was.

When Sallyanne first saw me, she shook her head, all oh-no and shit. I know. I wasn't much back then, and you wouldn't believe it now. I know.

She looked at me and said, "Honey, what can you do? Can you cook?"

"Yes, ma'am. I can cook and clean. That's what I'm here for."

"That and to stay sober," Sallyanne said, like I didn't know. But don't get the wrong idea. She's awright. She knew who I was.

And then I come to know who she was, and we have a good relationship today. I'm OK with Sallyanne today. She saw the wretch I'd been, and she said, "Girl, I will love you until you learn to love yourself."

At first I was like, get yer homo-lesbo hands away from me, but that ain't what she meant at all. That was just me being small. That was me not seeing the Hand of God working in my life.

I will love you until you love yerself. Y'all know what that means, right? That don't mean, I will love you and treat you nice and give you everything you want. That don't mean I will love you and won't tell you what's up and what's down.

That don't mean I will love you and never tell you to git the hell over yourself. That don't even mean I will love you and you're great, because you ain't.

Excuse me. I was getting excited. Getting ahead of myself.

She set me up in the kitchen. And I cooked break-fast, lunch, and dinner for them girls. Still do. Sallyanne set me up and I made cheesy eggs in the morning, a great big bin of them, spaghetti for lunch, and chicken fried steak in the evening. I cleaned that kitchen by myself in the be-ginning. I wasn't trustworthy, I know. But I could clean a kitchen.

Back even when Roderick and I were cooking crank, I used to keep that kitchen nice. Nice like we was going to eat in it. I'd polish the counters, disinfect the sink, mop the floor, just to get ready for the day. There weren't no need to do that, really. And eventually it all stopped. OK, that's the truth: soon enough, the filth was everywhere. It was all over the kitchen. The house. On me, inside me. Everything was like sick to me. 'Course, the kids were gone already. I forget when but CPS had done come and took them. That's when we found out my boy was sick. I didn't realize it. I didn't see it. I thought he just had the flu or something when they told me he was sick. But he was sick for months before I knew what it was. Because that's the kind of mother I'd become. Blind. And addicted. Lost. But now I'm found.

And then I come here, right after rehab, after jail. Six months. I don't remember much of those days. I remem-ber shuffling around and not remembering. It wasn't all that different from being out there, you know. Big difference was there ain't no pressure on the inside. There ain't junkies and dealers and kids and people needing you, expecting things from you, pissing and moaning about how you failed them every day of their godforsaken lives.

These girls. I keep an eye on them all. Watch over them. They're all soft, if you ask me. They don't know how good they've got it. Some got families sending them care packages and phone calls. They've got places to go to after now. Me, I ain't had nothing. There was nowhere I hadn't been yet. And I mean figurative-like. I ain't never been out of Texas. But now there ain't nowhere else to go.

Well. Now that ain't entirely true. I got one place left: death. Ain't that what we say in these rooms? I see some heads going up and down. Jail, institutions, and death. Well, I got two outta three. That ain't bad. Ha! Get it? Two outta three ain't bad! But I ain't ready to go for the home run yet. I ain't ready for the Big One yet. I got a couple over there on the other side waiting for me, and Lordamercy, if I don't miss one of them every day— 'specially now that I am living clean and sober—but I ain't ready to heed His call. No sir. I am here, taking it one day at a time.

So I got my job at Second Chance. And I look for the opportunity to be of service, as they say. Sure, I still make cheesy eggs and whatnot. But Sallyanne's got me training girls. She puts them in my care when they's needy. She don't say it—she just calls it kitchen duty. She calls it such so the girls don't know that they have a special assignment with me. They don't know that I am like their tutor, like their governess in one of them old stories. I teach them more than just cooking, though they's going to need that too. I teach them to watch. I am the seer of all, and through me they can see too.

I have been brung to the river. And the river is good. But it's as far as I go these days. I was lost but I am now found. See no evil. Hear no evil. Say no evil.

I have let go and let God Almighty have a hand in my life.

I have made a decision to turn my life and my will over to my God, who I choose to call Lord. I know it seemed like I'd done it as soon as I'd gone to jail, or rehab, or even coming to work at Second Hand. But no. I did not know what *turning it over* meant. I do today.

I came to the river, as they say. Yessir. I came and I knelt. I knelt when I saw the face of evil and saw how the Devil was a wily, clever one—almost too smart for ole Starlene, except that I got the Grace of God on my side. Like my special armor of Light. I have seen the Devil. I saw what he could do and then I knew. I had no choice but to let go and let God. Turn it all over. I saw what he could do. I said, Lord, Deliver me from evil. I said, Lord, I will only do your will.

I am clean and sober by the Grace of God. The Program works if you work it, so work it, you're worth it, y'all.

Thank you for listening.

Swords

April 18, 1986

I heard Tad talking to Miss Sallyanne in the kitchen this morning, and I heard them talking about the old house. They talk so weirdly. Like they are more than family, something else. I couldn't hear everything they were saying. I was supposed to be in the Group room with Terri, who is the laziest human being in the world. We were supposed to be dusting and cleaning that shit room, and she just sat around, talking all kinds of shit about Kimberly and her stupid crew. I guess Terri thinks we are friends. And I suppose we are. She's all lanky and awkward—like my insides on the outside. That's why I wish she'd stay away from me, but noooooooooo, she just thinks it's OK to gossip with me, as if she wouldn't be telling my shit all over the place too.

Anyway, Terri realized I wasn't really listening and she got up and left. Then I could hear Tad talking about the old house from the other room. He's going on and on about how in the old days when boys and girls lived there, Group was like two hours long. Two hours! What the fuck does anyone have to talk about for two hours??!!! But here's the thing: it was boys and girls. Boys! It was all one house, one glorious house, until Something happened.

Duh duh duh....

Now I know the secret. And it happened on Miss Sallyanne Prissy-pants I'm-in-charge's watch: a couple of her own disciples, a few of the girls got pregnant. And that's pretty bad—but not totally a surprise, right? I mean, make some girls and boys live together, and then somebody's going to do it, right? So they moved the girls to a different home. Separated them. So now we're here.

But now something else has happened. Another girl is pregnant.

The thing is, this one, sounded like she was special. Like ole Tad was looking out for her, Sallyanne too. One of these girls whose mom or dad dumped them here and forgot all about them. So Tad and Sallyanne separated her out, when they moved the girls to this house. They set this one aside to work in the office, keep her out of general population. She used to be a resident, and I don't know, it sounded like the money was running out and she'd have to go to state, so they put her in the office to work and *now* she's pregnant, too. Get it? She is pregnant *now*, after the girls and boys were separated. That's all I got, because as soon as that creepy Starlene showed up in the kitchen, those two were all quiet, not talking. So somebody's got a secret.

Second Chance Girls

Teach—bless her soul—had turned her back on the long table in the center of the trailer and was hanging up our self-graded exams.

"A wonder to behold," she said. "All 100s! All A's! Amazing," she cried, as if all of us hadn't been dropouts or failing out of high school before we'd gotten to Second Chance.

"*Jesus, show me the Way*," Teach sang to herself while she taped the fraudulent exams to the walls. She placed the papers side to side, as if she were wallpapering the trailer.

"*This is my prayer*
Jesus, show me the Way."

"What does that mean?" Lorilee asked. She was sitting at the table, the only one who hadn't copied an exam— the only one who hadn't done anything since we shuffled into school an hour ago.

"Why don't you mind your business?" Crystal asked her. When Lorilee didn't answer, she barked: "Why ain't you doing your work?"

"Hey! Teach," she said again, "What does that song mean?"

Teach twirled around, a dark-haired Glenda the Good Witch. "Who's asking?"

"Does it matter?"

Teach shrugged.

"Me." Lorilee smiled and Teach was charmed.

"Why, bless my heart. My girl Lorilee wants to know what all the way my Savior leads me. I'm not sure if I can explain it good." Teach fluttered over to our table, the rest of the pile of our fake exams curled up in her wake and softly descended to the floor behind her.

"You're singing something you don't understand?" Teach looked at her. "That ain't quite what I said, my girl."

Lorilee gazed right back at her, fascinated, staring like Teach was a creature from another world.

The rest of us were quiet. Crystal already had slunk back into her seat, after no one, especially Kimberly, came to back her up. The queen and the rest of us were still recovering from the surprise of Lorilee's voice. We thought she'd started to learn her place in the Order of Things. Her voice came to us now, new and direct, and we saw she needed a lesson. But we waited to hear what Teach said. We were curious too, but none of us thought to ask. None of us thought we had a right to ask half the things we wanted to know. The least of which was Teach's singing preferences. We wanted to know why we were at Second Chance—besides the reasons Miss Sallyanne always said: we were sinners, drinkers, drug users. Why here? What was this place? Anyone else we'd ever known went to rehab and went home. But for the thirteen of us, home was elusive. After Detox and a rehab, nobody ever imagined a place as isolated like this, a jail without locks, and certainly none of us expected to be here infinitely, as we seemed to be. Why were we never ready to go home? Why did we have to repent if God already loved us, like Miss Sallyanne said? Why were we guilty when so much had been done to us? When would all those boyfriends, uncles, fathers, teachers, mothers, brothers, sisters, who used us, hit us, slapped us, raped us, ignored us, yelled at us, stopped loving us, when would they have to repent? When would there be justice? What was wrong with us? Why were we different, special cases?

But there were other things we wanted to know. Now that we were clean, we had other, less profound questions. Simple things, now that we thought about it. Like can you pee when you have a tampon in? Can you get pregnant all the time or only some times? Is vinegar really a douche? Do girls really smell different when they have their period?

Who could we have asked any of these things?

We could have told all of our questions to Lorilee. She would've asked for us. But that was also why we hated her too: she was not afraid to ask. She didn't seem afraid of anything, and we, well, we were just too afraid to know what we didn't already know, because what we knew was scary enough.

We waited for Teach to answer.

And we seethed, hating Lorilee because she wasn't afraid and because she still looked good. She didn't look ancient like everyone else. Lorilee was definitely better dressed than any of us—and maybe that is what gave her the right to ask. Although there wasn't an ironing board anywhere near Second Chance Home for Girls, somehow that Lorilee always seemed to have her shorts pressed, and her blouses (who wears blouses?) were always creaseless, tucked easily into her waistbands. If it hadn't been for the scars on her arms, we'd have thought she was an undercover agent, dropped here to spy on us. We saw her and knew she didn't look, act, or sound like any of us. The longer we waited, the more of us saw the possibilities, the lessons that would teach her where she belonged. We didn't need to speak; we looked—eyes darting furtively around the room—just enough to share the same thought. Only death would set us free. The final frontier. Only one death for the many.

"Honey," Teach broke the trance. She spoke like she'd known Lorilee all her life, "If you look inside, I think you already know." Teach lowered herself into the empty chair next to her—nobody sat next to Lorilee ever, so it was free, same with the one on the other side of her.

Lorilee smiled. A small one, but it was there. "How do you know I know?"

"I see you, girl."

"No, you don't."

We watched this exchange as if we were miles away, unseen to both of them. But we were close enough to touch them. They were speaking in a language we could hear, but we knew there was so much more we were not understanding.

"Lorilee, girl, I saw you coming a mile away."

Until now, we'd all thought Teach was a simple-minded idiot, like she should have been in Special Ed herself and not teaching it.

"Hmph." Lorilee cracked her knuckles.

"The Lord believes you in you, girl, even if you don't."

"It ain't a matter of belief, ma'am." Lorilee said, sounding both as if she was beginning a sentence and ending it at the same time.

The two women gazed at each other, one older, the other younger, but older still.

"What the hell is going on here?" Kimberly stood up.

"Do you kiss your mama with that mouth?" Teach asked Kimberly, her eyes still on Lorilee.

"I was just curious about the song." Lorilee pushed back her chair slightly, still holding the woman's gaze.

Kimberly watched the two of them. She breathed through her nose. "Cunt," she said under her breath and slammed herself back down in her chair.

A big smile broke over Teach's face. The new dawn couldn't have been brighter. "Sure, my girl. I see what you're asking now," she said to Lorilee. "It means that Jesus always is there for me. He's always showing me the way. That's all. It means I gotta be ready, because you just don't know when the Lord is gonna show up."

As if on cue, the aluminum door flung open. "Where're all my girls at?" Tad burst into the trailer-classroom, sounding like leather, metal, and wood all at once.

"Tad! You know I'm teaching here." Teach's voice clouded.

"I'm just checking on my favorite girls." Tad stood there, bow-legged and balanced, his eyes scanned our faces until he found the one he was looking for. His black eyes settled and Lorilee shifted her stare. She'd been nursing quiet defiance ever since Teach didn't answer her right proper, so she had a full store of it to shoot back at him.

"You almost done here?" Tad asked Teach, but his eyes stayed on Lorilee.

"I s'pose so. It's almost the top of the hour. I think everybody's finished their exams. Look, Tad! These are the smartest girls in Texas. We've got them right here." She held up one of the answer-copied exams.

"Well, let's see how smart they really are. Smarts won't keep you sober, now will it, girls? Addiction is an equal-opportunity disease."

Yes, we nodded.

"It don't matter who you are: a hobo or a rocket scientist. Addiction can affect anyone. There's only one way out." He looked around at us. "Anybody know what?"

Kimberly's arm shot up. For a second it looked like Tad was going to ignore her, look past her, waiting for another girl, *the girl*, to answer, but he looked at the cheerleader-queen. "Work the Program!" Kimberley burst out. She beamed like she was on a game show.

"That's right. Work the Program. Work it. You're worth it. It's all about doing the right thing."

By now, Tad had nestled himself into a chair around the table. Teach was humming her Jesus song, back at her wallpapering, and all of us waited on him.

"Let's play a game," he said. "What song describes you? Pick a song that says where you're at today."

"Higher Love!" Maryanne perked up.

"What does it say about you, darling?" Tad had kicked back at the table, leaning his chair back with the backs of his boot heels up on the table's surface. The hate in the room receded like a wave on the beach—a temporary vacancy.

"It means I'm being cared for by my Higher Power, and everything is all right."

"Good girl! Who's next?" Tad was smiling. He looked around the trailer.

"Be Good to Yourself!" Kimberly said. We all knew she had no problem with being good to herself. Hell, nobody even knew why she ever got high. She seemed perfect all the time, not like the rest of us. How she wound up here, none of us could ever tell. She had even told her story at Group, and she told us all—the coke, the boyfriends, the fast cars. She looked a little tired for seventeen, but shit, it all sounded pretty good to us.

"Aw now, that's a good one. That's one we should all be singing to ourselves." Tad's approval shone on all of us.

"Love Walks In." Crystal was looking sideways at Tad.

"I don't think I know that one," Tad said.

"Van Halen? You don't know Van Halen?" Crystal, all of us, cracked up. "It's on the radio. Their new album's due out this summer."

"Oh, girls. Come on. Ain't nothing good came out of Van Halen once David Lee Roth quit the band. Give me a break!" Tad's answer saved us all the embarrassment of listening to Crystal explain why that's her song—we all knew it was because Tad himself had just walked into the trailer. Even though we were all half in love with him, we'd die before saying so.

"How about this quiet little lady?" Tad said to Lorilee. She was acting like she was reading her schoolwork, but we'd all been sitting there that whole time and knew she hadn't done any of it.

"Lorilee?" He said again when she doesn't look up.

"What?" Like she didn't know.

"Yer song, girl." Magda said. "What's yer song today?"

"What song describes you today?" Kimberly translated, speaking slowly as if Lorilee couldn't understand English.

Lorilee breathed in and somehow we all felt it. She thought for a second. "In My Time of Dying."

"Jesus Christ," somebody muttered.

"Freak," somebody else whispered.

"Zeppelin or Dylan?" Tad said. He heard no one but Lorilee.

"Zeppelin."

"Nice." Tad nodded toward her. Somehow Lorilee won. We weren't sure what she won, but Tad's focus was on her, as if she were a flower in a forest and we were the moss on the northern side of its trees. Tad metamorphosed from a bull to a butterfly. He softened right in front of us, before our very eyes. He saw Lorilee, only her. We all might as well have been taped to the walls of the trailer with our fraudulent exams.

Teach started to hum Jimmy Page's riff and Tad started singing. His voice wrapped like a blanket around the room, transcending Teach's notes. *"In my time of dying, I want nobody to mourn. . . ."* The words were not for us—we knew—but they held us, held our breaths and the space around us. We were taken up into the folds of his voice.

"Why now, what a fine voice you have, Mr. Tad. Lovely to hear it praising the Lord," Miss Sallyanne interrupted. Her formality chilled the classroom. No one heard her come inside the trailer. "I come now to gather our scholars. All that studying . . . makes a body ache for some talk therapy, don't it?"

We couldn't tell if she was kidding or serious. We never really knew. None of us had ever seen the woman really laugh, so she was probably serious. Tad stopped singing. Now he was in some distant place. Teach turned her back to us and finished taping up the exams. The shape of our papers on the wall made a L on the wall, on account of the tiny window in their midst. We collected our books and shuffled out, following Miss Sallyanne, who walked like she was leading a band in a parade. She'd have been holding a baton, if she had one handy.

On the way out, somehow Crystal's chair got shoved in front of Lorilee. The sound of its feet against the linoleum agitated us, but the unspoken threat excited us, too. We held our breath. Lorilee stopped and looked at her.

Neither girl spoke. Lorilee waited until we'd all emptied out of the trailer. She walked alone, separate, even though soon enough she was back in the middle of us all again. Goddamn that girl. Her pressed clothes earned our resentment, Tad's attention to her inspired our contempt, and her fearlessness made us hate her. But it was her separateness that made us feel small and unable.

Starlene held the backdoor open for us without saying anything. She had stopped talking to anyone as soon after Lorilee got to Second Chance, only breaking her silence to yell or insult us on occasion. And here she was now: all washed out and making grits and eggs every morning at Second Chance. Exhausted and empty. In her we saw our mamas and our aunties and our grammas when she held open the door. That same-oldness about her that was as familiar as our own misery.

She thought we didn't see her, but it wasn't like we could avoid her: she was there morning, noon, and night. If she wasn't out there polishing that cream-colored Corvette, she was cooking. If you were unlucky, you got kitchen duty and worked next to her, with her pointing and grunting. But she used to speak. She had a lot to say about what you wore, how you talked, and why your life ended up at the Second Chance Home for Girls. Now she was just spying and tattling on us to Miss Sallyanne—it was almost like we were her entertainment for the times in between meals, when she wasn't doing anything, after the washing and chopping and stirring and frying had all ended, after she did all the shining she could do on that old Vette of hers.

And who knows where she got that old Corvette? Once we heard her talking about some kind of accident, but it couldn't have been with that car. The Vette was pristine.

After her nighttime sobriety meetings, that car would come roaring down the dirt road and crackling up the gravel driveway to the house—sometimes we'd forget it was her and thought it was some hot guy coming by. Newer girls always mistook the car for that—it took them a while too to figure it out. Coming to Second Chance and having no boys around took some time to get used to, so that any of the usual signs of Man—cars, loud music— made them jumpy.

But then the Corvette would park in its usual space next to Sallyanne's Corolla. Starlene would peel her miserable self out from the bucket seat of her car. Her fake eyebrows drawn too high over where her normal ones would be, and the rest of her face fixed on empty, her eyes staring straight at the backdoor as she walked into work—like if she looked at something else—the dog, a cigarette butt on the ground—she might get too distracted and forget the straight line to the kitchen.

Starlene probably should've been a Second Chance resident herself, but she was too old and Miss Sallyanne started the girls' home and needed her to cook for us. She came with Miss Sallyanne when they opened Second Chance and brought a few of the remaining girls from the co-ed house, like Magda, Cara Bobby, and a few others who had no chance of ever going home or anywhere else. Starlene knew the routine: prayers, chores, and Group. She went to her own recovery meetings at night sometimes—we knew that. Once we had a couple of program people from her night meetings show up, and one of them called out, "Hey there, Starlene!" as soon as he saw her in the kitchen.

She must've forgotten herself because she busted out right away with an uncharacteristically cheery: "Howdy, Mac!"

Mac! We'd never seen her smile before. She even knew his name.

"How you making out?" This guy—middle aged, with a huge sack drooping over a leather belt barely able to keep his jeans up—broke off from his partner. (And what were they anyway? Missionaries? Emissaries? Why did ex-addicts think they needed to preach to the rest of us? Why did they act like they had always been the way they were now: clean, righteous, and fine—no pains, no worries?) But those two were harmless, lost types. A lot of the recovery program people were like that. Not that there were so many. They were people who'd thought they'd found their way, acting like they knew the Answer all along, even after living through the disaster of their alcoholic lives. When they came by, they'd tell us their stories of loss: they lost children, husbands, wives, boyfriends, girlfriends, parents, friends, co-workers, pets, jobs, education, promotions, houses, apartments, condos, cars, trucks, lawsuits, direction, freedom, choices, and money, money, money—almost nothing any of us ever had. Frankly, they seemed to have nothing, too. These program people were the ones showing up in the middle of the day to talk about sobriety with us and how it "gave them their lives back." None of us were sure what kind of job that was or what kind of life they must have had before, but all of these folks seemed not just fine now but in a constant state of relief, a release from thinking and worrying (or working) for the rest of their lives, one day at a time. Why we would be expected to ever listen to people like them for advice on living was well beyond our imaginations.

Starlene was just another recovery program loser— no different than the other adults from the nightly meetings who came to preach at us. But when she closed the door after we filed in, she was still standing there, staring at us like she knew. Her stare made us look away. She might've been a program loser, but her eyes saw through to our secret; she knew it before we did, and she seemed to glare at us if only because she was thinking the same thing.

Swords

April 30, 1986

Tommy and I used to go to the airport and park at the far end of the runway, on the other side of the fence. We'd lay on the hood of his car and watch the planes take off over us. That was where he finally told me he loved me. Well, more like I told him first—and then he told me. We were lying on the hood of his car, with our backs up against the windshield, looking up. The planes roared over us, loud and close, terrifying every time and sounding like rockets. The wind of the engines alone could have made us deaf. I'd hold his hand each time another plane went up. This time, though, it sounded like the plane was too close, like it might not make it up over the fence. I grabbed onto him and ducked my head into his chest, keeping down. He put his arms around me (though what would he have been able to protect us from, if the plane came down on us?!). The plane made it, of course, and he was still holding onto me, pulling me closer, like. So I told him. I told him and held onto him too in case he let go, but he didn't. Tommy didn't. He held me tight and said he did too. He said, I love you. And neither of us let go until after the next plane came and went. It was only once, but I will always hear him say it.

We'd been going out for a while, going out and nobody knowing. I don't know why now. I don't know why everything had to be a big secret, but it was. For the longest time, like all of tenth grade, Tommy was like, we're just hanging out. And I'd say yeah, cool, like, of course, as if that was what we were. Just hanging out.

And it was true, we were just hanging. But part of it was because I'd known him almost my whole life. Our parents knew each other—I mean, our parents knew each other. We both knew—and I guess a lot of people did—that my mom and his dad had a thing. I know, that is so revolting, but that's how we got together. So I knew him way before then. We used to play together as kids. Tommy was like totally obnoxious as kid, too. I used to tease him about it later, when we were older—alone, together. Back then, he didn't know how to play nice—he was used to playing with his sister and brother, and they were obnoxious too. And then they moved away.

He came back with his dad after his family split. And that's how we knew his dad had a thing with my mom. He came back to be near her. He came back because she was still there waiting for him, because his wife would no longer have him. Because my mother, crazy as she is, was better than nothing, I guess.

When Tommy came back with his dad, his hair had gotten long. He was still really skinny and he was still playing guitar. We were now in the same high school, but we'd pretend we didn't know each other in the halls, although every now and then I'd see him coming my way when classes changed, and in the crowded hall, he'd pass and sometimes give me a small push, small enough so that only I'd feel it and no one else would see.

I lost my virginity with him. And I can only see now, all this time later, how scared I was. I didn't tell him I was so scared. He knew it was my first time. He was super gentle. And I don't know why I was upset after. I got real quiet after and pretended I was sleeping—I guess I thought that was what people did afterward. But I was biting on my lip so I wouldn't cry. That's a long time ago.

Things I love about Tommy:

1. Super skinny. Like a straight-edge ruler. I never cared that he was skinnier than me. (OK, a little I cared.)

2. Music. And he started to love Rush after I turned him on to them!

3. Guitar (this is more of a subcategory of #2). Really good guitar player!

4. Wanted to be a police officer (which was really funny considering all the weed he smoked and everything else. I loved how he wanted to do good, but I talked him out of it—I mean, come on! A cop?!).

5. Funny. 'Nuff said.

6. *Hart to Hart* (a secret only I knew that about him!).

8. Outdoors. His major loves, besides me: the beach, the woods, trout fishing.

9. Cool hair. Long, halfway down his back, like a rock star.

10. Love. He told me. At least I knew that.

May 2, 1986

Lorilee saw me writing the other day. Jesus, she is spooky. She crept up behind me. I didn't even hear her. I was on my bunk, like I always am, writing in here. I disappear during smoking time, when the other girls are out on the patio smoking up, and I come in here where no one will bother me. No one does. Except Lorilee. It was like all of a sudden her face is right next to me at the top bunk and she says, What are you writing? Like she wants to read it or something. I told her, none of your business. And she says, you don't have to get in my face about it. Just say so. I said, I did just say so. Then she huffed (!) and dropped herself into her bed. She's underneath me now on her own bunk. But now I can't think. She wrecked my flow. I can't write with her breathing down there, not doing anything.

May 3, 1986

I will try to write now. I will try to write now even though Lorilee is here, underneath, on her bunk again. It was like she followed me in our room, like she saw me walk off when everybody went out for a smoke. She had a cigarette in her mouth, about to light up, but she saw me and dropped it back in her pack and came in. I saw her. And now I can't write about anything but her.

Oh fuck it. I'm going outside.

May 4, 1986

Lorilee is outside. Tad is here at the house (Mr. Bulllegs himself) and he cornered her, talking JesusTalk, so she ain't going anywhere. Not for a little while, anyway. So I'm in here on my own.

If I didn't know better—and I am sure Tad is JUST talking Jesus—I'd think he was in love with her, like everyone else seems to be. The other girls like try to ignore her, but it's more like they're super in love with her too, always watching her and trying to get up close to her, talk to her. Then they talk about her and say they hate her, but it's not hate, not really. It's like they keep scratching at her surface to see the stuff underneath. They all seem convinced there's something there. I'm not sure. I mean, she told that shit story in Group a couple weeks ago. Some BS about having sex with her brother, being with her brother and having his kid. The girls were like, Oh My God. They all shut up right fast, even though they had been egging her on, like pushing Lorilee out on a limb to share a secret. And I swear if she didn't look side to side as she begun to tell her story. She told it slowly, and everybody was all holding their breath, all being folded into this bullshit thread she was weaving, giving us all just enough juicy details until we couldn't believe it, except we could—we could imagine she and her brother alone, defying all decent things. I know some of those girls imagined it, like her brother was forcing her or overpowering her—because they knew that kind of thing; they didn't really have to imagine it. But I don't think anybody's been forcing that girl to do anything. That's all I'm saying. She told that story like she wasn't fazed by any of it. Like she saw it in a movie the day before. Missing something, like a feeling or something, as she told us. That's how I knew something didn't sound right. She didn't seem to be embarrassed or upset; she was more like a storyteller, telling someone else's story, telling our stories to us. Miss Sallyanne looked like she was going to cum from the whole thing: the story had all her favorite parts: incest and illegitimate children. That's like a home run to her. She loves it when one of us drops a brick that has some of that stuff. Guilt, she says, is our path to the Lord. And I guess incest and kids without fathers make for guilty girls. Of course, usually the incest is wayward uncles and stepfathers and sometimes male teachers— but there was a girl who used to live here whose dad got down her pants. When I look at the faces around the circle during Group, I doubted there was only one girl who had that story. Good thing my dad took off years ago. Ha ha ha.

Oh that's not even funny. He wouldn't have never done anything like that. My dad was a jerk but not that kind of jerk.

The other stuff is the rape stuff. Just about everyone here has a story like that—near rapes, over-and-over rapes, rapes with things, rapes with people known, people unknown, with mothers knowing about it, cops doing nothing, teachers saying nothing. We all got something like that. Well. Not all of us. Not me. Not me. Not me.

Jesus. They are getting into my head. I hate that I just wrote "we," as if I am one of them. As if I am not me and so totally separate from all those girls with their rapes and kids and incest.

I'll say one thing about Lorilee: she's not one of them either. She doesn't need those girls, which is good, because they don't like her anyway.

May 5, 1986

I'm starting to think Lorilee actually LIKES me. Like she thinks we are friends or something. She came up to me the other night when we were all settling into bed, and she was like, you writing tonight?

Writing what? that asthmatic bitch Crystal said from her bed.

Nothing, I said. Lorilee didn't even acknowledge her.

Should I keep the light on? Lorilee asked me. If you're writing, you're going to need light.

What is she writing? Is she writing a story? Is it about me?

Jesus, would you shut up? No one's writing nothing. I looked mean at Lorilee to make her shut up. I don't need no light, I told her.

Sure you do, she said (so much for making that girl shut up!). Then she shrugged, like I was the one who had a problem. My word!

May 6, 1986

It is hotter than FUCK here today. And I had Floors today. HolyJesusMotherofGod! I was sweating as much water as I was mopping up. My sweat was pouring off of me, dripping into the mop water, like becoming part of the floor, the foundation itself.

May 8, 1986

Oh my God! I couldn't wait to tell you what happened today. After chores today, Miss Sallyanne said, we have a special guest. And we were all like, Oh no, not more of those program losers. And she was like, Now girls. That ain't Christian. So she brings us into the Group room, which was set up like a movie theater with all the chairs in rows facing toward the front door. We file in and Miss Sallyanne says, I am honored to introduce our special guest today. She's talking like she's on a game show. Miss Josephine Dixon, a beauty pageant contestant in the state of Texas, now turned Soldier of the Lord. Girls, please give Miss Josephine a warm Second Chance welcome.

Miss Sallyanne was acting like Vanna White with her arm up. Then she glides away from the front door as it opens on its own. Miss Josephine steps in. I swear, these two must have rehearsed this a few times because their timing was perfect. Miss Josephine is now in front of us. She's—I swear—like 9 feet tall and wearing patent-leather red stiletto heels. She's wearing a denim jumpsuit. Jesus! A jumpsuit! Which would have looked ridiculous on any of us—or anyone else in the whole world, except that Miss Josephine should have won that pageant (I doubt that she did because she wound up here!)—her body was perfect in the model way: long and lean, a huge rack and round hips. Her shiny blond hair came down in curls around her face and she had huge gobs of pancake makeup. If we had her in miniature, she could have been a Barbie doll.

Miss Sallyanne hands her a microphone out of nowhere, and then the reverb starts in. Starlene is messing with the amplifier (and why did we need that??? It was only the 13 of us in there. We could hear her just fine.) until Miss Josephine says, OK, hun, OK. I got it from here.

The reverb stops and Miss Josephine calls out to us like she's yelling out to a football stadium, How're y'all doing today?

We all mumble something like fine and she says, Y'all got Jesus?

Nobody answers that because it's too weird.

So she says again, Y'all got Jesus? I cain't hear you!

And I don't know if anyone answered her that time, but I start to get some giggles like right away. And it's fierce.

No? she yells out to the stadium. She's not even looking at us. She's looking way out over our heads. Well, I'm here to tell you you're going to need Him. Yes, sir. You're going to need Him. You need to ask Him to come in your hearts, she says.

And that's when the first one escapes. I lean forward to keep it in, but I'm sure I look like I'm either cracking up or I'm throwing up—and Miss Sallyanne is wondering too, because she sneaks over and before I know it, she is whispering hard in my ear, her sour breath spreading out all over me, You awright, honey? But it doesn't sound like she's concerned. It sounds more like she's going to kill me.

I tell her I'm fine. And now I'm dying because she creeps away and I see nobody's laughing. I'm sitting next to Carla Bobby and she's looking straight ahead with no expression, no nothing on her face.

Miss Josephine is sort of like pacing in front of us. And I admit it, she moves kind of like a big cat, like a tiger. Back and forth. She's holding that mic wrapped in both hands, holding it up to her red mouth. She's got these super long fingernails that match her patent leather shoes and every now and then they click against the mic.

When she starts talking about Jesus and the football field, she raises one hand like she is calling down God Himself. Right. You heard me: the football field.

Miss Josephine starts telling us that life is like a great football game and we are all on Jesus's team. We play for Jesus. Some of us are offense and some of us are defense. Are you ready to play for Jesus? she calls out to the stadium.

No, somebody says quietly, and then I start shaking. But I have to keep it together: I'm trying to get discharged from this place. The giggles come back. I am trying to hold them in. I see Starlene giving me the creep-eye-stare like she is going to kill me too. So I manage to push them down and get serious again.

But holy shit! Then Miss Josephine gets caught up in the football field thing, and she starts talking about Satan's team and how his players are very Clever and Cunning. And I don't know about you, but that sounds a whole lot more fun to me, because she is saying they don't play by the rules. And Miss Josephine is getting all worked up about Satan and sweat starts to come in little drops from her temples. Her makeup runs two little rivers down the sides of her face. She is calling out to the stadium—I mean, this woman is yelling, yelling like now she is calling out the Devil as if he were in the room—telling him to Git Behind ME! Jesus in front of me, Devil behind me. I'll say only to you that I looked around the room just in case— it sounded like he was like right there. She keeps yelling, and then she's yelling louder and louder like the Devil himself trying to get a riot going.

DEVIL BEHIND ME! JESUS IN FRONT OF ME!

And I don't know why but then I think about this porn magazine that Tommy had once, and there was a photo of these two old guys dressed like they're in a nursing home and this naked girl between them: Babe Sandwich, it said underneath. It was so gross. And I thought of that, Babe Sandwich, with Jesus and the Devil and Miss Josephine, who's probably known a few Babe Sandwiches, and then I can't hold back anymore. I mean, I'm not even giggling, I'm like busting out and cracking up, holding my sides.

And now I'm here. In Time Out, I guess. Like I'm a little kid. Miss Sallyanne told me to go to my room, as if I'm 10 or something, and I'm like, fine. I guess she didn't want to send me out to kneel at that fucking fence in front of Miss Devil-Git-Behind-Me. She didn't want her to know what Time Out really looks like here at the old Second Chance Hotel. Fine with me. I would rather write anyway, you old bitch. I guess I deserve being in Time Out. I really couldn't stop laughing, to tell the truth, and the tears were rolling down my face, and it felt like I was bawling, crying,—and it looked like it too, so I think Miss Sallyanne got some satisfaction from that, because she says, that's right: Cry—because you know you are a sinner. Go think about that while you're in your room, girl.

And over my shoulder I hear Miss Josephine tell the other girls, See? See what the Devil does? He just comes up behind you when you ain't looking. Pray for that child, y'all.

And I cover my mouth to keep from laughing all over again.

It's night now. I can barely see, but the moon is full and giving me a bit of light. I just wanted to tell you that while I was in Time Out (Oh *that* hurt, Miss Sallyanne! I can't wait to get in trouble again and keep writing!), Lorilee came in later, after Miss Josephine was done preaching— and singing apparently—she told me the woman sang for nearly a half hour straight. I *thought* I heard something coming from out there, but it's hard to tell from the back of the house.

Anyhow, Lorilee came in here and she climbed up on the other bunk and was like, What was so funny? I didn't really know, but that brought the giggles back, and she smiled, and then she was like, I know. Please kill me if I turn out like Miss Josephine JesusFreak, she said. And we both cracked up. But here's the cool thing: she wound up telling me that she was from El Paso, and wasn't entirely sure how she wound up here, but here is where she was. She said something like nowhere really felt like home anyway, so whether it was El Paso, or San Antonio or Arizona or the moon, it didn't really matter. She asked me where was I from and I told her, Elizabeth City, North Carolina, and she was like, where the fuck is that? And I said, I know, but it ain't as small as it sounds. She said, how'd you wind up here, and I said, I have no fucking idea. But then I said, well, I sort of do.

My guidance counselor told my mom that I was fucking up in school—and that was true—but the counselor was sure that all the kids in school were getting high—and OK, I was too, but not as much as compared to some of the heads in school—and my mom was freaking out. She was freaking out anyway, because I was so defiant, she said, all the time, and maybe that was true. I just was upset. A lot. The thing with Tommy had happened. Then there was this open space, like a black hole that I could see forever through, and not the good kind of forever, the lonely, all-alone forever kind—and it was all too much and I was staying out all the time and being *contrarian*— that was my mother's new favorite word. She didn't seem to get that she had something to do with all that, what with her little AFFAIR with Tommy's dad that the whole fucking world knew about.

But I didn't tell Lorilee all of that. I mean, my God, who would believe me? I just told her where I was from, that I missed being home like crazy and I thought my mom was overreacting, *which she was*, though you wouldn't know it now—she seems good now that I am gone. (I mean I guess she's good because she's not nagging me—or even calling me or sending me stuff. Not that I care.) And then Lorilee rolled onto her back and looked up at the ceiling and said, do you ever feel like running away?

No, I told her. Come on.

No. I'm doing the Program the right way. I'm going to be discharged and get home.

She rolled over onto her stomach, propping up on her elbows and looked at me, the same way she had looked at Teach. Fascinated-like.

Really? she said. You never think about it? When she looked at me, it felt like she was holding me steady. I didn't move, her eyes seeing me for the first time.

Yeah, OK, I wound up saying. Sometimes.

Hmm. She seemed to think about that. Maybe you should.

I don't know where the fuck I am. Where would I go?

That made her laugh. You don't? She laughed out loud this time, hard. Girl, you're in *hell*! And that made us both laugh. I don't know, but we were laughing so hard after a while, that it felt like I was crying, like really crying again. I had to wipe more tears from eyes. They were springing up like from a deep, underground well.

Are you OK? Lorilee sat up. She swung her feet over the side of the bed and jumped.

And I said, I think so.

She got like really close to my face, and then she said, like almost in a whisper, Do you remember me?

And I was like, what?

Do you remember me? She said again—I mean, I know I heard her, but what the hell?

I said, no, I don't know what you mean.

Then she turned fast and grabbed her smokes. OK. Maybe you will.

And she walked out of the room. I stayed in Time Out, but I think Miss Sallyanne forgot about me. I guess she was all busy trying to get Miss Josephine-the-Almost- Beauty-Queen's autograph before she ascended into Heaven.

But this is the point—and oh man, I can barely see, I think the moon moved because there is like no light, but I have to get this down: the point is that I think Lorilee meant something I sort of feel like I knew, but I can't barely understand.

May 10, 1986

I can't find my silver necklace. The one with the heart charm. I can't find it anywhere. I am trying not to freak out but I am freaking out now. It's totally gone. I told Miss Sallyanne, and she was like, This is a hard lesson in taking care of your own stuff. THAT is what she said! And if that wasn't bad enough, I *swear* if I didn't see Terri staring at me when we were out back smoking—and Kimberly, Jesus Christ!, was glaring at me, like I'd kicked the dog or something. I think they knew I told it was gone. Oh man.

I think Terri took it, too. She was the one wanted to get a better look at it. I bet that stupid dirty girl took it. Now there is nothing I have from Tommy.

I fucking hate this place.

I fucking hate this place.

I hate this fucking place.

Second Chance Girls

Maryanne and Magda were the lookouts. They crouched at the edge of the driveway—too far from the house than we were normally allowed, but low enough that Miss Sallyanne or Starlene wouldn't see them right away. The boys were coming back. They were coming to do the landscaping, to fix the trees and the bushes and whatnot. They were coming to do the heavy lifting; we'd done the easier stuff, working as we usually did, between chores, school, and Group. Getting outside was a good way to pass the time and every now and then when it was hot enough and everything else was done, we'd lay out on the grass with our towels and bathing suits, tanning, trying to look good for God knows who.

We knew who today. We'd gotten all made up: makeup, jeans, tank tops, hair up, hair down. You could see who knew how to take care of herself now: For a regular Tuesday, we were looking Fine.

We knew they were coming. We heard it Monday when they just showed up. Tad drove a creaky old green pickup onto the property. It swayed side to side as it crushed the gravel beneath its fat tires. We might not have even noticed at first, except Maryanne saw them and yelled:

"Y'all, I see guys. Like a whole bunch a guys. If I am dreaming, do not wake me!"

"What guys?" Kimberly looked up from an old *People* magazine. She had her feet hanging over the arm of her chair. We were in relaxation time: the ten minutes after morning chores before Group, sitting on the chairs in the Group room, which was supposed to be a living room.

"Those guys." We could hear Maryanne breathe in deeply as she said, "Oh my word."

"Where?" Kimberly went over to the window.

"There! Holy shit. There!" Crystal wheezed and now held the sheer curtain in front of the window to the side. By the time we'd all crowded up by the front door, the truck had disappeared behind the house, but we could hear it. We charged to the back of the house, climbing over furniture and through the dining room to the back patio. At the kitchen station, we heard Starlene:

"What the fuck are all y'all doing?"

We ignored her. The truck had pulled up in the back and six boys—guys, dudes—leaped out from its back and over its sides. They looked like us but better. Better shape, not as skinny as we were. Work agreed with them. They'd been out in the sun. They were rugged looking, their shoulders were angled under their t-shirts, their jeans were faded and hanging from their waists, crumpling at the ankles.

"Lordy," somebody said.

"Do we git to keep them?" Magda said. Everyone laughed, but we were all kind of wondering the same thing.

"Where did they come from?"

"Is that—?" somebody else started to say but stopped.

Kimberly moved to the front of the pack and stood at the backdoor. None of the boys looked up. They were unloading equipment that had been riding inside the bed with them. Pruning tools and spades came out. They were focused. Nobody looked back at the commotion bursting just inside the screen door of this house.

"Hey!" Kimberly yelled.

Nobody looked.

"HEY!"

"You girls git back in here." We heard Starlene bark behind us.

Crystal pushed past Kimberly. "I just have to have a smoke." She took her pack out of the pocket on the plaid flannel shirt she wore in all weather, and pushed a cigarette between her lips. Out on the patio, she lit up, and unable to resist, we poured out around her like water seeking its own level.

"How do they not see us?" Kimberly said what we were all wondering. "I bet Tad told them not to talk to us."

"That's probably it." Magda lit up too, but her eyes fixed on the boys. "That asshole."

"Yeah." We all agreed, but to say it felt like blasphemy to criticize him.

"Girls! What are all y'all think yer doing? You got Group now." Starlene stormed outside. Her hands shone wet and red from washing dishes. Her eyes were also red but that was from the constant, stricken look on her face. Everything on that woman looked stressed all the time. She was thin like paper and she wouldn't have seemed like much except her voice was loud. "Git inside now."

We ground cigarette butts with the toes of tennis shoes and then dropped them in and around the empty coffee can outside the back door. One more look toward the boys made us know they were not going anywhere soon. They fanned out across the backyard with their different man-tools to clean up this sorry-ass backyard. We all looked at each other and knew we'd be ready for them when they came back the next day.

Tomorrow comes and we *are* ready. Even we know we're being ridiculous, but who cares? There are guys on the premises! Most of us hurried to get our chores done:

the mopping, vacuuming, scrubbing, and sweeping. The rooms looked shittier than they usually did, since we rushed through the work. Correction: *most of* us hurried, because *some of* us are constitutionally unable to move fast, especially when it comes to work. Some of us don't even bother with chores: Kimberly is in the bathroom during chores, doing her hair. Miss Sallyanne doesn't notice she's gone and neither does Starlene, who doesn't care as long as she hears the noise of work coming from somewhere. Crystal is vacuuming for Kimberly, so nobody with any say-so notices that it's not Kimberly (which is just what we suspect they think of us anyway: we are just bodies, replaceable by other bodies, filling the beds in this house).

Besides Kimberly, the rest of us more or less hustle. Then we melt away into the bedrooms to change. It almost feels like we're getting ready for a school dance, although not many of us really know what that feels like, since we were usually the ones hanging out outside in the parking lot, in backseats, or nowhere even near a school. But we do what we can. Out come the acid-wash jeans, the hair combs, the fringe, the black eyeliner, the clean white high tops. There is the annoying buzz-hum of hair dryers coming from the bedrooms.

We float onto the back patio. It is 10:30 a.m. We look like we are headed to an Iron Maiden concert. Kimberly emerges last—of course—and her hair is all teased out like she is skipping the concert and going right into a Poison video and then to hang out with the band. We all feel vaguely inadequate. Nobody thought to pack a belly shirt when they were sent away, but Kimberly did. But again, *of course*, she did: looking hot was her normal attire, and that was one of the main reasons she was Queen.

Lorilee comes out to the porch, too, but she looks like she always does. She's wearing pressed-looking shorts that come just to her knee and a white blouse. Her hair's the same as usual: sandy blond, wavy but neat. Even she, though, looks happy—even she is looking forward to the boys coming. She's happy, it seems, because we are happy. She's buzzing, we're all buzzing—though we all know without looking that she and Kimberly are near each other but in separate orbits. No matter what happens—a free trip to the moon, a visit from Bon Jovi, a group of boys, nothing—them two will never talk.

We're not sure what we are actually going to do when the pickup truck arrives, and truth be told, we're not even really sure it's coming. A couple of us had the job of eavesdropping on Tad and Miss Sallyanne when the boys were cleaning up to leave the day before, and it sounded like they'd be back. In fact, it sounded like they will keep coming back till the property is cleaned up: until all the shakes are fastened to the house and the pile of timber is moved from the eastern side of the house, and all the other stuff around here that makes this house look like a temporary fixture on the landscape and not the permanent home for us girls.

So here we all are milling around on the cement patio, with the mangy dog, which is weaving through our legs, as excited as we are.

They come. We hear them well before the truck makes the creaky turn onto the gravel. Cassie the dog starts to run toward the truck as it meets the driveway. Kimberly and a few others know to cluster and pretend to be talking about something important, but the rest of us look toward the side of the house where the driveway leads around. We don't hide our need. We haven't been around guys—boys our own ages—for a long time. Months and months. And most of us have a somebody we wait for at home—whether they're waiting for us or not— someone we say we're waiting for, anyway, but the expectation today is high. We are in our A outfits, though with the exception of Lorilee, who always looks like she's dressed for private school, we worry we aren't much.

"Jesus, Mary, and Joseph," somebody mutters.

Those boys are *fine*. We watch the truck drive up the back. They are finer today than they were yesterday. Old t-shirts, faded jeans. Lordamercy. They see us and don't pretend not to this time. Whistles, waves, and it is only a matter of seconds before Starlene is out here with a spatula in her hand, yelling, "What the hell is going on back here? What are you heifers up to?"

Not everybody is from a farm, so whenever she calls us this, not everyone gets the insult. But today, not even the farm girls care. The Boys Are Here. They see us. They are only six and we are thirteen—though we all know some of the dirty meth girls like Crystal are out of the running already, with their pinched faces and missing teeth, so that narrows things a bit. Crystal and Terri can push and shove all they want to get out to the patio, but they are not really competition for the rest of us.

The boys all notice Kimberly, of course. How could they not? She's got that smooth, blond hair that she's got teased out and curled at the ends. It drops down her back— and her back is turned to them, of course—just above her double-moon-perfect ass. Some of us do the loyal-girl thing (Why? It's just in our DNA) and say, "Look, Kim, them guys are looking at you! They think you're hot!" To which she says, "Who me?"

The rest of us who know that personality and blow-jobs can still get you far are already scheming—that's also in *our* DNA. We know we're on our own. Every girl for herself.

It's getting louder out here, and Starlene is screaming now. She's like a sheepdog nipping around the edges of the group, trying to move the whole mass of Female into the house. We hear her but we outnumber her. "Tad! Tad!" she is screeching. "You git them boys the fuck outta here. We got a bunch of horny girls here who need to do some self-reckoning. They's need to find themselves and you're bringing these boys here now." Jesus H. Christ! Then Starlene's voice drifts and she says to no one, "I swear. What a bunch of fucking idiots." Who she's talking about, nobody knows, and nobody cares. Because the boys have jumped off the truck and are now with us on the patio, a couple are lighting up cigs.

The backdoor opens and bangs closed. Starlene has raced inside.

Tad has moved into the swarm of bees that we are; he is lost in the buzzing excitement too. He comes over to Lorilee, who smiles at him and they're talking like normal people, normal adults, that is—nobody's worried about her adding to competition since Tad has immediately monopolized her. Even with girls like Kimberly—and Maryanne with her amazing boobs—our confidence rises: maybe we are a fine-looking bunch.

And doesn't Starlene know it. She busts out of the backdoor, leading the way for Miss Sallyanne, who calls us to Group.

"Girls. It's time to get honest and drop some bricks."

"It ain't Group time," somebody says.

One of the boys snickers. They know what this is too.

"Tad? Tad? Where are you?" Miss Sallyanne is on tip-toes, looking for him among the crowd of us all. Her eyes are watery and brimming red. "Tad! Tad!"

He must be ignoring her on purpose, because there is no way anybody could miss the high-pitch shrill Miss Sally-anne's voice has become.

"TAD SAMPSON ROGERS!"

"Sampson?" somebody says.

"Right here." He jumps to and turns from Lorilee, who's now turned her back on him to finish her smoke. "We was just fixin' to work."

"Working what, I'd like to know," Starlene huffs.

"Wouldn't you," Tad says quiet-like but we all hear him.

He pushes through the crowd that is us. "Come on. Let's go, fellas. We got work to do."

The boys start to peel themselves away from us. Nobody gets much out of them, a name or two, and soon all six of them will be remembered as John and Pete, since nobody can really tell the difference and we never see them again.

We are herded into the Group room, where nobody wants to be. We stare at the floor, nobody saying anything after the second time Miss Sallyanne chirps,

"Who'd like to start us off?"

But we have important information. These boys—whose breath we can hear from inside the house as they hoist timber onto their shoulders—are the boys from the other house. Nobody still knows where that place is exactly and nobody who lived in the old house remembers these six guys. But the house doesn't sound so different from the Second Chance Home for Girls and the boys are good enough. Better than good enough. They like us too. Even better.

III

Initiation

I got news for all y'all. Them girls. Them girls are hopeless. There ain't nothing anybody can do for them heifers. Just when we think we got them on track. Just when we think they ain't the same little she-devils they came here as, there they are, out on the back patio, looking like a bunch of sluts. Tight jeans, tight tops. Jesus. Makeup. Makeup! They's in a *home for girls*. Ain't nobody care what they look like. Especially now, with their wrinkly, too-old faces, and tracks and scars up their hands and arms. There ain't nobody on Earth who wants them now. They look like a bunch of middle-aged whores.

Except for those six idiots that bigger idiot Tad brung here try to clean up this yard. They were all over the girls as soon as the truck pulled in. Like white on rice. I spied them driving in, craning necks, looking for our girls. Looking around like they ain't never seen no girls before.

Nobody asked me, but I always knew bringing them boys here was a bad idea. When Sallyanne told me, all she saw was work—salvation through work. And there's so much work to be done at this house. Jesus, woman! What planet are you on? Just looking at the girls here tells you these kind of kids don't know what work is. None of them do. Not them girls or them boys. Look what they turn out like. It's why they are the way they are. If they'd a been working all their lives, they ain't surely would've wound up here.

It was all I could do to round our girls up and get them back inside. Weren't nobody moving. Like a goddamn ice cream social. And Tad standing there making time with that Lorilee. He's talking to her like she's the only thing in the goddamn world. All hell's breaking loose, his men and our girls breaking off into groups and what-have-you, and he's standing there talking to her like they're at a cocktail party.

There. I said it. Like a goddamn cocktail party. Because that is the behavior I was seeing: drinking behavior. Like I always say: if you're a drunk horse thief, and you take away the drink, you're still just a horse thief.

I seen it. A whole bunch of them out there behaving like the old days.

Anyway, I run inside to get Sallyanne, and she's like in her office with the door locked. And I am banging on the door—I mean, I don't see her nowhere else—and she's got to be in there, right? Right? Well, it's like ten minutes later—OK, not totally ten, but like a really long time it seems—and she opens the door and she says, What? Like I'm breaking up her own party in there.

She's moving so slow-like. Her little white sneakers padding through the house to the back door. The buzz out there gets louder and louder as I'm following her there, but that don't make her move faster. I'll give her that. She goes at her own pace. When she gets out there, it takes her a few seconds to think. Then it dawns on her what's happening. She says something that I will not repeat here. Something not Christian. Something that gives even ole Starlene the shivers. And then she orders all the girls in. She damn near draws the sky to the earth with her ordering and cussing.

Tad, he blinks a little our way, almost as if he's in some other dimension.

I know what dimension. Dimension Lorilee. He seen that wicked girl, and she looks all neat and clean. Dresses better than any of them. And I know: she's different. She's queer-like, ain't like the others. But she cain't be more than seventeen. We don't take 'em older than that. These girls seem like they know so much, and some of them do, but they's just girls. Even Lorilee.

I know. I was like that too. She thinks I don't know what she's up to, but it ain't that long ago that I cain't remember hanging out at Dudley's on Friday nights, when I was thirteen and had no business being anywhere near a bar. But back then, nobody cared. Parents drank with their kids, kids with their grandparents, everybody was drinking with everybody else. Nobody was carding nobody. Not that I was going to the dives where my daddy was drinking. No sir. I was going to my own dives! I learned real early which ones had the men who'd buy me drinks and talk to me, talk to me like I knew something about the world and knew what they meant.

That's how things happen. Bad things. But for the grace of God, I did not wind up dead. Bad enough a couple of times somebody got the wrong impression and thought I understood. Got the wrong impression and thought I knew and kept going. And you know how that goes. Became a woman the hard way. Lost my virginity. I know. It's my own damn fault: wrong place at the wrong time. Eighth-, ninth-grader has no business in a bar like that. No crying about it now. Cain't get back what's long gone. Lord knows it was just a matter of who was going to take it. Just happened it was that man, almost my daddy's age. And me stupid and drinking free drinks.

But for the Grace of God, is what I say now. I coulda wound up dead. All those brothers I had and nobody looking out for me.

The first time, well. It hurt, you know. Like ripped me in half. But it's the smell I remember, really. His breath smelled old. It got into every pore of me, like. His stubble rubbed me raw at the side of my neck, and the smell seeped into my skin. Sour-like. It was all over me. Like for days. I ached down below, and I had a headache that didn't quit, but the smell stayed longer. Way longer.

I almost told my mama, but the look on her face as I starting to tell who did it, and I hadn't even told what he did, she knew him, our town being small and all, and her face looked like she didn't know what I was. Looking at me like I was something from the moon. She slapped me first, and told me to shut my mouth, stop talking nonsense, she too busy, cain't I see that?

People, places, things. They will all lead you back to the drink and the drug. I had no business being in a bar at thirteen. You get what you get and you don't get upset, I say now. 'Specially if you go where you ain't supposed to be. You know what they say, "You don't go to a whorehouse to listen to the piano player." Like, if you hang out in a barber shop, you're going to get a haircut. You get the idea. Wrong place, wrong time, all wrong.

The second time—no, I didn't learn. It's true, there was a second time—I didn't try telling nobody, not my mama. She might of noticed my black eye from that time. But by then I was way out of control. Irretrievable as she goes. I was wild. Out all the time. No more school for me. After a few weeks of ninth grade I just disappeared and never went back. Again. Wrong places, wrong people. These old guys—and young ones too—just taking what they's want. Taking with force. I ain't afraid to tell you that I was high all the time after the second one. But for the Grace of God, I say now, but for the Grace of God, there I go.

After a while, it was just easier if I came onto them first, act like I wanted it and wanted it rough-like. Just get it over with. Them older guys—at the end of the day, they just so lazy—they just want some young heifer to climb on top and fuck them. It was just easier to go first, get that shit over with. It wasn't like I was feeling much anyways. I was running too fast back then. After we'd fuck, then I'd get my peace. Then none of that shit mattered for a while.

Roderick and I crashed into each other—we was still kids, really, but we was old kids. Old on the inside. I just needed somebody—I see it now—to fall into, to fold me into him. We met through some bikers, but we was in the same school, supposedly, though neither of us ain't never went no more. He was hanging out with his brother, who was in a club, and I was hanging out with any asshole there who'd have me, and we crashed into each other. Our lives collapsed, two empties, making one big, ginormous hole.

It ain't like it weren't no picnic. 'Specially after we started cooking and dealing ourselves, as I've told you. But at least I wasn't getting dragged out behind some shitty bar, some old pig pulling me by my hair to have his way with me out back. Shit, after a while, Roderick just left me alone anyway. Well. Leave me alone after he'd beat the hell out of me. You know married people. After the kids come, it just ain't the same, and we did all that real fast, used up any chance of togetherness real early. And the truth is, if a beating meant he'd stop bothering me the other way, well, I didn't mind that much. Just leave me alone. I could get through a beating—I'd grown up with a daddy. Me all black and blue sometimes, Roderick couldn't look at me. And I didn't care if nobody was touching me that other way. Real truth is, I was more than not just minding, I was just glad, because the smell done never really went away.

Jesus H. Christ. Would you look at me? I'm going down Memory Lane, and it ain't like it's a good Memory Lane.

I look at these girls here, and I know some of them know. I see that idiot Tad talking, making time, and he don't know I see him—shit, I *smell* him a mile away. I know he ain't no different. He sees them girls and he sees what is his. Their bodies are like open doors to him, and he acts like he gets to pick which one he can walk through. These stupid heifers don't know no better. They volunteer. They may as well wear signs. They don't live in those bodies no more, those wheezy, scarred up, skinny- ass bodies they walk around in. They suck down cigarettes like they might numb it all, but they's just waiting, even if they don't know it, to go back to the old ways because the smell don't ever really go away and you just gotta turn it off somehow.

Me and Sallyanne get them girls back in the house. Ain't nobody happy. Them girls sulk and drop themselves on the chairs in the Group room. Tad's boys slink off into the backyard, start moving timber and cutting down things like they're at war with the ash trees back there. There are a few other twiggy, skinny trees, and some of them boys swipe at them just because. I can hear Tad yelling at them, he's pissed off too, overruled by Sallyanne again.

Sallyanne sits at the head of the Group room and tries to get the girls to focus, and when she sees that they are just far gone, way out there, mooning for them boys, she starts to pray. She seems a little unsteady herself and she calls upon Lord God Almighty, Maker of Heaven and Earth. She calls upon Him and she is raised up. Like she ain't no longer interested in the girls, they too far gone. But she will be taken up. Ascended, like Jesus Christ. She is chanting. Over and over. Calling upon Him. The girls quiet down and stare at her. I admit it: it is creepy but ain't nobody can look away, she might just burst into flames at any point.

Sallyanne raises her arms up and then starts in: "Lord protect this house. Lord protect this house."

She says it with a force ain't none of us seen before. Not in her anyway. Long time ago, I seen it in church, but not since. Not in years. But there she is trance-like, chanting. And maybe because the girls know they ain't going nowhere, that the boys right outside the house might as well be ten miles away, they quiet up.

Then Lorilee starts in: "Protect this house. Lord. Protect this house." She syncs up with Sallyanne. At first, I'm thinking she's making fun, but it don't take long before the girls from her room start in too. They are looking at each other but not looking at each other.

I can't lie. It is like a wave. A wave that carries on and on, and before you know, the whole room is going. The chanting gets louder, and I won't chant, but I ain't leaving, neither. I am glued to the stairs at my usual perch, looking down at the folding chairs. The girls are in they's circle and they ain't slouching no more. They keep going and the room—I don't know, I don't know how to say this—changes. It just feels different-like.

And when it shifts, them girls are in it, they are chanting good. Sallyanne stops. Like she breaks out of it and looks at me like she don't recognize me or them. Then, it's like her face freezes and she don't know where she is.

"Girls! Girls! Stop!" She's in a panic now. "Girls! Stop! Mind yourselves!"

The waves slows, and the girls settle. Well. They settle but they ain't the same. They ain't the restless, mopey heifers they shuffled in like. They are something like whole. I can see that bothers Sallyanne. She ain't a part of it and it's like bugging her. So she calls on one: "Maryanne. You got a brick to drop. Don't you? It's your turn to get honest."

"No, ma'am," this one says. "It ain't my turn."

"I seem to recall, young lady, you have something to get off your chest. I seem to remember you saying something about your daddy's friend the other day, when you and I were having our one-on-one."

And there it is. Sallyanne kills the group. She has pulled out this girl's private pain. She brought it to light, and the energy in the room deflates like a punctured balloon zipping around before it splutters out on the floor.

Sallyanne knows she's won. "Go on, honey. Tell them girls what he done to you. Tell them how you were goading him on until he couldn't not do the wrong thing. Tell him how your daddy nearly killed you both—him for violating his girl, and you for making him. The truth will set you free." Sallyanne looks at me and sniffs hard. Triumph. She's got these little bitches, she tells me without saying anything. "Unless somebody else wants to take her place?" She looks around the room. "Well, bless y'all's heart. Maryanne. Looks like you're up, girl."

The room hushes. Eyes turned to the floor. Every one of them knows it could be her next, so they sacrifice Maryanne. Their silence volunteers her.

There ain't no protection inside this house. Not for nobody.

Sallyanne's got something on everybody here. She's got this sugar-sweet way at first. Gets you talking to her, like she's the first person who's ever listened. In your one-on-one with her, you wind up telling her about all those things you don't never tell nobody.

Well, almost everything. But you tell Sallyanne stuff you wouldn't even tell your own mother, because, well, it ain't like your mama's going to believe you.

Sallyanne knows about my son. She knows. She tells me my guilt is my reminder: the price I pay for my bad ways. She's right. I know. I done so many bad things. It's what I get. But it is my passport to Salvation, she also says. My holy passport. 'Course she don't know that one thing I done, the unforgiveable thing. And she ain't going to know. Everybody's got their limits. 'Specially Christians. They can say "Come all ye sinners" all they want, but even they's got their limits, where they's like, "Um no, We ain't taking that one. No salvation's going help that one." So like I said, Sallyanne don't know everything I've done, and I ain't sure which direction I'll be heading when my time comes. For now, I just follow the Program and hope for the best.

She says the same to the girls about they's guilt. But sometimes—

Sometimes I just ain't sure about that.

Sometimes I think, they's so young. What could they been up to, to feel so guilty-like? It ain't too late for them.

When I ask her, she says, no, maybe it ain't. But evil knows its home and it will keep spreading. That's the thing, she says. It's one thing to be evil, but evil being evil, means it can be catching like a virus. We got to get these girls to come to Jesus. Come to Jesus so he can absolve their sins. That's our real job, she says. When she ain't so perky, she admits, "Might be an exercise in futility, Starlene, but that is our cross to bear. Maybe best we can do is give them a place to take a break, a place where they won't be bothered by them other things out there."

A place where I won't be bothered neither. Amen, I say. That's enough for me.

Lorilee is fully at home here at Second Chance now. Like the other girls, she's got the routine: morning, noon, and night. Each day folds into the next so seamless it ain't easy to tell them apart. The only day that is clear is Saturday, when Sallyanne goes home to see her people. It's her day off, and I ain't even sure where her people are, since she's originally from eastern Louisiana, and that ain't like a day's drive. And frankly, Tad and her daddy, The Reverend, are right here in Texas. Shit. They're right here in this *town*. She's always back for Sunday service, which we have here now—we don't take the girls off to no church anywhere, but Sallyanne's daddy is a preacher and he's been coming here and giving the Word. Ever since the boys were here, Sallyanne has amped up the Salvation effort. I guess her daddy's too old to have his own parish and maybe the geriatric ward is all full up and she's keeping the old coot busy—because he's older than the Lord himself. He forgets what he's saying sometimes, and sometimes it sounds like he's just making shit up. And just little things he says, drives me crazy:

"Be afraid, little flock, for it is your Father's good pleasure to give you the kingdom!"

Or

"And you who were once estranged and hostile in mind, doing evil deeds, he has now reconciled in his fleshly body through death, but you ain't holy and blameless and irreproachable before him."

Them girls so stupid they don't even notice. And I know it ain't from not hearing scripture they whole lives. We are all raised the same around here. I know I was. Some of the best lines in the Bible and this old geezer is mixing them all up.

And I wouldn't care, but Sallyanne thinks getting her daddy in to preach could maybe redeem them girls. There might be a chance they could come to believe they could be saved. Like I said. Sometimes I wonder. I didn't always think so. I admit it. But they ain't to blame for some of what's been done to them. They's just girls. I know. I was like them too. Everybody out there acts like you just have to follow what they say. That you just are there for what they want to do. I remember. Like if you say no, they still say yes. If you say stop, they say go. People just think you're there for their pleasure and whatnot. I know. I been there. After a while, a body just gets tired of it, I think. A body just gets tired of being used all the time. And after a while, you just get mean, and nobody can tell why. You are mean on the outside because of the hurt and what have you on the inside. And sometimes you got to take matters in your own hands to make it stop. I know. I been there too. So maybe this is them girls' chance. Ain't nobody here to be bothering a body, wanting to use you just because you're there. You're left in peace, and maybe redemption. I really don't know.

So when one day this preacher miss-says something from Revelations, I don't say nothing. There ain't no harm in it. Them girls ain't really listening anyway. I wasn't going to be the one to say so. I seen Sallyanne closing her eyes while this old joker rattles on, coughing, clearing his throat, staring down at them girls with his crooked eye.

He yells out at them: *"I saw no temple in the city, for its temple is the Lord God the Almighty and the Lamb. And the city needs the sun or moon to shine on it, for the glory of God is its light, and its lamp is the Lamb. The nations will walk by its light, and the kings of the earth will bring their glory into it. Its gates will never be shut by day—and there will be night there.*

"You know what that means, y'all? It means if you don't do the right thing, the sun will die, the moon will die, and all a darkness will consume the earth. That means, the whole world is watching you, watching you girls to do the right thing, to come outta your evil ways," he says.

"No, it don't," Lorilee says from one of the folding chairs, which are lined up like church pews. "That ain't the line." Right in the middle of things she says it.

Jesus H. Christ, I think, this girl don't know no manners. She is right, of course, but doing the right thing is shutting up and letting the man talk. He is a preacher, for Chrissake!

"It doesn't make any sense the way you're saying it," she says. Which it doesn't, but now Sallyanne starts to open her eyes, her revelry done interrupted.

These days, I stay far away from this she-devil. I keep my eye on Lorilee, always making sure I know where she is in a room, but I stay way away from her trouble- making self. I know the girls still don't like her, but I see sometimes some of them talk to her, getting deeper into that devil's web. Miss Smartypants-Don't-I-Jis-Know- Everything.

That preacher draws himself up, and I swear if he ain't transformed like from the reed he was to a great wall. He gathers his voice like, and a great boom echoes through the room: "Silence, child! Know thy place!"

Sallyanne doesn't know what the fuck. She's looking around, and getting smaller and smaller. Suddenly she's looking like a little girl. She knows that voice. She knows that voice, like I know the sound of the belt. She knows what comes after the voice, and she is small, so so small, she cannot save this girl from what is coming.

I think, No, I ain't doing this. I ain't getting involved.

"Repent!" He yells at Lorilee, but she just crosses her arms. He don't know what he's up against, and as much as I know it would be better to stand up and get her out, I cain't look away, and I cain't help her. Ain't nobody here can.

"That's not what it says." She's stubborn-like. I'll give her that.

Them other girls don't say nothing. They know that voice too. They either know that voice or they just don't care—and really, it could go either way.

"Repent woman! Harlot! Daughter of Jezebel!"

"What the fuck?" she says.

Sallyanne comes to, out of her stupor. "Lorilee!"

"You will be dealt with, sinner! You will reap what you sow." He slams the Bible on a folding chair and it pops open again.

"Lorilee. Stop this. Church is over. The service is over." Sallyanne starts to get up.

"Sally. Sit your ass down," he says. "Sit your goddamn ass down, before I whoop you, girl. This is how these whores got outta control—from your leniency!"

"You can't whip her," Lorilee says.

The old man done spun around and he's staring at her now. "She is my flesh and blood. She done come from my side. I may do with her as I please." Lorilee rolls her eyes and looks around, but ain't none of them girls looks back, their eyes fixed on the floor. The old man's voice sounds like it's coming from somewhere else, like from outside, and he's got all these girls frozen to them folding chairs—if they didn't care before, they are caring now. I ain't the only one, but my hands, my fingers, get a little nervous-like, shaky. And he ain't said it yet, but I can feel what's coming next. I feel it like the electricity in the air before a Texas storm.

"Shut up, Lorilee," Terri says. "Just shut up already."

I got to stop this. I peel myself off the steps. I can barely get the old legs going, but I walk to Lorilee, who is leaning forward in her seat. She has grown tall even though she is sitting.

"Come on, girl," I say. "Let's go."

"No, fuck that. I'm not going anywhere this time. I want to see what this old asshole is going to do."

"Come on, girl. Let's go. You done enough for one day."

"I think Lorilee has a brick to drop," the Cheerleader starts in, but even she's not sounding all that sure this is the time to pick on this girl.

"I think she's gotta Jesus issue." Crystal tries, too, but she backs down when Maryanne tells her to shut up.

I'm pulling on Lorilee's arm and it's the first time I've touched her since she worked in the kitchen. Her skin is hot, like not-normal hot, and I let go when I remember who she is.

That other one, Summer, the one who's always lurk-ing around with her nose in that notebook, writing down everything we do, gets in it now. She yells like she's testing out a new voice: "Y'all leave her alone."

Lorilee pivots real fast. "Stay out of this."

"Shut up." Summer stands up and I'm not sure who she's talking to now.

"Sally," the old man booms and I don't know where that voice is still coming from because this guy is all skin and bones. "Sally!" He barks commands at her. "Heed your flock! Heed your flock! Devil behind us!" He turns to Lorilee. "Devil get behind me," he says. "Get behind me."

Well, that Lorilee starts cracking up, laughing out loud, like she's at the picture house or something. If you didn't think she was a demon yet, what with the Reverend screaming Devil and whatnot at her, calling her by her real name, the sound of that laugh made you know now. There ain't no question in ole Starlene's mind. This girl is laughing out loud, when every other girl, every other female, in that room is sweating it out, terror-frozen, that the old violences they left out there, way back home, that they trusted to leave them alone for a while, had finally found them again. The temperature in the room is hot— it's a hot day anyway—but this girl's devil laugh makes the walls bend. Some of them other girls are crying. But this one, she heads toward the door, still laughing. "This place," she spits through laughs. "You're all fucking crazy."

That old preacher man, he weren't used to no she-devil's disrespect. Not like that heifer. So he done roars "Repent sinner!" to nothing. Lorilee keeps walking like she don't even hear the old fuck.

"Daddy!" Sallyanne jumps up. And this is where everything goes wrong, where it all starts to go as bad as bad can get, where ain't nobody can turn back the time on this one and all that came after. Sallyanne reaches for him. Both arms out like she's gonna hug or tackle him. "Daddy!" Then he strikes her so fast I wouldn't've believed it with my own eyes. He strikes her quick and hard with his open hand like he's been doing it every day of his life, and she topples into some of the girls sitting on folding chairs. They don't know what to do. They's so wigged out, they push her off-like, trying to make her stand on her own, but as soon as Sallyanne makes it almost up, she loses her balance and winds up on hands and knees.

I will tell you this: I cain't even look at her. Seeing her there on the floor. Like a dog, hands and knees. Now Sallyanne's crying, Daddy Daddy Daddy. And I just cain't. Ain't nobody can. It's too much.

"Git yer ass up," he says to her. "Git up, woman. Git up before I whoop you good in front of this whorehouse. Git up or they's going to see what really happens to a fallen woman."

Sallyanne rouses. Somehow the horse picture on her sweatshirt got some gray smudge on it now. But she ain't moving fast enough for the old man who's come to life in front of us, yelling fire and brimstone and whatnot.

"Git up, woman. You won't heed your flock? Then I'll done teach you, girl."

Sallyanne pulls herself up, not looking at us neither, I'm sure. I'm just staring at her feet now. I just cain't look her in the face. That old man steers her out the hallway that leads to Sallyanne's office, on the other side of the house. He walks her out like he owns her. Them other girls are paralyzed. Stricken like with lightning. Pillars of stone and fear. Except for that she-devil. She's got her hand on the door knob up the steps on the other side of the room and never looks back. She don't care what is in that Group room behind her, don't care nothin' for the hope that starts bleeding out from these girls. There ain't no way to undone what she's done in there. Them girls ain't never going to be the same.

Lorilee is just about out the other door, and a young woman is standing there. Even Lorilee seems surprised because she jumps back a little. This woman has jeans on, but they're the maternity kind, with the stretchy part pulled over the huge, round ball in front of her. Her small t-shirt has inched up just at the waistband.

She's holding papers and folders and says, "I thought I heard y'all here." She's smiling, too, because she knows she's interrupting something. Looks happy about it, too.

And then I remember her—she used to be in the old house. She was young and they moved her into the main office as some kind of secretary. Some of the girls look up and cry out her name: "Marla!" They call to her not like a hello, more like a help-us kind of way.

Lorilee slips past her. Summer follows while everyone else is staring at Marla. I bet them two will have a good laugh out there, laughing at us all the way.

"I have some things to drop off." She holds up the pile in her hands. "Y'all having Group? Sorry—it sounded like a party." She's looking around at the disorder and sees she don't know what's going on. But this girl ain't surprised by nothing no more. She just waits. I'm standing there in the middle of the room. Somehow some of those folding chairs, which were in rows, got turned over. The old man has slammed the door at the other side of the room and he has drugged Sallyanne somewheres outside. I hear one more door slam and a woman's scream that I will hear in my ears till the end of my days.

Some of the girls are out and out crying now, and
some others have left—I don't know where, but the smell of
cigarette smoke coming through the windows tells me they
ain't gone far. And of course not: none of them ain't going
nowhere. They stay here, day after day, nobody leaves, ain't
nobody got a better place to go. They will stay here, even
though all hope is dead now. I peek out the back window
and I see Lorilee out there too, lighting up, and I know: this
is the beginning of the end.

"Come on, Marla," I say. "What do you want?"

Second Chance Girls

Why did she have to start something? She ruined
everything. Why'd she have to open her mouth? Everybody knew the preacher was making shit up and forget-
ting scripture. Why couldn't she just leave well enough
alone? Look what she did. Miss Sallyanne on her hands
and knees. Miss Sallyanne humiliated. Because of this girl.
Always have to open her mouth. Say the thing nobody else
would. And now what? What do we do? Who will save us
now?

We were all out on the back patio. Even Summer. This
time she didn't sneak off to write it all down. She thought we
didn't know what she did, but we knew. She recorded it all.
Back then, we had no idea why, but now we know. Now we
see why the words must come. But that day, even she was
outside, sucking down cigarettes like the rest of us, trying to
suffocate the despair.

Nobody was crying anymore. Nobody was doing anything. Just sitting. Sitting and smoking. Not talking about
what we'd seen.

Miss Sallyanne was still inside, placating that creepy preacher—creepy *father*, actually. We all heard her say *Daddy*! after he made her leave the room, yelling about hellfire and damnation and the four horsemen and the end of time.

"Wait till Judgement!" We heard him yell at her. "You will be called to account, woman." Then her scream. The excruciating scream that gave way to sudden quiet. Then things were silent, unnaturally so, and we couldn't make out what was happening.

Starlene shuffled us further to the edge of the patio, away from the house, like she was a cop, "Come on, girls, go on out. It's between Miss Sallyanne and her daddy. Mind your business. Have your smokes."

Marla came out too. She lay a manila folder stuffed with paper on the picnic table and started to light up, but then Starlene said, "Sugar, you smoking for two now?"

Marla put one hand over her huge belly and then dropped the cig back into her pack. "Look who's talking. The Great Mother."

"Ain't you got some business to get back to?" Starlene snapped.

Marla glared and picked up the bulging folder. She waddled back into the house. Her hands empty when she returned. She nodded to a couple of the girls without talking and loaded herself into a little green Chevette. Starlene watched after her until the Chevette reversed over the driveway gravel.

"Who was that?" Lorilee asked when Starlene disappeared through the back door.

"You say something?" Terri barked at Lorilee. "Ain't you done enough?"

"What?"

"You gotta just keep up asking things. You don't know? You don't see around you?"

Lorilee almost looked like she was smirking. "I ain't done anything y'all didn't do to yourselves."

"What the fuck?" Crystal said what we were all thinking. That Lorilee. Always speaking in crazy talk.

"Well?" Lorilee was waiting.

"Well what?" Magda had been sitting on the picnic table, pulling at loose threads fraying from the hole in the knee of her jeans. She yanked one off.

"Who's the pregnant girl?"

Some of us who'd been around a while remembered Marla from the old house, when we lived with boys.

"She's from the Ash House," Maryanne finally said.

"The Ash House," Crystal said. "That was the first place, before Second Chance."

"The *Ash* House? Jesus. That sounds grim." Lorilee dragged on her cigarette.

"Named for the tree," Kimberly butted in. "Duh." She rolled her eyes.

"I see somebody," Lorilee said to no one and got up and walked to the side of the yard, then out of sight. We were glad she walked away. We didn't care what she saw.

"Some of us used to be there, but they moved us to this house last year." Crystal bit off a fingernail as she said this and then spit it out.

"Since last year?" Summer's eyes opened wide and round. "Y'all been here since last year?"

"Not all of us." Terri looked up at her.

"Some of us have been. Yeah." Crystal looked over at Magda. "Not sure any of us are ever going to leave. It's like the Hotel California in Texas: '*you can check in . . . but you can never leave!*'" Crystal high-fived Kimberly. We laughed.

Summer was looking at Crystal. "Well, somebody's left. Somebody's had to have gone."

Probably someone had left, but none of us had, and nobody—not Miss Sallyanne, not Tad, and not Starlene—had given anybody any sign of when a body could go home.

"So y'all just wait?" The ash at the end of Summer's cigarette had grown long and looked like it would crumble off the tip at any second.

Kimberly lit another cigarette with the end of a butt. Streams of gray smoke spread softly from her nose. "Don't you cause fucking trouble too," she said.

Summer turned away from her.

"Girl. You are trying my last nerve." Kimberly stood up but faced Crystal as she said it.

"Me?" Crystal said.

"Jesus. Am I talking to you?" Kimberly pointed to Summer.

"Oh!" Crystal nodded.

"I ain't staying forever," Maryanne said. She'd been petting the dog this whole time. "I need to get home. And it just ain't possible that we cain't never go home. They cain't keep us forever. We ain't here forever."

"Oh, you're here forever," said Lorilee, as she re-emerged from the other side of the house. She was smiling. What was she up to? What was that girl ever up to?

"You're so fucking weird." Kimberly rolled her eyes.

"I know." Lorilee winked at Summer. We saw her.

"Marla left," Magda volunteered.

"We *thought* she left," Kimberly corrected. "She just got knocked up and they stuck her with the retard in the office. Then they moved the rest of y'all here."

"When did you live with her?" Lorilee ignored Kimberly. "Like, when did you know Marla?"

"I was at the Ash House, let me see, when she came in." Crystal had started drawing circles in the dust on the cement patio with her tennis shoe. "Marla was like totally scared, and tiny. Oh my word. Totally tiny. Not like now," she dropped her head down to study the dusty circles.

"Holy shit, she is totally not tiny now. Did you see her?" Magda jumped in. "I will fucking die before any man does that to me."

Some of us laughed. At least we were not talking about Miss Sallyanne.

"It ain't so bad," Carla Bobby said. "It feels nice in a way."

"What? *Getting* pregnant?" Kimberly slapped palms with Crystal.

Summer muttered something that sounded like "idiot."

"No. Being pregnant. It's beautiful."

"When was that?" Lorilee looked at all of us. Her hands were on her hips and she was standing, so she gave the impression that she was bearing down on us. No one answered at first. "When was Marla and y'all who lived at the Ash House there?"

"I don't know, last year some time. I forget," Maryanne said.

"Think."

"I lose track of time here. Days are like the flows in a river now."

"It couldn't have been a year ago."

"I'm thinking. No. It couldn't have been a year ago. You're right. What the fuck does it matter?" Crystal looked at Kimberly for support. "Ain't no sense of time here, but it's even worse when you're still not done detoxing."

"Well, now. Maybe it was a year? We've been here not quite a year yet. Is that right?" Maryanne said.

We were all shrugging. Maybe. The currents of time ebbed and flowed, one into the next, no beginning and no end, at the Second Chance Home for Girls.

"What holiday was it near?" Lorilee persisted.

"The Fourth of July. Yeah. I got in around then. I remember the fireworks we heard from across town got to my nerves. I couldn't sleep. But I couldn't really sleep anyway." Magda put one finger to her mouth.

"That was like 10-11 months ago." Lorilee counted on her fingers, still holding a burning cigarette between two of them.

"Sallyanne's boy didn't work at the Ash House back then," Crystal said. "He only came to work when the girls got moved into this house. They'd already moved Marla. Remember?"

"Oh my word. It couldn't have been him." Kimberly's eyes got big.

"Who then?" Summer was the first to ask it.

"She was hanging around that boy from Ardmore," Maryanne said. "At the Ash House. Not here."

"No, she didn't really like him. It was more like he was hanging around her." When Carla Bobby reminded us, the few that had been there had to agree: that boy trailed Marla like a puppy.

"Was it John?" Crystal asked.

We all got quiet when somebody said this, because we knew there was John who came with the other boys to work at Second Chance, the tall kid with the shoulders who "belonged" to Kimberly. Somehow she had a claim on him, though nobody got to hook up with anybody else when the boys had come by. Starlene had made sure of that.

"He didn't live there then, when we were there," somebody said.

"Who could it have been then?" Kimberly asked. "She didn't stay in the house anymore, once they got her working in the office."

"What if was Tad!" Maryanne broke out in a laugh. "Oh." The laugh stopped midway.

"I'm sure Tad did not fuck that girl." Kimberly blew her smoke out from her mouth. She held one elbow balanced upright in the palm of her hand.

"Why are you so sure? Because he doesn't want you?" Lorilee said to Kimberly.

"Am I talking to you?" Kimberly's eyes were staring upward, not at Lorilee as she spoke to her, not at anyone actually.

"OK, I'm out. See y'all later." Summer looked at Lorilee and nodded. She reached for the screen door but dropped her hand and turned back. Summer said to everyone, but she was looking only at Lorilee: "You know, there was another girl I'd heard. She got pregnant too."

"Where'd she go?"

"Don't know."

"Maybe they let her leave," Summer said.

"What about the baby?"

"I heard she gave it up and left the Ash house anyway," Terri said.

"That an option?" Lorilee turned to look at her. "Not keeping it?"

"Catholic," somebody else broke in.

"Who's Catholic here?" Kimberly asked. "Ain't no Romans here. Only Indians are. And they're all on the rez."

"Not all are on the rez," Magda said between her teeth. Kimberly did not see her glaring but we did.

"Miss Sallyanne?" Maryanne asked. "Maybe Miss Sallyanne made her get rid of it. Is that even legal?" Sallyanne's name hovered over us. We were not going to talk about what we just saw and heard.

"What about Marla?" Summer said. "What's going to happen to her and her baby?"

"Oh, they're keeping that one," Maryanne said.

"I heard she was going to marry Miss Sallyanne's boy," Carla Bobby, who'd been silent up until now, said.

"Maybe Marla was in love," Terri sighed.

"That girl ain't in love." Lorilee pushed off from the bench she was sitting in, making like to go inside. "And ain't nobody loves that girl either."

"How do you know?" Kimberly turned toward her, the edge in her voice.

"She look happy to you?" Lorilee then added, "she ain't staying."

"Where she going to go?" Kimberly wouldn't let up.

"Anywhere else. Just wait."

Summer poked her head out the back door. "Lorilee. Starlene needs you in the kitchen. Dinner prep."

"Well, ladies. It's been real." Lorilee put her cigarette out and followed Summer inside.

"That fucking Lorilee. I swear, everytime she opens her mouth, I just, I don't know, I get the shivers. She just rubs me the wrong way. Don't she? Ain't no telling what shit's going to come out of her mouth." Kimberly put out her cigarette butt with the tip of her tennis shoe. "She's fucking ruining everything."

Crystal's head bobbed as if she'd had the same thought all along.

"That fucking girl," Terri shook her head.

"Bitch." Magda spit onto the patio cement, and that's when we knew what we were going to do.

Swords

June 1, 1986

O God. O God. What I saw today. How do I say what happened? How do I write what nobody could say afterward?

The old preacher showed his real self. Just when somebody— some girl—no, not just any girl, but Lorilee started to stand up to him, just to ask him something simple—he lets loose and starts swearing Hellfire and Damnation at us. I know I heard a Jezebel in there too. Jezebel! Miss Sallyanne broke down and started to cry: Daddy! That old fart is her *father*. Yuck. All of a sudden she was crying like a little girl, begging him to stop yelling. But then she'd switch and start yelling at Lorilee to stop provoking the old man. But then. But then. Jesus. How do I say this? Did this really happen? Miss Sally-anne starts to go to him, like to put her arms around the old man or something and he hits her. *He hits her*. He hits her so hard that she crashes into Carla Bobby and Maryanne, and they like don't know what to do. They like try to get her up but it's more like pushing her off and Sallyanne falls onto her knees. She's on her fucking knees. And she looks like she is begging him, and he, this old skinny piece of shit, looks like he'd beat her senseless if he thought he could get away with it. So then Miss Sallyanne's on her knees, and she really is begging him. Seeing her like that, I don't know, I wanted her to beg, to ask, to make him stop. But the truth is, she wasn't asking. She was getting into a position. If that makes sense. Because—and this is where it started to get weird, or really weird (it was all already weird)—it looked like after he hit her, it looked like he was just getting started. And she knew it. He dragged her out of that room and he hit her—like he must've been her whole life. Weird with her being an adult and all. There was one loud scream and then nothing.

But it was Lorilee that started it. She did it.

She asked the questions.

She wouldn't stop, even though she knew. I think she knew Miss Sallyanne would break. I think *that* is what she wanted, why she kept pushing, provoking-like, the old man. The old, crazy man. She doesn't care about scripture, the Bible. She just can't stop herself from scratching at the surface of things.

So she did it. That Lorilee.

What do we do now? How am I going to get to go home with Miss Sallyanne like that?

All this happened and then a pregnant girl showed up. She like comes to the door like a ghost, and I swear if Miss Sallyanne nearly swooned like she'd seen one.

This girl's showing up seemed to add a new layer to the craziness. Something didn't seem right. She looked younger than me.

Later, out back, when we went out for a smoke, some of the girls who've been here a while said they knew the girl from the other house—the house where the boys are now, but it was like called something else back when they all lived there. The Ash House. I guess for all the trees over there. That's what somebody said. But it sounds like this place, a place where the elephants go to die. Or we do.

I think I am the only one who feels like she is dying here. I guess I am the elephant.

Jesus. What the fuck am I going to do now? Here comes Crystal. I have to go.

(Later)

Lorilee stopped me during clean up (somehow I always get clean up after dinner) while I was wiping down the dining tables. She says, What'd you think of that old man?

I said, I don't know.

You don't know? You don't have an opinion?

I said, no. I don't.

She looked at me queer-like. Jesus. Those eyes. I feel like she is looking for something hard, those eyes poking and prodding like fingers.

What? I said.

Nothing, she said. I just thought you knew. Knew what?

You know.

Fuck off, I said. I don't have time for your bullshit. I got to finish this.

Her face squinched up and I felt bad. What does that girl want from me? She keeps trying to hanging around, like we're friends or something, and I don't know, sometimes she's all right. But she's just going to ruin me having any friends at this place. It's bad enough these girls think she has already ruined everything (I do too). Nobody else likes her. She's like bad luck or something. But I felt a little bad for telling her to fuck off, though not bad enough to go up to her later and say sorry.

Nighttime

I can't fucking sleep. I hear Miss Sallyanne sobbing or moaning or something in her room—it's down the hall from ours. I can't think about her. If I do, I'll never sleep.

I don't know what Lorilee meant before, *she thought I knew*. Knew what? I stopped going to school once Tommy was gone. I never finished 10th grade. And the longer I'm here, the slower my brain seems. I don't know anything anymore. I used to like school.

I used to like school, and then I didn't, and then Tommy came around and I wanted to go to see him.

I loved to see him out in the world. I liked looking over at him during breaks between class periods, when we all moved down the hallways like fish in a stream to our next classes. I'd walk by him in the hall on my way to Bio, and he'd be hanging out with some guys, and I knew he saw me, that his eyes were on me, as soon as I passed. Sometimes I'd watch his eyes, our eyes connecting, and sometimes I'd pretend like I didn't see him—which is stupid, now I see, because of course I saw him, of course he knew. But he'd do the same thing sometimes, pretend like he didn't see me, like he didn't need me too.

It was like a game to play, because I always saw him after school. We'd be alone again in our own world and even though he pretended not to, I knew he could see me. He needed me as much as I needed him.

I would give anything to go back in time. Just for one day. Go back, way far away from this place.

June 2, 1986

Sometimes I wonder why I don't miss Tommy more. It's like I don't feel that much anymore. I remember things but it's like watching a movie of somebody else's life. It's not even like a whole movie. Just parts. The good parts. I guess what I don't get is how can I go from being with someone so much, and wanting to be around only him, to feeling almost nothing with a bunch of strangers?

It's not like I was getting high so much that I didn't feel back then. And same for him too. We weren't high *all* the time. I never thought Tommy would say he loved me, and he didn't say it more than once in words, but he did in other ways. Like when he found out I fucked that guy Chris—which was so stupid and lame but it was enough to bother Tommy. Tommy, who said we were just hanging out with each other, that *we* were no big deal, not a thing, especially since our parents were a thing. We were like them: on the sly, he said. Nobody could know. Then I hooked up with Chris, just because—insurance, I guess— and Tommy found out and put a hole in his bedroom wall.

I didn't know why nobody could know. I think about it now, and I don't know why he didn't want people to know he was with me, and not just in the hanging out way, but in the everyday way. Whatever happened in the day, he wound up coming by to find me—at my house, at my afterschool job. Sometimes at the dry cleaner where I worked, he'd come by, and oh man, Freya would be eyeballing him something fierce, and I knew she was thinking like, *Get that derelict out of here*. In his concert shirts and long hair. Tommy wasn't any dry cleaning customer! That used to make us crack up. That and the fumes in that place! We both would try to get high inhaling them, but I was there nearly every day after school and on Saturdays, too, inhaling the fumes, and nothing ever happened to me. (Well. Maybe something did. I wound up here, didn't I? Ha ha ha.)

One day Tommy was late and he knocked on my door. It was after dinner, and my mom was already out (probably with his dad!). I opened the front door and at first I wasn't sure because there was a shadow over his face, but when he came inside my house, I could see he had a black eye. It wasn't the worst but it was hard to look at. He hadn't been in school all day, which wasn't anything new, so I didn't really think about him not being there. But he got hit on the way into school, he said. Got into a fight with a black boy named Kevin Smith. And as soon as he said Kevin's name, I kind of shuddered because I knew Kevin could've fucked him up even worse than he did. Kevin was in awesome shape, like a boxer, and walked around like he was ready for a day like today. But Tommy never told me what they said, or how it started and I guess Kevin only had to hit him once for Tommy to walk away with his pride mostly hurt.

But that's how I knew he loved me. I could feel how embarrassed he was. He walked past me in the front hallway and into the den. Tommy didn't say much after that. He threw himself onto the old couch and started watching TV. Normally, I would curl up next to him, put my bare feet into his lap and my shoulder under his, but this time I just sat next to him, lit up a cigarette and stared at the TV too. Carol Burnett was on.

He came to me that night. That's how I knew. He didn't want to get high. He didn't want to fuck. He just wanted to sit with me and watch TV. And that's how I knew. There was nowhere else he wanted to be but with me.

June 3, 1986

Sometimes I get this feeling—it's an old feeling and it's a good feeling—like I know this place. Like I've been here at Second Chance before. It's more like I can remember this place, not the real place, but what I feel when I look at the ranch out back, the horizon, the Ash trees. It happens at dusk, at the change of day, when the sun starts to go down. I feel like I have always known this place, like I have come here and it feels almost like a relief, like I've been waiting all my life to remember this place. It's not the house itself (and don't get me wrong: I still want to leave!). It's in the dusk air that settles on the pasture beyond the fence. It's in the purples and blues that rise into the dark sky. One thing's for sure: there isn't any place with a sky like Texas. It stretches over the land and draws color up from it and then covers the ranches and highways and houses with the deepest blacks at night. I think there are more stars in the sky over Texas than anywhere else in the world. You don't really need any lights outside. The stars light up the night. They are busy, far away above us, and when the moon gets involved, the light that shines down is so bright, it looks like you can walk on its beams.

The night sky brings quiet like you've never known before—even if there is still some noise in the house, even if you can hear the cars on the road in the distance. The quiet isn't the kind that drives you crazy. When dusk comes, I feel a little cozy, because I know what is coming.

I stay up, here, writing, as long as I can—it doesn't matter how tired I am during the day. The days are the same anyway: chores, Group, sometimes church, sometimes school. The only real changes each day are what Starlene makes for dinner: chicken fried steak or spaghetti, corn or peas.

When I write at night, I can hear better. I hear the day, who I saw, what they said. I remember things, too. Like Tommy. I remember we were happy for a while. I remember killing all kinds of time, like we had forever, lying on his bed and him playing guitar sitting on that old kitchen stool he kept in his room. I wouldn't even be looking at him—it wouldn't matter, because he wasn't looking at me anyway, so into his playing. I'd just stare up at the ceiling, looking for patterns in the paint, a crack maybe, like I could see the future, if I stared long enough.

Sometimes I thought I did. I'd see pictures. They'd drift in and out of my mind—I didn't really see them. More like, I saw things that I didn't really see. Which is why I think I feel like I've been here, in this place, looking out at this horizon, before. It's happening again. The pictures and the feelings are coming back, like they are dreams and not real sometimes. The pictures just flash, kind of gently, in and out, sometimes over and over a little—and sometimes I remember and they stay with me, and sometimes they don't.

I saw the end with Tommy. I always knew. That's the truth. I couldn't see how, but I knew somehow that he and me would not always be together. I just never imagined I'd wind up stuck in a place like this.

June 4, 1986

It is hot as fuck out today. I packed mostly jeans and long-sleeved shirts when I came to Second Chance. I am never one of those girls who's like prepared for anything. I always travel light. (Like I ever go anywhere! Ha ha ha!) But shit, I don't have anything I need.

The other girls somehow knew to bring bathing suits and they're all laying out right now on towels. What the hell? Who brings a bathing suit to a place like this? They said, Group and work, that's what we're going to be doing. I was still scrubbing the toilet in the other bathroom, and everyone else whizzed through their work and stripped down out there.

OK, it's not like they were able to hang out for long. Before you knew it, Starlene had run out, yelling about what lazy heifers they were. It's like she took it really personal that they'd all given up doing their work for the sun.

(While the other girls were getting dressed again, Lorilee pulled me aside. She tried to tell me something. She said she met somebody on the road the other day. While we were all talking on the back patio. She tried to tell me, but then Starlene came charging and yelling at us too, telling me to get to work and not be a lazy heifer. So I have to remember to ask Lorilee the rest.)

I decided I will write down the pictures I see in my mind's eye, because I forget to write them down, and then they go away after a few days. They go away and I feel like I missed something important. I see the pictures when I am not trying, like when I'm looking out at the stars or staring in the almost-dried up stream at the far end of the yard, the one that divides us from the western pasture. I see when I don't try. I see and I don't know what.

A motor bike—like a racing motorcycle. I didn't see who was riding. But I saw it going. In motion-like. Going somewhere. Going somewhere not here.

That was last night's picture. I was staring at the stars from my bed—I can see them over the horizon, if I lay my head down. I was trying to sleep after writing.

I don't know what it means. I still see it. The picture stays with me for a few days and then it fades. Maybe writing it will help.

P.S. Nobody is talking about the preacher and Miss Sallyanne. It's like it never happened, even though she's walking around with a puffy wrist and dark purple bruises up her arm. Something's not right with her jaw, either. I hate looking at her now. I'm trying just to stay out of her way.

June 5, 1986

Maryanne was playing Ozzy this morning. Woke me up. I was mad at first, and then I realized that I had long overslept, which like never happens to me. She was already showered. And Crystal and Lorilee were already dressed and out of the room. I don't know how I missed Wake-Up, but there it is. I was late.

All day I felt like I was late, too. Like somehow the gears of the day were not catching my gears and I was off, my own gears turning on their own time. I wasn't slow or even late to everything—I mean, it would be hard to be late, since we don't ever go anywhere. But I was just off. My time, my inside clock, was just off. It felt like I was reset to somebody else's rhythm.

Lorilee seemed to know it.

You ain't never going to see him again, she said. Her face was like real close to mine.

Who?

That guy you're still thinking about.

I looked at her real close. What guy?

She looked back at me, waiting-like. I'm just saying, she said.

Saying what? I said. If you are going to say something, just say it out right straight.

I was on my stomach on my bed, propped up on my elbows, so I was eye-level with her. Then I sat up, way up higher now. Lorilee was just standing there. She didn't seem to care or be impressed that I'd grown taller just talking to her.

What are you writing? She asked.

Nothing.

Don't look like nothing to me. You write about him. Would you quit? No.

Don't lie.

This girl, I thought.

She just waited.

Yes, I said. OK. Yes, I said again.

You ain't going to see him.

I'm going to go home, I said.

Why? She looked at me. You miss home, she said after a time. You miss him.

All the time.

Yeah, she looked like she was thinking about something. I'm going out for a smoke. Want to come? She waited for me to tuck my notebook under my pillow. I jumped off my bed. I know she saw where I put it, but I don't know. I think it's OK.

I pretended not to care that Kimberly and her roommates were staring at us when we came out on the patio. I knew I'd hear it later.

We sat on the picnic table top with our feet on the bench, with our backs to everybody. So for a little while I wouldn't have to think about those other bitches talking and asking me what was up with Lorilee. Not like they couldn't have figured it out themselves. They just as easily could have talked to her. But they almost never did. Sometimes they included her, because it was the thing to do and we were all getting into something. Like the time we all wound up singing "Jessie's Girl." We were all out back that night having one last smoke and the song came on the radio, and we all started chiming in, all knowing the words, after pretending since junior high school like we didn't. Lorilee was there. I think she was singing too. I didn't really look over, but I remember she was out there, so she probably was. Anyway, nobody cared that she was. But usually they did care. Usually they all just seemed like hyper-aware when she was around. No one was going to exclude her outright. You could get time out—

like demerits, days taken off your discharge date (not that anybody ever knew when that would be). Usually, though, the girls just ignored her. They pretended they didn't hear her questions right away. They looked away from her eyes, which seemed like they could see right through everything. They waited until she walked away to keep talking about the days those boys that came to clean up the yard and when they were coming back.

So I knew I'd hear it later when I went out there with her. I'd have to think of something to say. And I would. I am good like that, with words. I can find them when I need them—which isn't bad for someone who hasn't been in real school for a while. I was always good at English.

Lorilee seems to get me, weird as she is. She like sees me. No, better yet: she sees Tommy. She knows. She knows I belonged to someone out there, and I don't know why but when she said that I wouldn't even see him, I didn't want to pretend anymore like I didn't know. It was almost OK, even though it isn't. So I went with her and I wasn't afraid of what other people said. For a little while, anyway.

June 6, 1986

Nothing, I said, when Kimberly and Crystal wanted to know what we talked about. I'd avoided them all night until vespers, knowing, of course, they wanted to know. They all wanted to know what me and Lorilee talked about.

Nothing, my ass, Crystal said.

Tell, Carla Bobby gave me a little shove.

It was nothing, I said. Talking about the dog or something.

We were heading back to our rooms for the night, and I heard Kimberly behind us say, I swear sometimes that Lorilee gives me the creeps. Feels like she's laughing at all of us, when we're just trying to do the right thing and get sober. Don't you think so, Summer?

Yes, I said over my shoulder, but I kept walking. Sometimes, I swear. I just wish she'd just disappear. Right,

Crystal? Like she ruins everything, Kimberly said loud enough for me to hear. Just sometimes, I don't know, I wish she'd just, like, leave or—Oh Lord forgive me—die or something. Is that bad that I said that?

No, I think the same thing sometimes. Crystal coughed up something and spit it to the floor.

You ain't going to tell her what we said, are you?

No.

Good. Because sometimes people just say all kinds of things.

Right. I just wanted to get in my bed then. I wanted the day to end.

But even then, when everyone else seemed to be asleep, Crystal started whispering from one of the beds down below, asking me again about what Lorilee and I were saying before.

Nothing! I said. Now, shush. She's right there. She could hear you. I pointed to the lump on Lorilee's bunk.

No, she's asleep. Don't worry. She cain't hear.

She could have, I said.

You know, Crystal whispered, if she'd just minded that mouth of hers, that old preacher wouldn't have done what he done.

You don't know that, I said.

Don't tell me what I know.

I felt the mound on Lorilee's bed move below my bunk, and I knew she wasn't sleeping. I just rolled over and stopped talking.

But I'd told Crystal basically the truth: Lorilee and I talked about nothing. Nothing and everything, it seemed. I know the basics about her now: she was doing H, like just about everybody else around here. Lorilee had been pretty quiet about what she had done, but she told me. It was H, all the time. The usual thing, she said: a boyfriend got her started. First weed, beer. The same old story, then coke, but heroin was just faster to the bloodstream, right into the veins. Didn't take long for her to get her ass into rehab—parents, big brother, especially, intervened. Threatened to kick her out on the street. She was the black sheep of the family, she'd said. That was kind of funny to me: what with her pressed shorts and white blouses. Who were these people anyway? What did her mother look like?

You don't want to know, she'd said. Your worst nightmare: perfect and unreachable. Forever bound in her own reality, she'd said.

Forever bound in her own reality, I said again. Sounds like a parental condition.

We both laughed. I think it was the first time I'd really laughed on my own and not under the influence. Dusk was coming and the day was done. Somehow we'd wound up on the back porch on our own that night, looking out at the stars.

She said, what do you see?

Out there?

Yeah. In the sky. I know you can see, she said.

I smiled. I see the Big Dipper, Venus.

No, she said. What do you *see*?

Oh. That.

Yeah.

How do you know?

She laughed when I said that, but I let it be.

I see things I don't totally get sometimes.

Like what?

Fast flashes. Pictures in my mind. Cars. People. Hills, malls. Then sometimes weird stuff. I've seen a castle. An island. Like stuff I've never been to, never seen before but I feel like I know sometimes. I almost said, I've seen the end, but I thought that was too weird—even too weird to tell Lorilee.

When does it happen?

I don't know.

She dragged on her cig. When she blew out the smoke, she stared at the burning embers at its end.

When I'm not trying, I said. That was the truth.

Do you ever see us leaving?

I got really quiet. I was afraid to say anything out loud. Was she tricking me? Would she go and tell Starlene or Miss Sallyanne?

No, I said. Just in case.

Now it was Lorilee's turn to be quiet. I do, she said after a time. I think we ain't staying here. If we stay here, we ain't going to *be* anymore.

What? Like we're going to die?

Not like Sallyanne is going to kill us or anything. But we will start to disappear. More than we are now.

I flicked my cigarette butt onto the grass. I knew we weren't supposed to do that. There were dozens of coffee cans around the house, meant for butts.

Oh, you mean like Kimberly? Blond and—Empty, she said. Them girls are empty. They started that way, and they are going to stay that way. We could be like them too after a while. That's what they want.

Who? I said.

Miss Sallyanne. Starlene. Shit. The whole world. The whole world.

Yep. Empty out them girls, that's what they want. Stop

Yep. Empty out them girls, that's what they want. Stop thinking. Don't ask. Don't want. Do as you're told. Come on. You've heard it your whole life.

I started to think about it. I'm still not sure. I'm just starting to fit in with the girls at the house, with Miss Sallyanne. It took a while. Part of me was afraid that I wouldn't fit in—it'd taken so long for some of them girls to come talk to me—but then part of me is afraid of exactly what Lorilee was saying: that I would fit in too much, be one of them. Shit, that was one of the sayings: *Be one of the many.* I didn't really get it until now.

You can't get out, unless you fit in, I said. They won't let us go home until we get the Program.

What is there to get? Lorilee said. I'll say this about her: she didn't take nothing at face value. Always asking questions.

You know, I said. Sobriety. The Program. A life with a Higher Power.

God as we understand Him? She started to laugh a little.

See? You're getting it. I gave her a little push, kidding-like. There's hope for you.

I know. I know. It's all the same, though. You know what I mean: fit in and don't resist. Get in line. That was the problem in the first place.

I don't get it.

You don't? You're telling me you always felt like you belonged everywhere?

Oh shit. No, of course not, I said.

Square peg in round hole, right?

Right, I said. Always. Always, I thought, and then I found Tommy. Or he found me. Another square peg.

Me too, she said.

We looked out at the pasture beyond the doghouse. The cattle had migrated near to it, on their side. They were all clustered against each other—which was kind of strange since it was so hot tonight. But you know cows, cattle, they're not the brightest beasts out there. They cling to each other winter, summer, doesn't make any difference. Dumb as shit.

Lorilee put out her smoke. You out? She held up her cigarettes toward me.

No, thanks. I waved my hand. I'm done for the night.

Right, she said. You got your writing to do.

Instead of feeling embarrassed, I just smiled. I don't know. I liked her tonight.

June 9, 1986

Something's going on. I just know it. Lorilee thinks so too. Miss Sallyanne and Starlene are both buzzing and hiding, talking in quiet voices. Miss Sallyanne was even late to Group this morning. Her eyes red and glassy. If I didn't know better. But it's probably just allergies. And while Terri was going on and on about how her mama and daddy got divorced and then how she moved around so much, she just moved away one day from both of them, and nobody noticed, Miss Sallyanne stopped her and said, Now, girl, tell us what your brother was doing. And Terri just looked at her for like a minute and then said, I ain't got no brother.

Oh, that's right, honey. I'm getting my stories mixed up. Miss Sallyanne took her glasses off and wiped them and went back to not listening.

That was one of the first signs. Miss Sallyanne is a lot of things—a lot of weird things—but I'll give her this: she's a good listener. She doesn't always have great ideas about what to do about things. I mean, like, she'll say, Pray, child, after some girl has said that her uncle has been raping her for four years, or she'll say, Repent, sinner, when somebody tells the Group that she was selling herself for drugs—that kind of advice doesn't mean anything, everybody knows that. But Miss Sallyanne listens with all she's got, nodding her head, usually, up and down, as if she's calling the words right out of you.

She hasn't gotten anything out of me, though. I'll be damned if I tell anyone here about Tommy or anything else that matters. For all they know, I am just a garden- variety alcoholic, as they say, boring as they come. A Juvenile Delinquent. And that is the way I'm going to keep it. But it was pretty unlike Miss Sallyanne not to pay attention—that was strange.

The second thing is that Tad has not been here in more than a week. A week! That also means that his boys still haven't been here either, and the job they started to mend the old wooden fence out on the western side of the house isn't finished. There's timber piled up still, some next to the house, and I guess they ran out of room over there, because some of it's also piled up near the dried-up stream, looking like it's ready to roll right in. That's too bad for a couple reasons. One is, obviously, the outside work isn't getting done, and now the yard looks a little like a junkyard, what with the wood and the table saw and the other tools tossed all over the place. But the other reason is the boys. I feel sad not to see them—and especially John. He was one of the ones who talked to me that day. He was from up north—St. Louis or something like that. I don't know how he wound up down here, if only because he wasn't sure himself, but he seemed kind of happy to be here—there, in the boys' house—where things were kind of mellow, he said. We talked about books and then, I don't know why, I told him about my journal. He asked me what was I writing. He thought it was stories, like I was a great writer or something, and I was sorry to say no, no stories, just a whole lot of frustration. His face turned a little down when I said I was just writing my thoughts, what I was thinking about and whatnot. But he said he'd like to read my writing some time, and then he seemed a little happier just thinking about that.

But now John and the other boys haven't been here in a while. A couple of weeks. I guess they're never coming back. Same with Tad, though it sounds like he calls a lot. Miss Sallyanne is always running into her office to answer the phone. She closes the door, but we can hear her from our bedroom.

This morning, Lorilee and I were up first. Crystal was snoring away like an old man. My word!

We were dressed and already outside on the back patio—we've got into this habit of going out to see the horizon first thing in the morning and last thing at night. I don't know why, but it feels good to see the sun rising (even when it's cloudy) and the moon rising later. It makes the days feel like they are wheels on a bicycle, turning and turning, getting closer to the day they let us go home.

What the fuck is going on here, Lorilee says. She's got a cig between her teeth.

Let me get some of that fire, I say and I'm leaning toward her with my own cig in my mouth.

She cups the match and bends toward me. After the end catches, she shakes out the match and drops it to the ground. I don't know why but everything she does seems like dance.

I just realize it when she lets the burnt match fall, and I almost say so, but then I realize how queer I'll sound—though I know she wouldn't really mind if I did.

I don't know, I say. Because it's true. I don't know what is going on. I don't know shit here. And I'm in one of those moods where I feel like nothing ever changes and I'm never getting out of here. I'm still the same as I came in and I'm never going to be allowed to leave.

Later on, Lorilee says to me in the kitchen: Why do you always pretend about your drug of choice?

What? I am scrubbing the pots from lunchtime. We both have kitchen duty. Well, I have it, and somehow Lorilee has shown up. Starlene is snarling over in the corner of the kitchen at some recipe that she peers over from time to time to look at Lorilee. For some reason, that woman doesn't come near me when Lorilee is near—which is F.I.N.E. with me. And it really isn't even clear if it's the recipe she's snarling at. Something is bugging her, but who knows? I'm sure not going to ask her.

She said, why are you pretending what you done?

Who's pretending? I say, but I don't look up from the pot. This thing is burnt like crazy and the black char is getting under my fingernails.

You are, she says.

Oh and you ain't?

Not about my drug of choice.

I couldn't argue with that so I just kept quiet. I mean, she came here to hang with me, I guess, so she could just talk. I didn't have to talk back to her. You ain't just an alcoholic.

Nobody is, I say.

What else are you?

What else am I? I didn't answer her. I am nothing, I think. I am not even sure what kind of music I like anymore, after being here so long. I was listening to Chaka Khan on Maryanne's turntable the other day. Chaka Khan! (Tommy would be cracking up if he knew!)

You're a junkie, like me, she says, which makes Starlene look up. The snarl-face temporarily melts away.

Like you'd know. I turn my back to her and drag the pot over to the sink.

What did you see last night? She asks. I know you saw something.

I am glad she stopped with the drug of choice stuff, although I really don't want to talk about seeing things either in the same room as Starlene, who has gone back to snarling to herself. It's better if Starlene and Miss Sallyanne think I'm just an alcoholic—I heard Miss Sallyanne say once that alcoholics have a better chance of recovery, not like people who've used narcotics. Much too hard to kick, she said—heroin addicts, coke addicts, they all almost never make it. I guess that means that we are all damned.

Starlene paces back and forth by the pantry like a panther, but she ain't going to bite us. She keeps her distance. Lorilee is like kryptonite.

Any cars this time? Lorilee asks me and rolls up her sleeves. She starts to play with the dough. She sprinkles flour on the clean counter and pulls a heavy lump from the bowl and starts to knead it.

No, not a car.

I know you saw something, she says. I could see it in your face.

I like this girl, I think. I don't know why. She is rude and too direct and dressed way too well to be friends with me, but I like her anyway. I smile. It's crazy, I say. I saw the wind.

The wind? You saw it? You are a crazy girl.

Starlene makes a sound from where she is in the corner. It sounds like a bark. Lorilee and I roll our eyes.

I know, I say, because I *am* crazy. I must be. My mood is breaking and Lorilee reminds me of the sun.

What're you heifers talking about over there? Ain't you two got work to do? Or is this just a lesbo love fest?

Jesus. Lorilee says under her breath and rolls her eyes. She turns to Starlene. What if it is?

Then you better pray to have those evil ways mended, my girl. Pray the Lord sets you straight. Girls were meant to be with men.

Lorilee turns and look at her. I swear if she didn't get taller. What the fuck are you talking about?

The way of the world, Sug, Starlene says but she starts to turn away from us. The way of the world, she says to no one.

I hold my breath, like—because nobody talks that way to Starlene and Miss Sallyanne. But I reckoned a while ago that Starlene and Lorilee had an understanding. They understood each other and they dealt with each other like equals. I wouldn't've dared. But that is the difference between me and Lorilee. She dares.

Starlene is about to say something, but Miss Sallyanne comes charging in. Starlene. I need you. Marla's missing.

Starlene turns to me and says, Finish up, heifer. She looks at Lorilee once and follows Miss Sallyanne out.

What is going on? I say when both women have left the room.

You heard her: Marla is missing.

Yeah, I say, but.

Yeah but what? She's pregnant. It's serious. Again, I say:

Like you'd know. This time I am kidding a little. She'd told me about her fib in group—the one to keep the vultures at bay. The one about her fake brother impregnating her—the fib that kept the whole house talking for weeks and that softened things around her for a little while. That was until she provoked the old man and he beat Miss Sallyanne. Now I'm not sure. The other girls don't seem so soft toward Lorilee anymore. They ignore her but something doesn't seem right at all. If I didn't know better—

No.

These girls are just pissed because Lorilee pushed the old man too far, brought back the old days too much. Like seeing their mamas beat, broken down. All too much, I think.

Anyway. I think I'm the only one who knows Lorilee's secret about her fake son, about him not existing. And who am I to judge her for lying? We all got secrets.

As if on cue, Lorilee returns to one of mine. It's OK to be a junkie.

Now I roll my eyes at her. Please.

Secrets keep you sick, Lorilee says. She's imitating Miss Sallyanne, who always says that.

Well. Looks like I'm going to be sick a long time—even if I can't get out of this place sooner.

Yeah, Lorilee nods. She takes the dough and starts to shape it into loaves. You have some secrets, she says.

I drop the pot into the sink and it makes a loud bong sound.

Jesus, girl. You're tearing up the place.

I can see Miss Sallyanne get into her little car, which is parked out back—I can see her from the back window over the kitchen sink. Her car is parked back, beyond the patio and grass, along the fence, the part that is still standing and keeps the cattle from wandering over here.

She zooms out backward, and she's zooming so fast, I don't think she's even looking. God help anybody who's standing in the way. But nobody is. Since nobody's in charge, the girls are all hanging out or finishing their chores like me. Some are sunning themselves on towels out back. There is no rush to do nothing, since Teach isn't coming today and now there isn't any Group, what with Miss Sallyanne burning down the gravel driveway.

So is she. I point out back with the rubber glove over my hand.

Look it how Miss Sallyanne tears out of here. Something is up, I say.

Glad you finally agree. Lorilee throws another loaf down into a bread pan.

(Later)

I don't know how Lorilee would know what I've done or not done. What my drug of choice was or wasn't. I don't see sometimes why she can't leave well enough alone.

Jesus. I cannot sleep.

I don't know how Lorilee knows, but all I can say is like recognizes like. Junkies always knows who's the junkies in the room. Even when we're not all shooting up.

The thing is, I wasn't always one. And I still don't really think of myself like that. You can't hardly see the track marks between my toes. That's all it was. And it was all for Tommy. I could've stopped at any time. I would have. I did. I did now. I always preferred beer, vodka. Mmmm. Vodka.

It was Tommy who was always trying something new.

Try something new for a change, he'd say, whatever it was: drugs, food, sex, movies, anything. He was always up for trying something, trying it on for size.

At first, we were casual. At first, for the first two years we were casual and a lot less dramatic than my mom and his dad, who were always getting into fights on the phone or in the house. But not me and Tommy. We just were. And we could walk away at any time. That's what he said. This we coulThis is not a Thing.

But then it was.

So were the drugs. I know. I could've walked away—from him, from the drugs. Any time. I could and I did.

Well, OK. It sometimes was more like *hobbling* away. Tommy shot me up usually. Not like he totally knew what he was doing. And it really fucking hurt the first time— and a lot of times after that. Worse than when we fucked for the first time, I'll tell you that. He sometimes got it right, and then sometimes really didn't. I could barely walk on my left foot once for like three days. My mother noticed after the second day that I was limping around. Took her to the second day. Huh.

He'd shoot me up and then himself. He didn't care much for it at first. First snorting it. H ain't all that but it's everything, he'd say.

We never had all that much money, so it wasn't like we could do it all the time. And I didn't really have the will. I just had Tommy.

I had the will to be around Tommy.

He's all I wanted. And now I have nothing.

Boy, I am just in a foul mood. And the moon is waxing, I see. This is dream time for me—my best dreams come at this time. If I could only sleep.

I'm going to try. Lay down and try.

Impossible. No fucking sleep. But I'm kind of glad I couldn't sleep. Somewhere around 3 am Lorilee got up to look out the window. I saw her staring out at the highway—it's way far off, and the cars can only be seen by their lights. I know what she was seeing. I think I know.

I see it too.

But then she does something weird. She's still looking out, but she raises her hands up at her sides. She's got them open-like facing up. I swear if she ain't mumbling something. I don't know what. I was so afraid that she would know I was awake that I didn't barely breathe out. She's mumbling something and then Crystal and Maryanne start getting restless in their sleep. Crystal is wheezing bad, and Maryanne is talking, mumbling-like.

Within a few minutes, the moon, nearly full as a disc arrives in the window. The beams are bright as regular light and it looks like Lorilee is calling them to her hands.

She, who is wearing her Donald Duck pajamas and furry yellow slippers. She, who is almost ordinary on the outside. She, who no matter what we think, is not like the rest of us. She, who calls the moon.

Do you remember me? She asks me. I am like too stunned to say anything, so I say nothing. I don't know why. No words are coming because they keep getting tangled at the back of my throat.

I know you, she says. I know you through time. You know what I mean?

No—, I start to say, but I just don't know what I'm saying, except that I'm pulling myself out of bed. My notebook drops to the ground. I leave it and I walk up next to Lorilee, who says she is showing me something and I don't know at first except that I see the horizon, the moon, the cars in the distance, and then and then and then I see so much more, and I know I have been in this place before and before I can turn it off, and not remember, the letters form with hard angles and points, catching on the soft places in my throat and I say, Yes.

June 10, 1986

Forget last night. Starting over now. Just too weird. It was like Lorilee was trying to show me outer space or some crazy shit. I must've been really tired. That's all. Tired and sometimes I think the drugs affected my brain. Like my perception is just off. Like way off. It feels like there are after-effects from drugs, like an earthquake but the aftershock hits months later. And that was last night. Like from H. From the acid, especially, although I only did that once or twice. OK. A few times. Definitely like from mescaline. But again, that was only a few times. I didn't like going that far out, tripping, like.

I only liked to snort H, anyway. We figured that out pretty quickly. The pain of shooting in my feet wasn't really worth it. And Tommy agreed—he was doing the same thing. Our parents would have freaked out if they'd known. Well, eventually they *did* know. And my mother, drama queen that she is, went nuts. I guess I get it now. I know. I know what I did. It is my fault, I know. I know. I know. It was my fault. I know.

June 11, 1986

I know what happened, Lorilee said.

I ignored her. I wasn't in the mood for her bullshit.

Hey. I know.

No, you don't, I said, although I didn't even know what she was talking about.

Yes. I know.

How?

I have my ways.

What ways? Sometimes, I mean, sometimes, that girl could be so annoying.

Do you want to know what I know or not?

Other girls started to come out on the back porch. Me and Lorilee had perfected breakfast clean up—we were done so fast that we got out back to smoke usually before anyone. But today was pancakes, it being Sunday and all, so there was a bigger mess and that took us a little longer. Less time to ourselves to smoke in peace. The other girls started to come out, everybody with a cigarette already in their mouths.

Know what? Kimberly asked.

Lorilee looked Queenie up and down—that's what we started calling her behind her back—I knew Lorilee didn't like Kimberly much, but she wasn't scared of her like I was.

Who invited you? Lorilee said.

I froze. I wasn't sure what this was about.

Ah, come on. I want to know, Kimberly said.

Other girls had come over to hear, and soon we were right in the middle of the pack of them. Know about what? somebody said.

Marla. Lorilee winked at me and I breathed out. Not telling my secrets today. She and I were sitting on top of one of the old picnic tables out there, with our feet on the bench next to it. The other girls were standing in front of her and sitting next to us on it, too.

Oh like you know, Kimberly snorted. Man, sometimes I really hated that bitch. She had to know better than everybody. Kimberly started to walk away.

Lorilee looked like she was smiling when she rolled her eyes. I know who the father of Marla's baby is.

Kimberly stared at Lorilee, and for a second there, I thought they were going to fight or something. But Lorilee wouldn't. I don't know how I knew that, but I knew Lorilee wasn't about to fight anyone for anything.

Kimberly went on. Everybody knows that.

This shut all of us up, even those girls like Crystal who were snickering, hoping for a fight.

I don't know that, said Carla Bobby. It's Miss Sallyanne's son. Kimberly's revelation moved out like the dust waves of a bomb.

Wait. Miss Sallyanne is the father? Crystal said. So fucking stupid, that one.

She has a son? I asked. Who?

He works at the boys' home now, but he was at the Ash House. He does the books.

What books? Crystal. She could be dumb as shit, too.

The bills, idiot. Kimberly flipped her hair. He worked in the office. He still works in the office, but in the boys' house now. Didn't we talk about this already?

Where is the boys' house, anyway? Terri asked, but I think we were all wondering the same thing.

It's like less than a mile from here, Lorilee said. I looked at her. She winked at me.

Who's the son? I mean, the father, now? I still didn't get it, like.

Now Kimberly was getting into it. Wait, she said to Lorilee. How do you know where the boys' house is at? You just got here. You weren't ever there.

The other girls waited.

I just know, Lorilee said.

How?

I have my ways.

I bet you do, Kimberly said. Bitch.

Lorilee dropped her cigarette and put it out with her tennis shoe, but she didn't stand up.

Will someone finish the fucking story? I said.

Lorilee looked at me. Sallyanne's son is Zach. You know, Zacchaeus.

Zacchaeus? That is his real name? Kimberly laughed out loud.

I thought you knew everything.

I didn't know that was his real name. Holy shit.

I know. Lorilee smiled at her for a second. It's a ridiculous name. She lit another cigarette. The boys are still *in* the Ash house.

They moved the girls to here when they realized the problem. That's us, Kimberly said, we're a problem around boys, they said.

That's *before* us, Lorilee corrected. Well, she said, before most of us. She nodded over at Magda and Terri, who both seemed to have been here for years, never leaving, never seeing their families again, watching other girls come and go. How come they didn't know where they were just spoke to how long they'd been in the same space.

Who? Kimberly butted in again.

Who, what? Lorilee glanced at her at first, but then looked at Kimberly as if she were seeing her for the first time.

Who moved who?

Miss Sallyanne and Tad, Lorilee slowed her words down.

Mister Tad, Maryanne said.

They own the houses, with their dad.

The Reverend. Crystal said, and that might have ended it all right there, because just mentioning him drew fear up our spines.

This is a family business? I asked. I needed to know. I needed to find out how I was getting home, and this was all a little too much to take in.

Yeah, Lorilee said to only me. They are all working it. Now Marla is in the family, in the family-way, at least. She started to laugh, but we both knew how not-funny that was. They put her to work in the office. Now she is with Zach.

How old is he? Maryanne wasn't smiling like she normally was.

He's out of high school, but not by much, I think, Lorilee said.

What the hell's going on out here? Starlene busted out of the backdoor. I swear, that woman.

Quiet.

What y'all yammering about? Look like all y'alls up to something. Come on, she held the door open. Time to repent. Git your lame-sinner asses in there.

The Reverend was in.

Git yer lazy asses in gear. Starlene glared at us.

Everybody looked around. I looked at Lorilee, waiting for her to say something. But she just ground out her cigarette and walked toward the door, like she was going to vespers or something.

Move, heifers! You know what's good for you.

That started other girls to move like the cattle out back, going to the slaughterhouse, slow and brainless.

Well, Kimberly muttered as we all walked, but loud enough so Lorilee could hear. I guess you do know everything. Amazing, since you ain't never condescended to talk to nobody. Nobody but your girlfriend there. Kimberly nodded toward me.

Shut up, I said.

Lorilee turned and smiled at her big and wide, like she was just meeting her for the first time. She let the cheerleader and Crystal walk inside in front of her.

Kimberly stopped fast and looked at us. Don't neither of you lesbos cause any shit today. Keep your fucking mouths shut.

I stayed back with Lorilee until Kimberly and the rest were inside.

How'd you know all that? I put my cigarette butt out on the patio cement. I mean, who told you all that?

Tad. She smiled—and man, it was a smile like the whole world was in her mouth.

There's more, Lorilee whispered to me. I turned to look at her, but she was already inside, way ahead of me.

Tad. I thought. Son of a bitch. How'd she ever manage that one? But I never got to ask.

Starlene started yelling again.

Come on, Summer. Git yer scrawny ass in here. I followed in through the backdoor just to shut her up.

IV

Ripening

I seen that ole mudsill Tad coming a mile away. He must've thought I was some kind of idiot. Some kind of desperado, me being here with all them girls. Like I never knew men before. Like I didn't have my pick out there. He tried putting the moves on me, but I saw him coming.

He struts into this place like he's the only cock in the henhouse. And he usually is, but he's way too old for these girls he's pecking around. Miss Sallyanne, man, she does not see what is right in front of her. That's what started the trouble in the first place—she don't even see it with her own son. Zacchaeus knocked up that little girl back in the old place and she still don't wise up. Zacchaeus. She named him a Bible name and it don't make any difference. She could've named him Jesus Christ, and he still would've knocked somebody up. That boy. Well, let's just say that boy can't find his ass with both hands. Dumb as rocks. And Sallyanne—bless her heart—she can move them girls all she wants—a couple of miles or all the way to China, but it won't make a damn bit of difference. They's men. Boys. And boys will be boys, as they say. Even the mighty dumb ones. And these boys are all family: a son like the uncle, and I know what I seen: like the

Reverend father himself. It runs in the family. Boys will be boys, yes, indeed. They just can't help themselves.

I say, No thank you, mister. I am clean and sober today, and I choose the Lord above. After the last one, I don't need no man hanging around me. I say, if I could be one of them nuns like the Romans, I'd a married God Himself. There is no other protection from men. They just take and take. It's in their nature. There ain't no earthly protection. No. There ain't. Any grown woman tell you that. Any goddamn idiot tell you that.

I swear Sallyanne ain't got a bit of sense sometimes. She and Tad left that little girl over there while she was in her time, working the office. Zacchaeus is probably over there too, but Lord knows he ain't done a stitch of work in his life, with his mama looking after him and giving him a job in the family business. Zacchaeus is a grown man now. He's easily twenty-three, twenty-four. If he were my son, I'd had him enlist by now. Keep his sorry ass out of trouble, and his dick away from these girls.

Marla ain't but fifteen, sixteen. No idea where her own mama is at. And maybe that's why she's still here: her own people don't want her now. She come to the Ash house to sober up and find Jesus, and she just gets knocked up. Shit. She coulda done that out on the street.

When that little girl shows up at Second Chance last week, she ain't so little anymore. She's looking like the full moon herself. Except she wore the face of misery. I know what that's like. She ain't just wearing the Pregnant Miserable, either. She's got the teenage misery and the I'm-trapped misery. She's working for Zacchaeus, who looks after the office, while Sallyanne and Tad work the houses. They've got it all organized nice, except that Marla. I don't know. She's not happy. I don't know who's looking out for that girl, but I guess she's got Zacchaeus, who's both boss and boyfriend now. No wonder she tried running. She's looking down the barrel of life with that loser, who is riding his mama's—and his uncle Tad's— coattails. Jesus. What a life she's going to have. What a life that baby is going have. Thank God, Sally-anne and her cousin—the deputy sheriff—brung her back. Found her trying to hitchhike up near I-35.

I just mind my own business now. But for the grace of God, there I go, I say. I keep my pants on and my hands to myself. I don't need no man coming around me, taking my freedom away. I am happy on my own, thank you very much.

I ain't one for keeping secrets, neither, but for Marla's sake, I don't gossip and such about that kid. She's young. She's kind of a sly one, too, but still. That don't make it right. But I seen now that them she-devils knew all along. I guess it was inevitable—most of them started back at the old house. You can't pretend that didn't happen and they don't know what went on over there. Then they was moved here, but we don't talk about the old house much. The girls remember things, even though we are here now. We live for today, one day at a time.

Ain't nothing you can do about the past, and I say Amen to that. Amen!

But then, shit. Marla shows up—I guess she was going to sooner or late. I ain't sure anybody's talking to her about pre-baby stuff. I tried asking Miss Sallyanne, and now that she is going to become a grandmother and all, I'd thought she'd know, but she just says it's between the Lord and him now. And I say, him who? And she says, why Zacchaeus. He's taking care of that girl now. He's gonna marry her.

"Ain't he already done enough?" I say like real quiet.

"What was that?" A cranky schoolteacher voice come up in her. Like I'm in trouble or some such thing.

"Nothing," I say. I need this job, this house, as much as any of them heifers. So I swallow it.

"Why bless your heart," she says.

I am already decided I'm going over there to the office later to check on Marla when I hear Lorilee holding court on the back patio, talking about everybody's business to all them other girls. How the fuck she knows, I don't know. Not at first. But I figure it out. I got it. She can fool Sallyanne (that seems easy enough, even that dumb shit of a son got her fooled), and she can fool them other girls, but I know who she is. And now I know what she's been up to.

There's a rule in the program: no relationships in the first year. I'd been such a wreck when I first got here— which ain't that long ago—that I didn't care about no relationships. I didn't care about no men. Shit. I was just glad not to have some fool pawing over me. And I was real glad not to be nobody's punching bag no more. Once my son had passed and I'd paid my debt to society, I was done. D.O.N.E. with men. My whole life I'd been holding my breath since they was finished doing what they were doing. Since those days outside the bars, didn't matter who it was, even if he weren't being forceful and whatnot, I just held my breath, thought of night, and hoped I'd be able to breathe again when it was over. A great big wall grew up around my softer inside parts and no matter what else was taken from me, he'd never get near my inside space.

Once my boy had passed, the sad spread over me like spilled oil. Ain't nobody even want to touch me no how.

Even rough ones didn't come near. Nobody messed with me anymore. 'Course, it coulda had to do with the fact that I never showered no more, and I was living under the bridge for a short while. Had ole Roderick's car, but at one point I didn't realize my papa done took it away and kept it at his house. I guess he thought I needn't be driving myself to an early death and whatnot.

It wasn't just me being dirty, though—nobody's safe on the street. Plenty of women get attacked, dirty or not. It was more like I'd grown that great wall and it was not defense no more, but offense. The oil was too slick to come near. And that was just fine with me.

So ain't nobody need to tell me about no relationships in the Program. Sallyanne started giving me that long talk in the beginning about men and evil thoughts that keep us from getting sober. She started on about the jeans I wore and my hair and then stopped after a time when she saw she might as well be talking to a goose. We were sitting in her office and she had on her white sweatshirt with the tree and gray horse on the front, the collar of her shirt underneath sticking out from under its neck. Sallyanne's reading glasses had slipped down the round top part of her nose while she was reading my file. Then she looked up at me over the desk. The glasses now off.

"You don't need my advice, do you, honey?"

"No ma'am," I said. "I'm good."

"You just need a little rest, some time down."

"Yes, I do." And that was the truth: I needed the rest. It had all been too much. Too fast. And now I had nothing left. "Yes, ma'am. Imma empty well."

"*An* empty well," she said. "Yeah, I reckon I see that. Can you cook?"

Back then, when I first got to Second Chance, Tad was on me like white on rice, as they say. As soon as he seen me in the kitchen that first time during one of his weekly visits, he was on me, asking where I was from, what was my drug of choice, all the usual Program stuff. And I knew he ran the other house—I didn't know that he was Sallyanne's brother yet or that he'd been in jail and the whole kit an' caboodle too. But then he told me he'd been into H, and that it'd taken everything from him: wife, child, job, and home. He'd had a normal life once back up in Ardmore, he told me, and then H took it all, took over. People, places, things got to be too much, and he was running with the Devil day and night. Oh, I knew all about that, too. He'd seen my own tracks, though it weren't H done it to me, brought me all the way down. But he knew I knew. He took one look at my bad arm but didn't ask who'd done broke it. And then Tad said that he'd found God again, that his sister—God bless her—had shown him the Light, that they'd grown up as a preacher's brood, and it didn't make no bit of difference in the short run but now he'd seen the Light and everything was awright.

"God is good," he said that first week. "You'll git this Program, Star," he said. "I'm calling you Star now, because a star is what you are."

I was just acquainting myself with the kitchen that day, poking around to see what I had to work with. He was leaning over the counter that separated the tables from where the girls ate. I couldn't see the half of him, but I could feel him watching me—but how stupid of me, thinking he was a man of God. The way he talked, he sounded like a preacher himself.

"Many are called, Star," he said, "but few are chosen."

And how stupid I was to think he was talking about God's calling.

Sallyanne walked into the dining area. The girls had their free time to do what they wanted. "I see you met Starlene. She started yesterday," she said to him.

"I know." Tad dipped his head and tapped his finger on an invisible hat. "I've had the pleasure of making her 'quaintence. The Light of God is shining on her. She is a joy to be near, to bask in her sunshine."

Sallyanne's face broke open with a light-smile of her own. It was all going to be OK, I thought then. I was safe. I was finally home. I wasn't one of the clients, but I was getting my second chance (more like my ninth chance, but who's counting?) here at the house with the same name.

"Trinity," he said. "We have Trinity here now." He looked from Sallyanne to me. "We will make a great team." He said it and I swear it sounded like he was only talking to me. Even after what I'd done. What I still could do if I had to.

It only took once. I think ole Tad didn't realize how tired I was. How the oil comes right back, pouring out fast like a rig accident. I think he had no idea what he was dealing with.

He come up from behind me one day, this was now weeks after I started. I was pulling out some biscuits from the oven. I got my mits on and I'm trying to be careful because the pan is so hot. I know he was there at the counter, leaning like he always done, talking about Jesus and shepherds, and this time he even made a joke about loaves of bread, because I was making biscuits. But he come up from behind me so fast and reached his spider arms around my waist and all of a sudden I felt my breathing stop. I was gasping for air. Ain't none of it was coming into my lungs. I dropped the pan and swung so fast, I still don't think he knows what hit him.

"What the fuck?" he said. "You fuckin' bitch." His hand went to his chin, but then he swung fast at me. I ducked. So much for that Jesus talk, I see now. Just takes a woman saying no and the cussing starts. Right before the fists.

I was scared. I admit it now. I was scared. And maybe in another life I might have cussed him out too, or let him do it or I don't know what, I woulda done something, anything else. But this day, my biscuits were all over the floor and one of my oven mits had fallen too and I couldn't breathe and I couldn't speak, so afraid he was going to fire me or tell Sally-anne and she'd do it, and even more afraid that if he hit me, it would be the last time he'd hit anybody. And this time, they would know it was no accident.

This time, they might just know.

"You are crazy," he said. "That's what you are. I'm just trying to be nice here, and you get all up and crazy. You a lot sicker than you know, girl. A lot sicker."

I got on my knees and picked up the biscuits. I still weren't breathing. My head started feeling all light.

"You got a bony ass, too, girl. You know that? Ain't nobody want a piece of that. What you thinking? You're way too bony."

His words falling around me. Little bombs dropping. Not landing. I heard it all before. My great wall up. My plans for moving on already started turning gears. The air coming in a little now.

Sallyanne came around the corner. "What happened here?"

My breath got stuck again.

"She dropped her biscuits." He shoved a toothpick between his teeth. "Detox is a bitch, ain't it? Don't miss those days, right, Sally? All that shaking and unsteadiness. But for the Grace of God, there go I."

"Oh honey," she said to me. "I know. It's all too much."

She must've seen the tears come up in my eyes. My hands damn near shaking at that point. That fucker must've seen them too. But when I seen he weren't about to say nothing, my body got out of my control like, and the shakes come back.

"See? She's shakin' like a leaf. Ain't she supposed to be over that yet? She must be real fucked up."

"Ain't you got a bunch of boys to look after?" Sally-anne said.

He looked at her. "Right." Then he looks at me. "*It works if you work it. So work it.*"

If Sallyanne hadn't been standing there, I'd a been sending another pan his way soon if he kept that shit up. But he ain't never come near me again. I'm sure of that. Ain't nowhere safe. I'm sure of that too. As long as I know that, I am OK. But for the Grace of God, there I am.

I am. I see.

And I seen now where Tad's been sniffing. Like the dog he is.

Lorilee, that she-devil. If it were anybody else, I might step in. I might tell him finally to fuck off and stop trying to fuck my girls. But it's Lorilee. Let her see what it's like, she knows so much. And Tad. He ain't got no idea what he's up against, that stupid man, that stupid, low- life motherfucker-fake. Let him see on his own. She's young, but that's all a disguise—the devil's wily and knows how to pass for innocence. Tad's such an asshole, such an arrogant fuck that he thinks he's gonna win. Well, let that asshole chase a teenage skirt. If she don't get him, Sallyanne will, blind as she is sometimes. And if neither of them do, then it's in God's hands. Judgement awaits us all.

Second Chance Girls

Of course, we knew something was happening. How couldn't we? Starlene was slinking by doorways and peering in windows from the outside—slinking and peering more than usual. Miss Sallyanne was fragile, jumpy-like, sometimes even in Group. Sometimes she was distracted, calling girls by different girls' names— sometimes by names of girls who weren't even in the room. Once she burst out, Marla! to no one in particular. And a couple times she nodded off.

Miss Sallyanne's ghosts starting showing up that day her daddy nearly beat her in front of us and then finished the job in her office. The day we lost all hope. The day Marla appeared at the Second Chance home for girls and kept coming back, always with papers to be signed, things to be filed. Flaunting the rise in her belly. Seeming to like how her presence rattled Miss Sallyanne, unnerving her every single time she appeared in the doorway. Miss Sallyanne's only peace was when she locked herself in her room and emerged hours or a day later, bleary-eyed and dull.

"I can come by the office to do that," Miss Sallyanne said to Marla one of those times she showed up at Second Chance. "You don't need to be coming allaways here."

We were all in the dining room that time. She had us filling out personality tests; she was in some school, we knew, and this was for one of the courses. We'd been having fun with questions that asked us what we saw in blobs of black ink on the page—we saw the usual, of course, poop, puke, so we almost missed Marla creeping into the house through the back door. But she slipped over to Miss Sally-anne, and before you knew it, Starlene had skulked over, and was now standing over all of us, eyeballing Marla.

It would have been funny, especially because of the poop silhouettes on our pages, but Miss Sallyanne perked up and got that razor edge back in her voice.

"Honey. Marla. Bless your heart. Really. You don't need to drive allaways here," she said. "It's too much. Look at you. You should have your feet up."

"My feet up." Marla's voice sounded softer than you'd expect, like she was imagining what a rest might feel like. She was a tiny girl when things were normal, when she wasn't in the eighth month of pregnancy. Her wrists were still small, her elbows, bony, and the cheekbones in her face jutted out just a little under her skin. She wore her long brown hair in a ponytail with a bow, which made her look like a little girl when she turned her back to walk out of a room. But when she faced forward, she looked around our age again. Our age, carrying a full-sized basketball under her t-shirt. Marla carried not only a nearly term baby but whole-sized impatience, which traced the edges of her words every time she spoke in that soft voice.

"It's just easier, ma'am," she said to Miss Sallyanne, who was already reaching for the folder in Marla's arms to speed things along and get her out of there.

"Let me carry that for you." Starlene grabbed it first.

"It ain't heavy. I can do it." Marla took it back.

"What are you all looking at? Finish those question-naires." The edge in Miss Sallyanne's own voice sharp and ready. Then a sunshine smile broke across Miss Sallyanne's face. "Teach is coming for school."

"Where she's been at?" somebody asked.

"Ya'll are still in school?" Marla says like she's telling us something, not like she's asking a question. "Not done for summer yet?"

"Yes, they're doing their learning." Starlene looked up from the folder she was snooping through.

"I remember school," Marla said to no one in particular.

"Give it here, Starlene." Miss Sallyanne held out her hands. "Marla, I'll drop it by later. Go now."

"OK, ma'am." Marla smiled broadly. "I'll be back."

"No, honey. Don't come back here." Miss Sallyanne gave her a hard look. "It's enough."

Marla stopped moving toward the door and turned again to face Miss Sallyanne.

"OK, honey? Don't come back. Stay in the office and let Zacchaeus mind you." Miss Sallyanne's mouth bent almost like a sneer. "Bless her heart," she said when we all heard Marla's car drive away. "Pregnancy ain't done nothing for that child's stubbornness."

Later on, when we talked about it out on the patio, some of the girls swore Marla had said "Fuck you" under her breath, but not all of us were sure. Like Maryanne, who would naturally see the bright side in everything, said she heard, "Yes ma'am."

"Why she saying 'Yes, ma'am,' to her mother-in- law?" Crystal tossed her cigarette butt on the grass.

"Hey! Watch out. You're going to burn the place down." Carla Bobby pointed to the smoking butt in the grass. "Look. It's too dry out here." Crystal dragged herself over and picked up the cigarette end. She dumped it in the coffee can on the patio. It kept smoldering there on top of a pile of overflowing cigarette butts.

"Yeah, right? Miss Sallyanne is going to be the grand-ma to her baby. Why is she calling her 'ma'am'?" Maryanne dragged on her own cigarette.

"Wonder what she is going to name it," Terri said.

"Zach Junior!" Crystal leaned over to laugh. She looked like she could have been throwing up.

"Ew! Who would fuck him?" Kimberly swung her hair over her shoulder. We knew *she'd* never fuck that slow, dull boy. But some of us might have. We knew that, too. Not everybody had her options. But to stay in the group, to be able to hang out on the patio, we all nodded. No shit, we nodded, he's like totally gross.

"Do you think they fuck now? You know, with her all preggers and shit?" Terri exhaled cigarette smoke. Magda blew rings through her stream of smoke.

"I don't think you can," Kimberly said.

"You can't or you wouldn't want to?" Maryanne asked.

"Ain't nobody would want to fuck that guy."

"Yeah." We all nodded again. "Amen."

"You can, I think." Summer leaned forward. She had looked like she was conspiring in the corner with Lo-rilee, who was quiet this whole time. "What do you think?" Summer asked her. "Pregnant women can have sex, can't they?"

"Of course," Lorilee said.

"Like you'd know," Kimberly muttered so we all could hear.

"She does know," Magda whispered just as loud. "Ain't she got a son?"

"Yeah," Kimberly said, her voice flat, not interested. Discussion ended.

Summer snickered and picked at her fingernails.

So we just waited the days. Some of us were actually excited, half hoping the baby would come to live with us, and we were talking about having a baby shower.

"A baby shower!" Starlene said, while we were all waiting for Group to start. "With what money?"

"We don't have to buy anything," Maryanne said. "We can make things."

"I don't know," Terri said. "We like don't even know her."

"You might not know Marla, but there's still a little baby coming." Maryanne sat up straight on her folding chair. That girl was smiling till tomorrow. "She's going to need stuff."

"Yeah, and we want to celebrate." Magda looked up from her nail file and stopped scraping her immaculate nails.

"Celebrate what?" Kimberly tossed her hair. "Getting knocked up by a monkey?"

Crystal laughed.

Summer walked in—she'd been doing something in her room this whole time.

"I think we should have a baby shower. It's the right thing to do." Maryanne leaned back in her chair.

"Who's friends with Marla anymore? Who was ever friends with her?" Summer sat down at the circle.

"Not sure anybody was," Crystal said.

"Right," Summer said.

"Tell you one thing," Kimberly said. "I wouldn't let no sperm ruin my life. That girl's life is over."

Nobody answered her. Some of us shifted around in our chairs. More than a couple of us knew the pains of aborting or abandoning little ones. Or really, not having the choice in the first place.

"Who's life is over?" Crystal broke the silence. "The baby's?" She was sitting right next to Kimberly, leaning away from her as if to see her better.

"No, Marla's, you stupid wench!" Kimberly pushed her a little. "But now that you mention it, yes, the kid's too. Who'd want to grow up here? With that dork as your dad? With a bunch of drug addicts running around the place?"

"I don't know, I wouldn't mind growing up over there at the boys' house. I could get used to seeing boys, addicts or not, running around. I damn near forgot what guys look like until a few weeks ago." Terri leaned back on her chair and looked at us all.

"Mmhmm," Magda agreed. "Maybe one of them boys could come change my diapers!"

We all busted out laughing. Even Lorilee started to laugh.

"What are all y'all laughing about?" Miss Sallyanne came down the stairs, her eyes rimmed red.

That stopped the laughing right fast.

"Nothing, Miss." Maryanne spoke for us. "We were just talking about Marla's baby."

"The baby." Miss Sallyanne's face pulled a little at its temples. "What about it?"

"It?" Somebody mumbled.

"Well," Miss Sallyanne sat down in her chair at the top of the circle. "We just don't know what it is. Girl or boy."

When nobody spoke, she said, "Who's got a brick to drop?"

Quiet.

"Nobody?" She said. "Y'all recovered? That's it?

Last I checked y'all were *recovering* from your addictions. You ain't *recovered*. No way. Your secrets keep you sick."

Our eyes moved around the room, away from where Miss Sallyanne sat.

"Summer? How about you, honey? We ain't heard from you lately. Drop your brick, honey. Lighten the load."

"I ain't got nothing today, Miss Sallyanne." Summer crossed her arms.

"I think you do."

We held our breath.

"No, ma'am. I don't." Her head tilted down a little.

"Summer."

We all got real still. Miss Sallyanne had that razor in her voice again—fine and really sharp, like you might not even know you got sliced by it at first.

"Why don't you read from your diary?" Kimberly said.

Lorilee's chair pushed back a little.

"What?" Kimberly said to us. "What are you looking at me for? She writes about us everyday!"

"No, I don't."

"Sure you do." Kimberly tossed her hair and Crystal sat up.

"Fuck you," Summer snarled.

"Don't act like it ain't true. You know it is." Crystal got into it, too.

"Fuck you—"

"*He loved me. He was everything.*" We held our breath as Crystal recited the lines she'd read to us the night before, while Summer was on dinner-clean up duty.

"FUCK YOU." Summer screamed, but her hand then shot to her mouth. "Ma'am," she said, looking over at Miss Sallyanee, "I'm sorry. I'm real sorry. It just came out."

"Ladies. Ladies. You are children of God. That is not how we speak to each other." Miss Sallyanne grew a little in her chair. "Starlene! Come here. We need you."

Starlene crept down from the stairs that led down to the Group room. She came over like a turkey vulture, looking sideways at each of us.

"Starlene, why don't you get Summer some air? She needs a lesson in how to speak right. A lesson in a doghouse, she don't know how to talk like a human."

"Wait—"

"You got it, ma'am." Starlene stood in front of Summer. "Come on, Sugar."

"No," she said. "I just said it one time. It was an accident."

"No, my ass. Get up and come."

"I'm coming too, then," Lorilee stood up and turned to look at Miss Sallyanne. "I am going to help her, be right back."

"Sit down."

"Come on, Summer. I got you." Lorilee ignored Miss Sallyanne.

"I told you to sit down, girl."

None of us were sure if Lorilee was ignoring her on purpose or if she really didn't hear the woman. Her arms were already around Summer, guiding her out, her whole attention on her.

"Starlene! Get that girl to sit down."

"Ma'am, I'm working on it." Starlene tried to move her body in between the two girls, but they were clinging to each other, moving toward the steps like Summer was wounded and Lorilee was dragging her off the war field. Starlene wedged her bad arm between them when they got to the doorway at the top, and then Lorilee said something under her breath, something nobody else could hear.

Starlene started to back away.

"Starlene!"

Starlene looked at Miss Sallyanne and then looked around the room then, her eyes moving to each girl, like she was looking for something we didn't see. She might have turned to walk out, but Lorilee and Summer were heading out that same door, so she dropped down where she was on the steps. Sitting quiet, like.

"Girls." Miss Sallyanne spoke. "Where were we? Starlene, I will deal with you later."

Fear

I'm Starlene and I'm an alcoholic and addict.

Fear's a big topic. It's a good meeting topic. Where do I start? There's things I'm scared of and things I ain't.

I'm scared of going back out there. Yes, I am. Real scared of that. Scared of waking up in strange places—jail, rehab. Just a few steps before waking up dead. No, thank you, I say. I want to know where I'm waking up.

Yes, there are some things I'm scared of. I ain't ashamed to tell y'all that.

There are other things, too. There are things that when you see them head-on and there ain't no hiding no more. *That* is fear.

Let go and let God help, they say.

Git out of the way and let it pass you by. When you see it eye-to-eye and you know it will be too big for you, may kill you dead, even, get outta the way. That is fear. To me. That is fear.

When there ain't nowhere to hide, then it all comes out. The pain takes over. It's like when my husband would start punching, after he got me by my hair. There weren't nowhere to go. You gotta just close yer eyes and pray you stay alive.

That's fear. When you ain't sure you're going to live through it. I'll tell y'all one thing: I ain't never going let nobody make me that afraid again.

Thank y'all for letting me share.

Swords

June 11, 1986

I need to never let this notebook out of my sight. Those fucking bitches.

When can I leave this fucking place? When is this fucking hell over and I get to leave and never come back? When does it end? How could I just get dumped here with all of these assholes? I wasn't nearly as fucked up as them out there.

How did I get in trouble, when these bitches were singling me out?

I guess I should just be happy. One minute I'm in trouble and Starlene's dragging me out to the fucking fence. Next thing, Lorilee's got her backing away like a dog with its tail between its legs and we're out smoking on the back patio. That Lorilee.

But still. This fucking place.

It's mom's fucking fault. She never calls me. She blames me for everything. She'd leave me here forever, just out of convenience. She is home, drinking her wine, crying, crying, crying, as if she had nothing to do with any of it, as if she didn't make her own boyfriend go away. Like she should get to have a boyfriend, a love, and not me. The only one who loved me is gone.

I didn't mean none of it to happen. I never meant it. I didn't even know it had happened until the next morning. None of us knew. We were just playing quarters on his stomach, not knowing. I woke up and it was all over.

I would take it all back.

I didn't know it would be gone so fast and then I'd be here.

Stop. Stop thinking about this. Stop.

It's pushing, pushing, pushing through, like a tidal wave behind a dam, and I can't hold it back anymore.

June 11, 1986, start over

Starlene is scared or something of Lorilee. I can kinda see why, but I don't get it. Lorilee seems like a regular girl, and then like she seems much older, like way older than all of us. Not that she knows shit but somehow she does know stuff—she knows more than any of us about the things that go on around here, like that drama, Miss Sallyanne's neanderthal son and Marla. (YUCK! I still can't believe she fucked that guy. Talk about punishment for a mistake! Now she's got that guy's kid in her and ... and ... she has to *live* with him. Probably has to fuck him again. VOMIT!).

And fuck Starlene. All pretending to try to make things better for me, fronting for Miss Sallyanne, I'll take care of this, she says in front of all those bitches. That stupid bitch Kimberly pushing me—I don't think they've really read this journal. That's crazy. It's safe where I keep it. Anyway, Crystal was being too general—it didn't seem like she'd read anything. Sounded like she was making shit up. I mean, that is seriously crazy if they read it. But they wouldn't. No. They just like to push me. They're always trying to get a rise out of someone. This time it was me. I could see if it was Lorilee they were really picking on, but not me. They wouldn't do that to me. But I'm keeping this journal on me from now on, just in case.

Anyway, Starlene pulls me out of Group, like she's going to talk to me, but as soon as Lorilee stands up, she turns to ice like she's seen a ghost or something and won't even look at either of us. Lorilee said something. She said something, but I don't know what it was. Starlene sits back down on the stairs and we walk out of the Group room. Nobody stops us. Nobody says anything. So weird.

Later, when we're still out on the patio, Starlene follows us and parks it on the bench and tells us to sit, to stay. Like we are dogs. Then she starts giving us a lecture, well, more like giving me a lecture—she still won't look at Lorilee—anyway, she starts telling me that I need to drop a brick, that ain't nothing going to get any better as long as I keep it all way inside. Like she knows there is something inside me, and then I'm like wondering, are they all reading my journal?

So I say, what are you talking about? Keep what way inside?

The pain, Sugar. The pain, she says.

Shut up, Lorilee says. I'm not sure if she's talking to me or Starlene.

Don't nobody talk to me like that no more, Sugar. Starlene stands up.

Just shut up with that shit, Lorilee says. You don't believe any of that crap.

At first I think those two are going to fight, because Starlene stands up like she's challenging Lorilee. But she leaked out of her mouth, and that is when I noticed not just how skinny her lips were but that they were quivering. Her busted-up arm shaking a little too. And then I realized that Starlene WAS scared. She was like totally scared of Lorilee. It looked like everything that woman had was mustered up in that minute. Because it only lasted a minute.

She manages to squeak out something like, I know who you are, to Lorilee.

Then Lorilee laughs. Good, she says. Then you know I'm right.

I'm watching all this like it's TV, but I don't know what is going on—it's almost like they are on the Spanish station and I don't know what they are saying but I can see their body language.

I got your number, Sugar.

No, daughter, Lorilee says, you don't. (Daughter!) Those two are standing eye to eye, and neither one of them sees me at all. I might as well be invisible or dead, because nobody seems to care that I'm sitting there—which was A-OK with me, thank you very much. They were starting to scare me a little.

Here's the thing, I'm thinking Starlene is about to freak out as soon as she hears the word "daughter," but she doesn't. She doesn't! Crazy, right?! I know! She calms down. That's right. She just calms down. If she had a sword, like a medieval knight, she would have laid it down right there. She rests, she lays down her own load, casts it, is how Miss Sallyanne might have called it, and starts to cry.

And just when I think nobody can see me, that neither of them gives a crap about me, Lorilee turns and says to me, it ain't your fault.

And then I think, *now* I know who's been reading my journal, but just as if she has heard my mind, she says, I didn't read nothing. I just see you, too, Summer.

I'm staring at her and then Crystal pops her pointing beak head out the back door and says, Come on, love fest is over, you lesbos. Get inside. Miss Sallyanne wants you all back.

I'm not sure why Crystal has to go and say stuff like that because it's not like we are hugging or anything. We're all just standing there, just real close. Starlene is sobbing, face in hands, and I—well, I don't know what I looked like. I was standing there. Not smoking anymore. I don't even remember putting my cig out. But my arms were down. There was no more fight, no more nothing in me either, though I wasn't crying. Not yet, anyway.

Daughter, she'd said.

What the fuck?

June 14, 1986

Where do you think you are going to go? Lorilee asks me tonight. We snuck out and sat on the back fence to see the stars when everyone had gone to bed. In the night, the fence by the doghouse didn't seem so ominous-like. Tonight it felt like a gate.

We were smoking in the dark, but the night was so bright, and I could see her real well. She looked younger. She had on her nightgown—some white thing with pink and green flowers—with her jean jacket over it—and somehow, leave it to Lorilee, her hair was still perfect, even though she'd been laying in bed, pretending to sleep, like me.

When?

When we leave here.

I'm not running away.

OK, she says. Just pretend you can. Where do you want to go?

Home, I guess.

Why? What's there?

Um. Duh. *Home*, I say.

I am listening to the air. I hear it carry the sound of the distant cars on the highway—I see them better than I can hear them. I feel them better than either seeing or hearing. I am moving with them. I don't answer her.

I'm not going home, she says. Lorilee has been pulling at a hangnail with her teeth and is able to peel it off. She spits it out into the grass. Ow, she says.

Why not?

There is no home. Nowhere is home.

I am shaking my head. She's so crazy sometimes. I have a home, I say. It's 199 Dogwood Road, Elizabeth City, North Carolina.

No, you don't.

You're so weird, you know that?

I know, she says.

OK, I say after a time. Now why don't I have a home?

You *have* a place to go to—a place everyone expects you to go to, and technically that is your home. It's where your stuff is, your bed, your posters, books, albums.

You are one odd cat, Lorilee. I know.

We sit there for like an eternity. The whole time I'm thinking about it. Thinking about home, and what is there—and what's not there anymore. She's right about that. Shit. My mother doesn't even want to talk to me here, what makes me think that she wants to talk to me or even be in the same house as me?

I keep thinking and then I say, So I could go anywhere.

Exactly. Her smile lights the night. You are free.

June 15, 1986

Marla's baby was born. I feel like I should write that down, record it, like, but it doesn't mean anything to me. It's an event that feels like it should mean something.

June 16, 1986

Lorilee walked back into the room tonight, and I realized she had been out. I mean, I couldn't have known she was gone—everybody was sleeping, me too. And then I woke up when I heard her changing her clothes.

I rolled onto my elbows. Where've you been?

Out.

Out. Like we are allowed to come and go as we please. But she wasn't answering any questions tonight. And if I tried, I just knew I'd get one of those answers that gives me a new question.

June 17, 1986

Miss Sallyanne is out today. She's out too! Why's everybody out all of a sudden? Where does everyone have to go? Why can't I go out???

Second Chance Girls

Miss Sallyanne's car was parked in the driveway, but Starlene kept saying she wasn't at the house. We looked too, peeked into the windows of her office and her room, and they were empty. Is it really possible she went somewhere without telling us? Starlene decided to take over Group. She called us all into the Group room after morning prayers, and she'd already set up the folding chairs into a circle. She was like, "OK, we're going to share our shit."

That's how Starlene does Group.

She says, "OK, don't want any y'all crying that Miss Sallyanne ain't here to make you feel better. Don't think anybody's going to be sitting there quiet, while some other poor soul carries the load. You think I don't see what goes on here? You think I don't see who the brave are and who the cowards are? Well, we ain't going to have none of that today." She looks around the room and sniffs hard. We would all be petrified, but we have a secret— and not the kind you share in Group. "Y'all going to talk the talk and walk the walk today."

She looks around the room again with pencil point eyes. "Don't nobody hide today," she says. "Go." But none of us know who she's talking to. "Do I got to call on someone?"

Lorilee coughs. "I'll go."

"Anybody else?" Starlene's pencil points move around the circle. We hide in our hair, in our hands. Our eyes on our laps, on the floor, on the ceiling.

"I said, I'll go," Lorilee says again.

"Oh," Starlene says, "I bet you got a lot to confess." She rolls her eyes, but she's not even looking at Lorilee.

"Confess? No," she says. "I have no sin."

"Yes, Sugar, you do. We all know who you are." Now she is facing Lorilee, but her eyes fix on the ceiling, still not looking at her.

Lorilee laughs a little. "Do you want me to go or not?"

Starlene sniffs. "OK. We got no other takers, yet. Yes, Sugar. We're all waiting on you." Starlene then adds, "As usual," but we don't know what she means at all, except we kind of do. Somehow we are always waiting for Lorilee. Like Starlene, we hate this girl, but we can't stop talking about her, talking around her, talking to her, either.

"You want me to tell them about the drugs."

"Yes. The truth. I can see the tracks."

"I started using drugs when I was fourteen," she says. "I started using them the same way most of y'all did. I started with weed, beer. Then it got to bigger things. I didn't get into hallucinogens like some people did. The trips, the head-movies that shit makes was too much for my mind."

"Mmmhmm." Starlene nods her head. "What else? Tell them the rest."

Lorilee's breaks into a broad smile. "Then, I guess you know, right? You sound like you know already. That makes sense." She was only looking at Starlene.

"Yeah, Sugar. But tell them girls. The truth will set you free."

"I'll tell them, but I am already free."

"You will be free when I say you are free, heifer."

Instead of fighting back or arguing, Lorilee's smile grows even bigger. She smiles in a way now that makes us feel like there is room for all of us, as if maybe we are already free too, and nobody needs Starlene's or anyone else's permission.

"She says the weirdest things." Kimberly whispers, but of course, we all hear the Queen. Her voice is ours.

"By tenth grade I was already using crank. Shooting it up. Mainline. My boyfriend helped me at first, but then I got the hang of it. Wasn't too hard."

Lorilee pauses, and now it feels like she is bullshitting us. It feels like what she is saying is true and not true at the same time.

"And then what?" Starlene sounds like she's taking notes.

"Then, I hit bottom. You know. Same old thing. Lost things. Kicked outta school. Kicked outta my house. And now I am here."

"That's it," Starlene says, "ain't it? We lose it all to drugs. We hit rock bottom." She starts nodding her head like a bad imitation of Miss Sallyanne. "People, places, things, y'all. They'll get us every time."

But Lorilee's pause absorbs us. We are all quiet. Thinking-like. We've heard the slogan, *People, places, things*, over and over, but today it hangs there like a jail sentence we will never outlive. There is nowhere to go to be free.

"You done, Sugar?"

We are still.

"Yeah." Lorilee leans back. Smirks. That bitch.

"What are we supposed to do, then?" Crystal breaks the silence. "I mean, we can't stay here forever."

"I wish we could," Maryanne says. A bunch of us make agreement noises. But not all of us think so, that's for sure. "What?" she says when some of us roll our eyes. "It's like totally safe here. Like a safe house."

Magda nods. Of course, she thinks so. Before she got here, her ole man never thought twice about smacking her around.

"I'd rather be here than out on the street," Carla Bobby says. "Much better here."

"There ain't nothing safe anywhere," Starlene butts in, and we don't know what to say.

"You're right," Lorilee says. "But we are still safe."

"I ain't got no idea what that means," Starlene says. "Y'all can't be unsafe and safe at the same time. And I'm telling you what you need to know: nowhere's safe. You are never alone—and not in the good Jesus bullshit way. I'm just telling you straight. Nobody's got yer back and there's always gonna be somebody on it. As long as you know that, y'all got a chance."

"That's not what Miss Sallyanne says," Terri says.

"I ain't Miss Sallyanne. I'm telling it to you straight, and I'm telling you the ways of the world. That is what it is."

"Where's Marla?" Summer pipes up. Nobody knows where the fuck that came from. But we look at Starlene.

"I don't know," Starlene says. "I don't know, Sugar, but good for her. God bless her."

"What's that: 'good for her'? What the hell does that mean?" Kimberly leans in.

"Kindly watch your mouth, heifer," Starlene chides. We snicker at the word "heifer."

"Where is the baby?" Summer asks. The morning sun is bearing down on the house and the roof feels like it must be made out of aluminum foil. Our hair sticks to the back of our necks and foreheads.

"Tell them," Lorilee says to Starlene.

"At the office house," Starlene tells us.

"The baby?" we ask in our ways.

"I don't get it. What is going on?" Kimberly looks at Crystal—not that Crystal, or any of us, for that matter, know anything.

"Marla's already working?" Summer asks.

"No."

"Where is she, then?"

Starlene holds her breath and her cheeks puff out. "Miss Sallyanne's at the Sheriff's, and she's bringing the baby here."

"Where's Marla?" Maryanne asks.

Now nobody's talking. Not even Starlene.

"What're we going to do with a baby?" Crystal asks, but no one answers her.

"*We* ain't fixin' to do nothing with a baby," Starlene says.

"Wait." Carla Bobby sits up in her chair. "*Where* is Marla?"

"She done left, Sugar."

"Come on," Kimberly says. "Let's smoke."

This time Starlene doesn't chase after us, calling us lazy heifers. She doesn't come with, but she's not resisting either. Group, we guess, is over.

Swords

June 17, 1986

It's time, Lorilee said to me. It's time to go. If you're going to go, it's now.

I thought we talked about this. We are in our room, and the roommates are on laundry duty. I'm not running away, I tell her.

Yes. But I'm not joking. It's time to go, she says.

I'm not even sure there's anything to go home to, I say.

I didn't say we're going home.

Lorilee says with Miss Sallyanne all upset about Marla gone and now a baby here to look after, that she is not paying attention. It's now, she says. Now or—

Never? I say and she says, no, you got forever. Lorilee. She says the funniest things. It's not like she's got so far to go to get home, but she makes it sound like she's got to travel eons or something. Eons. Like I even know how far that is. She could be going home at night for all I know.

Let me know if you're in. Lorilee's hair is pinned back in a tidy bun. She tucks a loose strand of her hair behind her ear. I'm going out for a smoke. Wanna come?

No, I say.

Don't forget, she says over her shoulder as she leaves the room. Let me know.

She was out again last night. She doesn't know I saw her come in. It's not like she is even subtle about it anymore. She comes and goes at night. And truth be told: I couldn't sleep. I was up thinking about running away. Thinking about leaving this place. Just the thought of leaving makes me feel like I'm going to explode. I didn't realize how badly I want to go home until now. It's like the idea of maybe being able to run opened up floodgates and my wishing and homesickness started to flow out, pushing out all the things I tell myself to not to feel so that Miss Sallyanne will say I look like a normal girl and I can go home. All of my longing has bled out, dragging rage with it: I fucking hate waiting for Miss Sallyanne to decide when I can leave. I hate her, I hate this place, I hate that I am disappearing the longer I am here.

I want to leave. Go. Run from this place. Get away before I forget everything and stop feeling everything.

When? I want to ask Lorilee. When can we go? I don't ask, though.

Tonight I swear I heard a motor. It was far off, and I think it was a motorcycle, but it left before she came in. And I don't know. Maybe it was way far away. With the pastures around here putting distance between roads and highways, sounds carry and seem closer and farther away from you knowing where anything really is.

V

Reflection

The sun, the moon, and the truth. Cain't keep none of them down. That's what they say. That's what I say. That child Marla done surprised all of us. Scared the holy bejesus out of Sallyanne. Panic mode, is what she is in now. Lockdown is what all of them girls is on. But they kind of were already, anyhow. It ain't like anybody was going anywhere nohow. Ain't none from here. Oh, they're from Texas all right. Mostly. Some are from Oklahoma— I guess somebody's gotta be. And one or two are from further—like the Carolinas and Louisiana. Same with the Indian girl here. That Magda. Living off the reservation ain't done nothing for her, but it's still better than living on it. But the rest. Born and bred Texans, I believe.

Not that *that* is helping any of them. They're more like the Texas Rejects.

Now that Marla. I think she's telling people she's Texan—and she is, don't get me wrong. But I know her blood. It's way older. I can see it in the shape of her face. She's Indian, too. No doubt. So it shouldn't a surprised nobody when that girl done skipped out on her kid. Done skipped out on the chance Sallyanne gave her—to marry her only son.

Not that he is such a gift. Zacchaeus is one lazy boy. You'd think that Sallyanne and Tad are bringing in the dough, that that child has been sitting in the lap of luxury his whole life, the way he takes everything for granted. The way he gets by doing just barely nothing at all. I'm supposed to call him when things at the house go haywire. Like that time I needed somebody to fix the pipe that cracked. It ain't that hard to do, I know now. How do I know? I will tell all y'all. I wound up doing it myself. Wrapped that plumber's tape right straight around and thank you very much. I've got a brand new pipe now, more or less. So that kid—by the time he'd a gotten around to calling a plumber for me, we'd a been outta water for days. It mighta been easier to get Sallyanne to get Tad's boys over here to do the work, but we know what havoc that will wreak.

Still. Sallyanne gave that girl her only son.

I should of known something wasn't right. I DID know something wasn't right. I could feel it, but I was watching them she-devils right here at the house. With Sallyanne trotting back and forth to the Ash house, running to the Sheriff's office and whatnot the last few days, somebody had to keep an eye on them girls. Like a bunch of man-eating sharks, they smelled blood in the water, and they just attack.

First it started with laziness. Ain't nobody wants to talk about feelings. So fuck it, I say. I can see that as soon as Lorilee starts bullshitting again us with some story in Group. I try to do the right thing, and look it what I get. I try to get them girls to get real, to get honest, to save they's own lives, and she starts some crap about using, and I already know it's bull. Fool me once, shame on you. Fool me twice, shame on me. She knows I know, but she keeps going. The other girls, they are with her, half believing, the other half, who the hell knows what goes on in they's heads? Their brains, I swear to the Lord Almighty himself, are just little marbles rolling around glass jars up there.

So the Queen announces they's all going to lay out in the sun. I don't know why I done it but I just let them go. I just let them. It's a whole lot easier than if one of them start talking real about the hurts she carries. Because truth be told: I can't bear the loads no more. With each story, each brick one of these girls drops, I get a little heavier, and I just can't do it. Ain't nobody around here notice that Starlene is carrying it all in her own two arms. I know I am just the cook, but I am also the carrier. The bearer of all they hurts. The one who watches and bears the witness.

Somebody has to be. It ain't Sallyanne. Sallyanne who's been living on Planet Jesus way too long to even notice that her son was fucking one of the underage clients. She don't even notice that nobody cares about Jesus here and Jesus ain't helping these girls.

All right. I know. I ain't being Christian right now. I know. I will let it go.

Live and let live. That is what I say today.

So I let them girls go out. Not all of them understood Marla's running, and that was fine. They shouldn't see a mother, a young mother, abandon a baby like that. They's going to see their own mothers in her, some of them. Or they's going to think that it's all right, that a mother ain't got to stay with her child.

But that ain't all right. That ain't all right, because I've been on both sides of it. And when you ain't there, when you do things that make it impossible to be there and you can't go back, well, that's a burden you ain't never going to drop in no Group therapy, no matter how many times you talk about it. There ain't a program, a counselor, nothing in the world that is going to make that all right.

So I let them heifers go outside, and we had no more Group.

Sallyanne done let these girls down. She knew I knew. That ole Tad. He's a wily one. Like a fox. A dumb fox, is what I say. He thinks ole Starlene don't see him. Don't see what he's up to. Don't see what he makes his sister do to keep everything fine. Fine on the outside. But I knew. And I wasn't the only one. Lorilee knew. I wasn't sure at first how. No—that ain't true. I didn't believe it at first. I couldn't believe it. But she's just as much a con artist as that Tad.

She sneaking in and out of the house in the middle of the night. The way them two look at each other when he comes over. And it ain't like I didn't notice that he'd started coming twice, thrice a week. Now what is he doing over at this house full of girls so much, I ask you?

I know what he's doing. He's up to no good.

And it ain't like Sallyanne weren't hip to it. She got hip right quick. She knows her brother. Thinks anything with a hole is his to fuck. Just like her father.

Oh, she don't know I know that neither. But I can feel it. She thinks she's the only one who knows that kind of shame. At least her brother weren't bothering her too. But he brung it somewhere else. The father—I seen him coming a mile away with his righteousness and fury. Thinks ain't nobody see through his lust.

My Jesus knows what's up and what's down.

Maybe that's why Tad never left her alone. He stuck by just to keep an eye on his sister, because that ole geezer weren't going nowhere. He was staying right close, preaching like he knew the Word, like he wrote it. He wrote it, my ass, is what I say.

He's old now, but he ain't dead. He didn't mind spewing righteousness at them girls. Shit, he got nothing else to do. Them girls, who bless their hearts, are still spilling out of their tank tops, wearing tight jeans, putting themselves on display like they're in a store window, having no idea what kind of lust they're inspiring in an old man.

Sallyanne didn't mean it all to happen, but she was still in it—not knowing the way out, because she was still in the cycle, feeding it, going round and round, reliving all of it, past and present, past and present. Now she was her own mother, not protecting these girls, exposing them to harm, they's now getting pregnant in her care. She got to face her own done-to or there ain't no break from the cycle. I seen it before. Oh hell. I *lived* it before with my own mama.

I let them heifers go outside. Let the sun care for them. I can't offer them much. I got my own pain in a bundle by the door. I carry it as soon as I leave the kitchen every night, take it back to bed with me, and it keeps me up at night. Let the sun care for them. Let them lay out and take in the sunrays, a nice little what-have-you in a desert of hurt.

I stay with them girls. I know they don't know it and they probably don't 'preciate it, stupid heifers that they are. I could've left any time. I can only hope they will look back and see that when things fell apart, ole Starlene was there.

I stayed.

I watched.

And when they all are gone, I will remember them as light and I will forget all the rest.

Swords

June 19, 1986

I heard the most incredible thing tonight. I can't seem to get my head around it. Lorilee told me her secret. Not her past secret. Her now secret. I just can't get it. I mean, I get it, but I don't get it.

I'm not sure she was going to tell me, but I caught her. I caught her—sneaking out again, and sneaking back in. I saw her go out this time. She got dressed in the dark, it was about 1 in the morning, and she had her clothes laid out on the bed like she always does. Her hair in a net. She was all ready to go out.

I waited this time before she came back. She was gone a few hours, till about 4. I barely stayed awake. She came right through the back door—I could see her out the window that looks over the patio. The moon lit the night and she was a shadow until she entered our room. She got undressed, re-folded her clothes and stood in her underwear by the window that looked out back.

Where you been? I asked her.

She turned and I could see her face in the dimness. I've been to see my beautiful boy.

He's out there now?

Ha. She said. Yes. Heading back home.

He's not a boy, I said after she wasn't saying anymore.

OK. Not a boy, you're right. A man. Yes, I guess so. A man-boy. Yes, she said. That's what he is. He's got the sweetest face. A man-boy. She like glided over to my bed, making no sound. All you could hear was Crytal's snoring cutting the air.

You're going to get in trouble.

Only if you tell. You going to tell on me? No.

He's the way out, she whispered. He'll take us.

Who? Tad?

She burst out in a laugh and covered her mouth. Tad?! No, Summer. A good guy.

Her face was like real close to mine. I was still up on my bunk, and she was leaning her head on her hands. I swear she looked so beautiful in the dark, and I couldn't help it, I'd have said yes to anything right then.

We can go. It's now, Summer. He will take us away from here. We can go.

Where we going to go?

Anywhere. San Antonio. Corpus Christi.

Texas? Oh, right, nobody'd *ever* find us in Texas. I rolled my eyes. What about North Carolina?

North Carolina? We could go to North Carolina, if you want. She shook her head. He's not going to drive us that far, but he can get us on our way.

What would you do in North Carolina? I said to her.

What are *you* going to do in North Carolina? she shot right back.

She was right about that. I'll give her that.

South Carolina's better, she said. Beaches, sun. Let's just head east and see what happens.

Wait. *Who* is this guy?

She smiled at me, and I got the feeling she was like Einstein, waiting for all the average-intelligence people to catch up every time he said something. I waited. But she wasn't answering.

Her hand moved over my arm. So you ready?

Crystal wheezed in her sleep.

I don't know, I said, but I meant yes.

We'll work it out in the morning. She patted my elbow like a mom. Get some sleep now. Don't worry anymore. Her hand moved to my temple and stroked it real slow, and that was the last thing I remember.

Early morning, June 20, 1986

How does she know? How does she know what I think, what I feel? Am I that obvious? She makes it all right, though. All is well, all is well, she says, all will be well.

She makes everything seem possible, and now I can't sleep again. I am already imagining us catching a bus to the east coast. Starting new in Virginia or Myrtle Beach. Somewhere warm and sunny. We could get jobs at restaurants, waiting tables. Be roommates. Jesus. We could even change our names.

Terrifying. But not really. She makes me feel like I can do anything.

She's definitely right about one thing: there isn't anything for me in North Carolina. And I already know if I go back there, I will look for Tommy on every corner, in every store, in every place I go. But he isn't there, of course, and if he isn't there, there isn't no home anyway.

Second Chance Girls

We heard the baby before we saw her. Even over the torrential rain, rain from like the Bible, we heard her. Even a Texas rainstorm couldn't drown out the sound of that child. Later some of us would say we felt her at Second Chance before we even heard her, but that's neither here nor there.

Miss Sallyanne brought her. Helpless and lumbering, Zacchaeus had left for good. He'd left to find his woman and left the baby in the office—alone—The Reverend was nowhere to be found. We heard later the preacher had gone with his grandson to track down Marla, to bring her home and teach her a lesson—to show Zacchaeus how it was done. But in the meantime, Tad found the child wailing when he stopped into the office for some paperwork. He took one look at that baby and called Miss Sallyanne. Nobody could say for how long that child had been alone.

We were in morning affirmations, still sitting at the dining tables after breakfast.

"Today, I am a good person!" Maryanne announced her affirmation.

"Love you, Maryanne," we all responded like we were supposed to.

"I can be one among many, I can belong!" Magda sang.

Terri started to say, "Today, I am ready to—" A baby's cry interrupted.

"What was that?" Crystal asked, but she of all people should've known. She had one of her own back home.

We knew we heard it. The wail came from inside the house.

Miss Sallyanne looked at Starlene like the baby's cries were her fault.

"I'm going," Starlene's feet were already moving toward the western side of the house, where Miss Sallyanne's office was.

She emerged in a few minutes with a white care package wrapped in a knit blanket. The baby's dark hair spread from under her pink cap, a sharp contrast. Her face puckered, and her black eyes widened to absorb a room full of sound and energy.

"Oh my word." Kimberly jumped up to see. We followed her and circled around Starlene.

"Did you have to bring that child in here?" Miss Sallyanne glared at Starlene. Even watery and bloodshot, Miss Sallyanne's black eyes were still penetrating, and Starlene turned away little from her like she was protecting the baby.

"You can't hide her in your office, ma'am." Starlene drew the blanket around the little shoulders. "Back up, you heifers. Don't you see this is a newborn? Stop yer breathing all over her. Yer germs are going to kill her dead before she even walks." The elbow of Starlene's bad arm sprang out and we backed up.

"Is that Marla's baby?" Summer said. We were surprised she wasn't writing all this down already.

"Settle down, girls. Spectacle is over. Sit down and finish your affirmations. I know all y'all ain't well yet." Miss Sallyanne took the baby from Starlene's arms. Her own arms made an awkward cradle, stiff and unmoving, like she was cuddling a stone. The baby started to cry again, and Lorilee stood up.

This time Miss Sallyanne didn't insist on anyone settling down and she automatically handed the child over.

Lorilee whispered something to the baby, which sounded something like, "We've been waiting for you," but we weren't sure. She held the baby close and moved her index finger in a shape over her forehead. The baby kept fussing. "Somebody get this child's bottle," she said looking right at Summer, who had already started to head to the kitchen.

"I got it, Sugar," Starlene said to Summer. "Sit down."

"What's her name?" Crystal asked Miss Sallyanne. "Abigail," Miss Sallyanne said after a moment.

"Abigail?" Lorilee said. "Yuck. Sounds like an old lady."

"I used to have a cat named Abigail." Terri nodded. "It's true."

"I beg your pardon," Miss Sallyanne said.

"I'm just saying—," Terri began.

"Did anyone ask you?" Starlene butted in as she walked back across the room with the baby's bottle. "I got her now." Starlene reached for the baby to feed her.

"I think your name is something else," Lorilee said to the baby, even as Starlene was pulling her away. "Abigail is not your name, is it?" Lorilee whispered. "Tell me your name."

"Rain," Summer said from the corner of the room. "Her name should be Rain. Like the storm she came in."

"That's like your name," Lorilee looked up and smiled. "Earthy-like." The two of them having their own discussion like nobody else was in the room.

"Yep. An earth name."

"I like it," Lorilee said, as if it were up to them to decide.

With the baby in her arms, she walked to the far end of the room, away from every other person in it.

"What the hell is going on here?" Kimberly stood up. She looked around the tables. "That baby ain't all y'all's."

"Settle down," Miss Sallyanne said, but she seemed to be lost in her thoughts, not directing it at Kimberly, or anyone in particular.

"I mean, who the fuck do you think you are? You don't name somebody else's kid." Kimberly stood over the table where she'd been sitting at. "Seriously. What the fuck? Somebody tell me."

"Kim, there's a baby—" Crystal began to say, but Kimberly wasn't done.

"I *know* there is a baby. I am aware, thank you very much. But somebody's got to say something and stop this bullshit." Kimberly didn't have to say it, but we knew she meant Lorilee herself. She was the bullshit—having her in our midst was so much more than the assumption that she and her loser friend would name that child. All the liberties Lorilee took, all the freedom she seemed to have, to say and do what she wanted—Jesus, it wasn't like we didn't know she was leaving in the night and coming back whenever she felt like it. Of course, we knew—her restlessness had become ours: Almost nobody had slept normal after she'd come. And if we knew, Miss Sallyanne and Starlene must have known too. Yet nobody said a word. Small offenses that would have gotten us on our knees at the back fence or bigger ones that would have gotten us a night in the doghouse didn't carry the same consequences for Lorilee. She spoke freely, did what she pleased.

Entitlement. That's what Lorilee exuded. We wouldn't have said that word at the time, but we knew it when we saw it. It was her entitlement that made us hate her. Her simple assumptions: to speak as she wished, to wear different clothes, to ask for what she wanted, to leave and to return as she pleased. We recognized it the minute she'd pranced into the Second Chance Home for Girls that first day. Her very presence had reminded us all of what we were not, what we would never be. There would never be any release from our lack until she was gone.

"Her name is Abigail." Miss Sallyanne stood up. "She is her father's pride and joy. That is her name."

"Oh yeah? Where's her daddy now?" Lorilee turned to look at Miss Sallyanne. And none of us were sure we'd seen it, but we thought—we just *thought*—we saw Miss Sallyanne shrink back a little. Even if she didn't, she had nothing to say. She got really quiet; because we all knew that Zacchaeus was out searching for his woman, that he'd never come back without Marla. If that lumbering idiot believed anything, he believed Marla had been given to him. She was his woman. Not even Jesus could bring him back.

Miss Sallyanne pushed her chair back and started to walk out of the room.

"Where are you going, Miss?" Terri asked. "Don't we have Group in a few minutes?"

"I'll be in my office. Don't disturb me," Miss Sallyanne said over her shoulder as she drifted through the door that led to the western side of the house.

"This shit has to end." Kimberly scooped up her cigarettes and lighter and charged out of the dining room. We followed. We had to. We shuffled out and found her on the patio outside, pacing and puffing. Nobody believed she cared about the baby. She knew we didn't care all that much either. We'd walked away from our own children, and we could easily walk away from this one. But we'd just seen the only mother some of us had ever known drift away from us, into her own private ether and there was nowhere else for us to go.

The baby stayed in Second Chance Home for Girls for the rest of our days there, numbered as they were.

That's when Miss Sallyanne moved in full time, seven days a week, the visits to "her people" now over. Being in the house all the time did not make her any more present. We guessed she felt obliged to be at the house, what with Rain living there, although she almost never held the child. You'd never see her feeding or changing her. Starlene took primary care of the child during the day, so Miss Sallyanne could still be our counselor and spiritual leader—that was what she was calling herself now, when in fact she did leave her office, which was more and more rare these days.

Tad stopped coming by Second Chance after an argument one day. We heard him and Starlene in the dining room screaming something fierce, like two old married people, when they thought no one could hear them. During Group, Maryanne had been crying, going on about her parents' divorce ten years before, but Tad's and Starlene's voices penetrated the walls, and it almost sounded like Maryanne's parents had come to Second Chance to act out their divorce. Baby Rain started crying (yes, we started calling her that, since Miss Sallyanne seemed unable to call her Abigail or anything else after that first day), and the arguing stopped. We heard a door slam. Starlene appeared at the top of the stairs with the baby in her one good arm. She was rocking her gently to make her stop crying, but she was staring at Miss Sallyanne like she was waiting for an answer to a question she didn't ask.

Maryanne was still talking when Miss Sallyanne started to speak over her: "*And now, Israel, what doth the Lord God require of thee, but to fear the Lord God—*"

"Ma'am?" Maryanne's tears had streaked lines over her cheeks.

"To walk in all his ways, and to love him, and to serve the Lord thy God with all they heart and with all thy soul."

"Miss Sallyanne, I—"

"We are done, girls. Go to school. Praise be to God."

There wasn't any school that day. Teach hadn't been around in a couple weeks—nobody knew why she'd left again—but we could see Miss Sallyanne wasn't in a reasoning kind of mood. Lorilee had disappeared—maybe to her room, maybe to the other side of the house, we didn't know—but the rest of us shuffled out to have a smoke.

"What the hell was that?" Crystal said when we were out on the patio. She lit one of those nasty old lady cigarettes she liked, the 100s with the gold filters.

"She's like totally checked out," Terri said.

We'd all see the liquid, runny eyes rimmed red. Ever since the preacher had beat her in front of us, broke her in front of us, Miss Sallyanne had never come back together. We saw Miss Sallyanne's detachment and then her temper, which flared at the most unexpected times. We knew she locked that door to her office for more than just to do paperwork—we knew it even as we were no longer invited to talk to her one-on-one anymore. We'd all seen it before, lived it, breathed it. We saw it in the way she no longer listened to our stories in Group, the way she sighed nothingness, no longer optimistic or chirping about Salvation. The difference between Miss Sallyanne and us now had narrowed to one point: while all of us were headed back to the endless road of using, Miss Sallyanne had just beaten us there. She showed us what we all inwardly suspected: Jesus himself couldn't keep any of us, not even her, his last true believer, from getting high. We all knew the name of our one and true god, and he was coming to claim us one by one.

The weight of this realization had doubled our despair. The hopelessness we carried ordinarily had now become full-blown. It wasn't just the obvious that worried us: that the one person who held the keys to our freedom had now checked out and would forget about all of us, forget to discharge us and let us return to where we came from. It was way more—because not all of us wanted to go home, even though we said as much—it was the loss of the one person who claimed she loved us. The only person on earth who hadn't left us, had now left us, if not in body yet, definitely in heart and mind. Miss Sallyanne was gone, as far as we could see. Now there wasn't anyone who might believe that we were good, loveable, redeemable. Not one person nowhere.

And it was Lorilee's fault. She set everything in motion.

It's hard to say who had the idea first, but when Kimberly called Summer over the next day while we were all smoking on the patio, we knew what she was going to say. We could breathe the very words as her own breath formed them.

"Hey, girl," Kimberly said to Summer. "Is this yours?" She held up a small heart charm on a silver chain.

"My charm." Summer put her cigarette between her lips and reached for the necklace. "Where'd you find this?"

"I don't know. Somebody found it."

Some of us looked over at Crystal, but we were careful not to distract Summer. She fastened the silver chain around her neck.

"We were going to play a game."

"Now?" Summer's fingers played with the charm.

"No, not now," Terri said. "Later, like at night."

All she'd have to do is get Lorilee outside. Just like they did sometimes, sitting out back while everyone's asleep.

"How did you know we went out there?

"Girl, there ain't no secrets here."

Summer got quiet. "I don't know," she said after a time. "She's kinda funny."

"You can say that," somebody said.

"Come on, girl, it'll be fun," Kimberly beamed a Barbie smile at her.

Summer turned the charm over between her fingers. We knew she was thinking about it.

"I don't know," she said again, this time more decisively. "Maybe," she said, but it sounded like no.

A motorcycle roared to life on the other side of the house. We could hear the gravel fly out from under its wheels and then its tires hitting the pavement of the road.

Lorilee came around the corner of the house, back from the driveway.

"That girl is so fucking weird," somebody said as we watched her walk toward us.

"Total freak," Kimberly said and turned her back on her. "OK," she said to Summer. "It's cool. Whatever. Your girlfriend is back."

"Where were you?" Crystal asked Lorilee.

"Doing chores." Lorilee lit a cigarette and winked at Summer.

"Down the road?"

Lorilee rolled her eyes. "Did I interrupt something here?"

We all turned from Summer and started talking about Marla's baby. Terri came out from the house. The back door banged behind her. "Hey," she said to Lorilee, "Starlene said you left the mop in the wrong place. Go back and put it right."

"Kay," Lorilee put out her cigarette with the toe of her tennis shoe. "I'm coming back in." Before the door closed behind her, she turned back at all of us and beamed a smile.

"Gimme a light," Terri said once Lorilee was inside. She cupped her hands around her cig while Maryanne lit her up. Her eyes looked left to right to make sure we were all listening. "Baby Rain ain't Zacchaeus."

"Wait. What?" Carla Bobby moved closer.

"It ain't his."

"Aw, bullshit," somebody said.

"No, really," Terri said. "I know *for sure*."

"How do you know?" Kimberly asked for all of us. "I heard them. Miss Sallyanne and Starlene were talking about it in the kitchen last night when y'all were out smoking. Remember I came back in to get my lighter because my other one died? They didn't know I was inside. But I heard them. That baby ain't Zacchaeus."

"I told you. Who'd ever fuck that guy?" Kimberly reminded us all that she would never, even if he were the last man on earth.

"God, he is like so gross." Maryanne's eyes still looked teary from Group, but the thought of Zacchaeus' repulsiveness seemed to cheer her up.

"He was always nice to me," Magda said.

"Ew. That fucking figures. You love him." Kimberly, again. "Maybe you'd fuck him."

"Shut up," Magda turned her back on the Queen.

"You do love him," Kimberly said. "You want to have his baby?"

She was half kidding, we knew, waiting to see, like a cat tapping a fallen bird, testing out what it would do.

Magda walked away.

"Sometimes," Kimberly shook her head after Magda hedged to the far side of the patio, "that girl too. A fucking weirdo."

"Shut up," we heard behind the screen door, after it slammed behind Magda.

"I know. Totally weird." Crystal lit another cigarette.

Miss Sallyanne tried—we'll give her that—she tried to keep things together. But with a newborn in the house, one abandoned by her mama, a mama that her own son impregnated and did not marry—at least that was the story she was still sticking to—it was like pushing a big, heavy rock up a steep hill, over and over. Not all of us knew about kids, but a bunch of us did. So instead of school and book learning, and because nobody seemed to know where Teach went anyway, we babysat, all thirteen of us at once sometimes—to keep an eye on the girls who'd get distracted easily—or on our own, because some of us already had kids back at home and knew a whole lot more about what to do.

We kept Baby Rain in her bouncy seat during Group. Almost always she'd be quiet. Never quite sleeping, but watchful. She wasn't a baby who preferred a binky shoved in her mouth. Instead she had this old-man look on her face, like she'd been studying us for a long time, observing-like. Most of the time. Then she had her normal newborn moments, when she'd just cry and cry and no one could get her to settle down. It was almost like she was screaming out for how we felt all the time.

Before it all fell apart, Miss Sallyanne called on Summer in Group one day—during the last Group it turned out, but nobody knew that then. Summer, who for all her quietness, her gentleness, her smarts, was more stubborn than anybody'd anticipated. Because there was no way, no how, she was getting honest, dropping a brick, in Group. She never said shit—even when she was talking, she didn't say anything important-like. As far as she was concerned, there were no unsteady bricks in her house to drop.

But we all knew *that* was bullshit. That girl carried some shit in her heart, just like the rest of us. We can say this now, because it turns out Miss Sallyanne was always right about it: Nobody came to Second Chance Home for Girls by mistake. Summer belonged here like the rest of us, just as fucked up. She only thought that writing shit down and not talking about it would make it go away, get her discharged sooner because she seemed like she had no problems. She didn't seem to know what all of us already knew: ain't nobody was going anywhere. Crystal had been stealing her diary every week and copying out parts until Summer began carrying the thing with her everywhere. Us girls on the other side of the house would read them—those of us who could read—like bedtime stories to each other. So she wasn't fooling any of us: her past was as much a prison as ours. We knew some guy Tommy was hanging her up. We knew she had some kind of mother hang-up. Of course, all of us did, so that wasn't all that interesting. Her father was gone, so she had Daddy issues too. We were all the same.

So when Miss Sallyanne called on her in Group, we waited. We could all see that Miss Sallyanne was belligerent-like, almost prowling for a fight with someone. We saw why in those red eyes and in her teeth- grinding. So we sat back and waited to hear the stories, to listen to the pain that grew like ivy around this girl's heart.

"I'll go," Lorilee said instead.

"Jesus H. Christ," muttered Terri.

Maryanne rolled her eyes. Even she was getting sick of Lorilee.

"Why, bless your heart. I wasn't asking you, honey." Miss Sallyanne spoke slowly, deliberately, like she was careful to pronounce the right words correctly, in case the narcotics reformed them in her mouth. She glanced at the baby in the bouncy seat across the room.

"Summer ain't got nothing to say," Lorilee said.

Miss Sallyanne ignored her—which was something that took tremendous will. None of us could ignore that girl, even when we were ignoring her. But we figured Miss Sallyanne had gotten ready for today's Group. The pills she was taking (yes, we know that now) mustered up the will to break Summer—if only because there was no breaking Lorilee. And the pills narrowed her attention, made it easier-like to pretend Lorilee was not speaking and zero in on Summer. Because somebody had to pay something for the broken house she had on her hands. Second Chance Home for Girls was not supposed to have an abandoned baby in it. And she used to say *we* were off the track! She had tried to make sure we were going to the same place every girl in Texas knew she was going: church, married, children, house. She knew no other benchmarks of a righteous life, even as she had none of these things herself. Miss Sallyanne used to say that we could be anything, if we lived a sober, godly life, but anything was only really one thing to her. A life of surrender, she'd say. But already most of us knew that *anything* was bullshit, and surrender, well, we all knew something about that. We'd seen that *any-thing* came with the price of everything: as soon as some God-fearing boy saddled you with a kid, there wasn't going to be time for nothing else we might have wanted. All we had to do is look at the baby in the middle of the Group room, and we knew all too well that surrender was the last thing we'd do.

Now Miss Sallyanne knew it too, so in her drug-induced fury, she came harder at Summer.

"Honey, I ain't sure you have a place here at Second Chance, if you don't drop your brick." That sugar-sweet venom voice. She might as well have said, Bless your heart, while she was at it. "Do you know where girls go if they ain't ready for change? If they ain't ready to accept Jesus, the Son, into their lives?"

"Hell?" Summer asked, but she sounded a little like she was going to laugh—or cry.

"Hell. Well, yes, honey. I have no doubt that you are on the path to Hell. Your resistance to change tells me that. You are powerless, girl, over so much: alcohol, drugs, sex. But so much more. As soon as you admit that, you will be on the road to recovery. That is where Jesus will meet you, on that road. And there ain't going to be nobody, no Lorilee, to help you then." She glanced toward Lorilee, who was leaning back, disinterested. "Where you're going, there ain't going to be nobody to help you."

"Sally—," Starlene started to say from her perch over us.

"Come on."

"Starlene, why don't you go straighten up the kitchen. We are OK here. We don't need your commentary today."

"Sallyanne, it's just—"

"Please, Starlene. This is my House. Know yer place."

Starlene turned around and left. Cabinet doors and pots banged from inside the kitchen.

A loud sigh sound came from Baby Rain.

"Somebody get that child's binky," Miss Sallyanne spat.

"She don't like it, Miss," Maryanne said.

"All babies like pacifiers. Y'all should know that. You've been pacifying yourselves with drugs and alcohol for years because you ain't growed up."

Terri put the pacifier in Baby Rain's mouth. We watched as the baby sucked on it like she was studying it.

"Now, Summer." The razors sharpened. "Drop your brick. Set yourself free. We ain't leaving here until you do."

Baby Rain spit the binky out.

We didn't breathe. Crystal went to pick up the binky but a look from Kimberly made her leave it on the floor.

Forty-five minutes of staring at the ground. Baby Rain had had a change and a bottle and was passed halfway around the Group room, held in our arms. The sun bore down on the roof and the heat in the room stifled us.

Some girls had to pee, but Miss Sallyanne wasn't letting nobody leave the room. "This is your last chance, child," she said to Summer. By now, Miss Sallyanne had transformed from ominous to nearly exhausted. Her will to break Summer was still strong, though, and when the girl—God, so stupid, we thought—said a defiant: "NO!" Miss Sallyanne surprised us all. From zero to sixty in two seconds, she leapt to her feet, stretched across the Group circle and slapped Summer's face. "You get the fuck in that doghouse and stay there until I tell you to come out. We ain't going to be tolerating no talk-back here, girl."

Probably from sheer surprise, Summer sat still, her hand to the side of her face that was now bright red from Miss Sallyanne's open hand. Stunned, she sat tall with a stiff back and both feet on the ground. Not moving.

None of us were moving, since we were all just as stunned as Summer.

"Get her out of here." Miss Sallyanne's black eyes were wild as they circled the room. "Get her the fuck out of here before I kill her dead."

Lorilee jumped up, but Miss Sallyanne told her to shut it before she got hers too. Lorilee took one step forward, but Crystal and Magda held her back while a couple of us grabbed Summer. Carla Bobby and Terri squeezed Summer's arms behind her back, both pushing and pulling her in opposite directions as they shoved her out the door.

"*Remember therefore from whence thou art fallen, and repent, and do the first works; or else I will come unto thee quickly, and will remove the candlestick out of this place, except thou repent.*" Miss Sallyanne gave a final word while we were wrestling with Summer and then left the room.

Miss Sallyanne had turned the corner down the hall toward her office. Magda stood in front of Lorilee and punched her in the stomach. Carla Bobby and Terri, who were already out the door with Summer, writhing and twisting in their grip, looked back to hear what the noise was. Lorilee dropped to the floor and threw up. We might've all taken another shot at her, because seeing her on the floor like that, holding her guts, felt better than salvation itself. But Starlene raced in, Baby Rain in her arms.

"What in God's name is going on here?"

We backed away from Lorilee, some of us looking like we were just seeing her for the first time. Starlene charged down the steps but stopped in front of her and said, "Git up. Git up, and all y'all get out of here. Something's gotta give around here. Something's gotta give." Baby Rain started to cry and Starlene tightened her grip on the child.

We melted into the walls and poured out into the backyard, but still savoring the taste of violence. In our minds, we would save the picture of that girl who once waltzed into the Second Chance Home for Girls curled up in her own vomit. We would replay the punch, the sound of it, and then the sight of her hitting the floor, the vomit in her hair, on her face, over and over and over until the desire for more overtook us, and made our secret, futile dream a reality.

Surrender

I'm Starlene and I'm an alcoholic and addict.

Letting go is a good topic for a meeting. If you don't surrender, your disease will control you. It'll bring you to yer knees. Give up control or it will control you and you ain't gonna like it.

Surrender is like something soldiers do on a battle-field. When there ain't nothing left to fight for and it's give up or die.

Yeah. Hmm. I don't know about all that. Let go and then what? What will save you? What will protect you? Surrender and you're dead. That's what it seems to me.

Surrender's for sissies and assholes. I ain't got much more to say about it. Not sure how much I like this topic.

Thank you for letting me share.

Swords

June 21, 1986

Miss Sallyanne doesn't have to waste her time trying to convince me that the Glory of God the Father is eternal. I'm not worried about the glory of anything. And God hasn't done much besides hold me in the space of time, where nothing moves forward and the past is as present as the present itself. And I don't need some phony woman in an office telling me about righteousness to make me tell the truth. My truth. I know who I am. I decide how and when this story is told. And if that old bitch thinks that she is going to make me tell a group of other bitches who and what I am, she can lock me up in that shithole doghouse till the end of my days. Lorilee tells me all the time I am free. I thought it was a joke. But now, I see what she means. I have always been free, whether I am here in this godforsaken shithole or some other one. She kept me chained to that fucking doghouse all fucking night. I saw the stars open the sky and the moon carve an arc through it. I witnessed the dawn as the sun grew long arms—a thousand arms—and held up its hands to me. I know who I am.

I live in the last day. It is a choice. I never forget it, but I live in all it was and could have been. If I could have changed it, if I had one more try, I would not hesitate. I would change everything all over, start it all over right. But there is no second chance. Don't let the name of this shitty place fool you. There is no second chance for anybody. You get what you get—and what do they say?— and you don't get upset. You shut up and you stay in eternity with what you did, with what you are. This now, is all there is. Does anything move forward? Does anything ever change? We stay with all we are and all we did and all that was done to us. Everybody here knows that better than anyone. You can cry all you want, drop all the bricks you want, but none of that will change what already is.

I loved Tommy. I know he loved me. He didn't say it much, but I knew. The drugs were there, and yes, we were up to it all—way over our heads. I don't know why. It feels so long ago now, but it wasn't—but that's what I mean anyway: there is no such thing as time. The past, the present, and shit, the future for all I know, all collapse into the same minute. The drugs are just a way to slow it down. You know what I mean. Everybody needs something to slow it down, to push back a little from what is now.

Tommy and I just sort of happened. It probably wasn't a great idea, but that's how love goes, doesn't it? You don't plan it. You don't go out and find it—it finds you and decides that it's your time. So it was our time. And—as disgusting as it sounds—my mother's and Tommy's dad's time too. His dad was still married. My dad was long gone. It was complicated. But my mother loved the drama. She would never tell you that, but she did. And she never worked. The only thing she did was wait for Tommy's dad to visit. He'd come over and things would be great. But then Tommy's dad would leave to go back home, and it would be a whole thing: *Why do you stay with a woman you don't love? Why do you have to leave me?* All that kind of thing.

Tommy wasn't like his dad. He didn't fight with me for no reason. He didn't test me to see if I loved him. And I didn't do that to him. We didn't see each other all the time. Not at first. At first we were just hanging out. We didn't even real- ize our parents were having an affair. That was weird. When we found out, I mean, it was weird. But it wasn't that sur- prising. Because I loved Tommy. I really loved him. And he loved me. So it would make sense that my mom and his dad would get along as well as they did— when they were get- ting along and when he wasn't at home, with his own wife, Tommy's mom.

I would have loved him whether our parents knew each oth- er or not.

I know this isn't about them, but they're in it too. The fights they'd have when Tommy's dad would leave—you could hear them out on the street. There wasn't anybody on our block who didn't know they were having an affair. How Tom- my's parents stayed married back then is a total mystery. His mom must've totally known.

But who cares about them now?

Tommy and I could hang out talking on the couch for hours. We'd hang—he'd play his guitar too—and kill a whole af- ternoon sometimes. He was funny too. God, he was fun- ny. He had this way of saying something funny but keep a straight face until I realized he was joking and started to laugh.

He was the only person who got me. He seemed cool with the quiet times. We didn't have to be out all the time. My friends were like that: going out every weekend. The parties, the music. I can only do it a little at a time, but then after a while the noise, the people, it all gets to be too much. Tom- my seemed to get that. He was totally cool just being alone with me.

We weren't alone that last night. We were out, hanging with his friends Andy and Mike and Mike's girlfriend Lorna. We were at Andy's place. He was already on his own. He's eighteen. Working at a garage, paying his own rent, so we'd go there. We were all doing H that night. Snorting it, though. Trying to slow it all down, stay away from needles. I remember Rush was on the hi fi. If I never hear *2112* again, I will be grateful.

We were laughing. Tommy was on the floor, laying down. I was lying next to him—my head on his shoulder but then I don't remember why I sat up. We were all laughing. Tommy nodded off. You know how you do. I had done a little coke too, so I wasn't so tired. So did Mike and Lorna. We were up. I don't know what Andy was doing. He was there, but I don't remember. The three of us were sitting and goofing off and it seemed funny at the time, so we started playing quarters. Bouncing quarters off Tommy's stomach—points for hitting his belly button. His belly curved like a pool under his t-shirt. We played for a long time. The quarters and bottle caps piled up and started sliding off to the floor. Then we stopped. After that we started to pour beer on his stomach.

We must've woke him up. Tommy sat up. First on his elbows, then all the way up. The rest of the quarters and bottle caps slipped off his stomach. He was awake again. He was awake, and he grabbed Lorna and was kissing her. Right in front of me. I was watching and then I saw it and I yelled something or pushed her. I don't remember exactly. It happened really fast and really slow at the same time. One minute he's out cold on the floor. Next thing, he's kissing Lorna. So I yelled. Or punched. Or hit. I don't totally remember, but I did something. And Tommy swung hard and fast—that part was fast. He broke my nose. Blood spilled everywhere. My blood was all over the floor. All over my hands. My shirt. I don't remember it hurting. It must've hurt. I remember the blood. It was everywhere.

You fuck, I think I said. I threw something at him. He had an arm around Lorna. She was smiling like she belonged.

Fuck you, he yelled back, but I could only see his mouth moving. I only remember it without sound. He said fuck you to me. That's what he said. I wanted to swing back. I wanted to hit or kick and hurt him. But Andy or Mike, I don't remember who, dragged me out. Dragged me to the bathroom for towels. The blood was everywhere. My shirt was sticking to my skin. That fucker, that motherfucker, I was saying.

He doesn't appreciate you, Mike said. It was Mike then. That's right. Andy was somewhere else. He never appreciated you, Summer. Come on, he said, forget him.

I wiped the blood across my face with the shoulder part of my shirt. I looked back at Tommy. He had his face in her lap. I didn't realize. I just didn't know.

Fuck it, I said. Let's go.

I woke up with dark half moons under my eyes. The inside of my arm ached. I could feel the dried blood under my nose flaking. Scales of blood had dried over one hand. I was on the bed in Andy's room. Mike slept on the chair. I woke up and it was quiet. It was late morning. I looked for my clothes.

They were already laughing and drinking beer again. The bottle caps bouncing. Tommy was lying sideways, sort of on his back. We did more lines. I don't know. I don't know how we didn't know. I thought I would have known. I thought I was connected, body and soul, to Tommy, but I didn't know. He was fucking blue-gray and I didn't know.

None of us knew. Well. Somebody figured it out. Because the paramedics came. My head was on the floor then and I heard their radios and watched their black boots move across the tiles.

I remember the taste. There was still blood in my mouth and under my nose. I can still taste the taste in my mouth. They cleaned me up too, but that was after.

And if I could stop time I would go back, just a little bit before. If I'd known that it would all stop right there and I could never forget, I'd have stopped it before the end started, when Tommy was still laughing and playing his guitar. I might have let him kiss Lorna. I don't know. Or I wouldn't have done any of it maybe.

So you can take your Jesus, and salvation, and shove it. Because I already know that time doesn't exist. There ain't no going backward or forward for me. There's sure as hell no going home. My mother will never forgive me, because Tommy's dad will never forgive me—for being there, for playing quarters and doing lines while Tommy was already dead—for not getting help, for not knowing we needed help. Tommy's father stopped coming around, and my mother wouldn't even look at me.

I don't care about that.

I don't care about her stupid dramas in her otherwise boring, lame life.

I just wish I could go back.

I wish I could have just stopped time a little earlier, when Tommy was still here. I didn't know we had a choice. That part I didn't know. And if dying was the only option for him, I'd stopped playing quarters and laid my head down on his shoulder and gone with him.

But here I am.

And there is no going back, never. So fuck you and your bricks and your stupid Group and that fucking doghouse. None of that makes a fucking difference because this pain is forever. It never goes away. There is no way out of what is.

One Day at a Time

I am Starlene and I am an alcoholic and addict. Thank you. This is a good topic and I try to remember to take all things one day at a time now. In sobriety, I've learned that if you got one foot in yesterday and one foot in tomorrow, you're just about to piss all over today. So I have learned to take things one day at a time.

Back when I was out there using, it was true, there never was no sense of time. Getting high made it feel like there wasn't nothing to worry about. All that worry came after-like, when I was worrying about getting my next fix or about getting busted by the cops. All that future-worry stuff kept me up at night, so I told myself I needed to come down sometimes, needed the drugs to shut it off.

I see some heads nodding out there. Y'all know what I'm talking about.

Over at the Second Chance house, we take it one day at a time with them girls. We done gone through a lot lately. I reckon it's kinda like a family, yes sir, kind of like that.

But those girls, they settled down some now. I guess everyone, even Sallyanne, needed to calm the fuck down and regroup—though we ain't had Group these days. It's probably better we stay away from those deep hurts and let them girls settle down some more. Quiet up and get serious about getting sober again. Refocus-like.

I'm sorry. I am getting a little distracted off the topic. Apologies, y'all.

What I'm saying is that the only thing, the only thing any of us has is now. There ain't no yesterday no more, and there ain't no such thing as the future. We are here now. Yes? You know what I mean. This is all we got. Just breathe it in and breathe it out, because it's all anybody's got. Ain't no such thing as time, Sugar.

I guess that's all I got to say. I just stay in the moment. But for the Grace of God, there I go.

Thanks for listening.

Swords

June 23, 1986

I have stopped talking. I will not say one more word out loud until I leave this godforsaken place. I will make sure I remember all of this. I will make sure I never forget what happened here. I will remember it all, as it was.

The only person I was talking to after the doghouse was Lorilee. She was the one who'd told me I was free. She was the one who stood up for me, though she got hit pretty hard for it. She puked, she told me, right after Magda punched her gut.

I had just started talking again, after spending that night outside in the doghouse. I smelled like pee when they brought me back in. The rope imprints starting to lift off my skin. I had just started talking again but I was only talking to Lorilee. She was the only one. We were out by the western fence, away from the house, away from the doghouse, talking about running.

We have to go, she said. They are going to kill us.

Kill us? I said. No. That's insane.

We have to go. You need to listen to me.

You're scaring me, I said.

I mean it, she said. How come you don't feel it?

I just looked at her.

You hate this place anyway. Miss Sallyanne would love to send you away to lock-up just for spite.

She took my hand. Girl. I'm telling you. It's time.

She lit a cigarette and turned toward the road. My guy can come get us. He's got a motor bike, and he can fit us, one at a time. He was just going to come get me, but I told him you need to go too. He knows, he gets it.

Your *guy*? Jesus, Lorilee. You really do have a guy?

Yes. I told you already.

Yes. But. I looked at her. Her hair was pulled back off her face into a neat bun, and her white blouse was tucked into khaki shorts.

I'll tell you what night and just be ready. He'll come get us. She looked at me. Listen, she said, Tommy is gone— he ain't coming back. It ain't your fault, neither, she put her hand on my arm. Let him go—he's gone. That whole life is gone.

I was shaking—I will admit that here, in these pages. I didn't know where we were going to go, but I knew she was right. We needed to go. But that wasn't what was scaring me. It's not what's scaring me now. The thing is, there isn't anywhere else *to go*. Tommy is gone, and my mom—. Forget it. She might as well be gone too. We have to go somewhere, but I'm not going back. There is no home for me.

OK, I said. But I didn't get what she was saying, how she knew about Tommy.

So you wait, all right? Wait till I tell you when. Lorilee started walking away, heading toward the road.

Lorilee—

She kept walking, but over her shoulder said, I'm coming back. Just be ready, OK? Just be ready. Don't say nothing.

I watched her disappear down the road. I was too terrified to follow her right then and too terrified to go back into the house.

I am ready, I guess. I have no idea what that really means. It's not like a can pack my clothes and nobody would notice. I just have this notebook and my heart charm, though somehow, now that it's been in other people's grubby hands, I don't know, it feels different-like. Kimberly must've thought she was fooling me, that's all I can say. I know Lorilee is right. These girls are nasty. And they must think I'm a right good idiot if they think I don't know they took my necklace—but that doesn't matter now. I need to think. I need to get ready. I need to leave this place and never come back.

June 25, 1986
This time I was glad to work in the kitchen. I was glad Starlene and I were peeling potatoes without talking. Just the sound of the peelers against the skins.

But then she does speak. I know what you girls are fixin' to do, she says.

I keep my head down.

You heifers are up to something. You ain't fooling ole Starlene none.

I don't look at her. I don't know what you're talking about, I say. I keep my eyes on the peeler in my hand.

That girl ain't what she seems to be, Starlene says. She puts her potato down.

I'm not up to anything, I say.

Starlene gets really quiet. I can feel her watching me.

Your boyfriend ain't coming back, she says after a time. There ain't nothing for you back there, Sugar.

I don't know what you are talking about. I reach for another potato and keep peeling.

She takes a deep breath and then she says, It ain't your fault he's dead. They all die, and sometimes it's just an accident. It ain't your fault.

Now I'm looking at her. I can't believe what she is saying. How she knows.

It ain't your fault Tommy OD'd. He had it coming. He hit you, girl. Take it from ole Starlene, once they start swinging, it ain't never going to stop. He did you a favor by dying young.

She says his name like she knows him. Like she's known all along. Starlene says my secret out loud. But this is my secret. Mine.

How do you—?

Starlene looks out the kitchen window, and the other girls are out there already smoking—I am sure nobody else bothered with their chores today. She sees them, breathes in really slow, and says, She done read the parts to us.

Read? Read my diary to you all?

She glances out again, like she's thinking about it, and then says slow-like, Yes. Them girls like the stories, and since you weren't telling nothing in Group, she'd read your diary to them. Kept them entertained and whatnot.

No way, I say.

Ask them. She points her peeler toward the window.

But I can't. I won't. I can't even think right anymore. Starlene knows my secret. I can see that. She knows, they all know. My love, my loss, *entertained and whatnot*. A joke to them. There is no one, not one single person on this earth, who is safe. I should have known Lorilee would betray me too.

I hate this fucking place.

June 26, 1986

I am just writing to say that I am not going to write anymore. I see now that there isn't a goddamn person on this planet you can trust. And I'm not sure what made me think otherwise, but now I know, thank you very much.

So fuck you to you who is reading this.

That's you, Lorilee: Fuck you. Fuck you because I know what you did.

Now you will get yours too.

Second Chance Girls

"Watch therefore: for ye know not what hour your Lord doth come."

Sometimes Miss Sallyanne, when she did come out of her office, said that. But most times, she just stayed locked inside. That was fine with us. We didn't want to see her old red, slippery eyes with the tears leaking out of the corners or her horse sweatshirts drooping off her bony shoulders.

We passed those last days smoking cigarettes, laying out in the sun. Just waiting for the right time. Waiting, waiting—we were good at that.

We didn't have to wait all that long before Summer came out and said tonight was the night. She would be getting Lorilee out back. They'd be looking for the stars or some lesbo shit.

"Star gazing?" Crystal said. "Homo—"

"Perfect." Kimberly interrupted her. "That necklace looks good on you."

Summer made a face. And we couldn't be sure, but it felt like we were all in trouble. Like she wasn't just leading Lorilee to her death, but all of us. But that doesn't matter now. Everything in Divine Order.

Swords

June 28, 1986

I

I

I am here. In this place. For now.

Everything is gone. I didn't mean it to happen this way.

I am so very sorry.

June 29, 1986

I slept here all day. But I can't stay here. I won't stay here much longer—this guy, this boy with the motorbike, is not a boy but a man. He is, he was, that is, Lorilee's man- boy. He is a young man—a guy—and rents a room at this ranch down the way—way down the way, actually, from Second Chance. He used to drive by the house all the time. He is the one we wished for, the one who would take us away and give us new life. It's him. He used to come for Lorilee at night and take her away. He's not all that much—tan neck and working arms, lines pulling at the corners of his eyes from the sun on his face all the time, nothing like we imagined. He saw the fire but he waited. He was waiting on us. Me and Lorilee. Well. He waited for her. I was just there. He took me away. That was the plan. He took me and came back right straight for her, even though he knew she was already gone. She was gone.

They are all gone.

June 30, 1986

Nobody knows I'm here. I have to figure out what I am do- ing. I need to make a plan. I cannot stay hiding in Lee's room forever. He lets me sleep in his bed and he sleeps on the floor. He seems to know I just need a little time. He doesn't bother me, but I see he is sad, too. I am too. We are both sad for Lorilee. Sad and not sad. How can you mourn somebody you never really knew? She was here and not here always.

Like she was living here and living in some other space or something at the same time.

Lee says I can take all the time I need. I think he wants me to stay because I'm the only link to Lorilee. He cries at night sometimes. I can hear him. He went back that night after leaving me up the road, where nobody could see me, but the house was totally burning up by then. He told me he saw the Corvette tearing down the road, but didn't think about it. He was just trying to get to Lorilee again. It was too late. That house with all that timber piled up outside went up in flames like a book of matches. Like the earth couldn't wait to consume it all, take it all back to itself again. Lee says I can stay as long as I want, but we both know (not that we say it out loud) that I can't stay here. This ain't no home for me. Texas is not my final resting place.

Well, then, Lee said last night, Go where you got to go or stay here. He spit a wad of tobacco juice into the paper cup he was holding. I can see why Lorilee liked him. He's easy, accepting of what is, even as he is hurting inside. You're free, he says.

And he's right. I'm free now. Like she always said.

July 3, 1986

I am going today. I cleaned Lee's room while he was working and I set up a dinner for him for when he gets back.

I have a bus ticket, but I'm scared to death. I have never been to the west coast before. Shit, I've never been this far west—to Texas—before, so I may as well keep going. But I'm not going to California, like they say. I'm going to Portland.

Some place real different. Some place where maybe I can just blend in and start from the start.

I'm going to leave this behind. All of this. I am going to leave Texas and start new. I need to leave Lee, though he's said I can stay and live here, but everywhere I look out of these windows, up at the sky, over the pastures and fields, I see Lorilee. I see her everywhere and the feeling comes back.

I didn't mean for all of it to happen. I was mad, sure. I told those girls to come out back that night. Lorilee reading my journal parts to them was more than I could do. She had it coming to her. An eye for an eye, like they say. It was just too much—too much to know that I didn't even have her anymore. But those girls. They were all riled up. Ready. I heard them punch her before I was even out of I opened my eyes. Get her up, Kimberly said. It wasn't the plan. We were supposed to meet outside. Lorilee was stunned and moving to get away. Crystal dragged her off the bed by her hair and let her drop to the floor. And then they kicked her and kicked her.

No! I think I said. This isn't what we said. I jumped off my own bed. No.

Starlene came tearing in, like she always did, but this time it was the middle of the night, and Baby Rain wasn't with her. No. This time she's got a kitchen knife in her hands. You get the fuck off that girl, she said to Crystal. And you, she said to Kimberly, you get the fuck out of here and take these bitches with you before I cut you all to pieces. She waved the knife wild-like at all of us. At me too.

You wouldn't, Kimberly started to say. You can't even use that thing with your good arm. But then Starlene swiped the blade up toward her face. Kimberly jumped back. You couldn't—

Let's try, she said.

You're just—

This time the blade made contact with the Queen's cheek. Starlene kept the point pressed into Kimberly's skin, and the girl stopped moving. A drop of blood slid to her jaw.

I am Chosen, Sugar. Ain't nobody noticed Ole Starlene here. The Lord has chosen me to carry out His justice. Don't nobody mess with Starlene no more. See this arm? The man who done broke it don't walk this earth no more.

I ain't afraid to do what I have to do and the Lord knows it. I know what you heifers are fixin' to do, and you ain't going to do it on my watch. So git. Y'all move.

I didn't know what to do. I stood there like everybody else, not moving, feet iced to the floor. I'm not sure what they were waiting for. Maybe they were waiting to see what Kimberly said. Maybe they were waiting to call Starlene's bluff.

Starlene then swung around and glared at me. What the fuck are *you* doing, girl?

Me? I said.

This girl is your friend.

No, ma'am. She is not, I said.

Heifer, you are. Starlene pointed the blade around the room. These girls. They's too much. But you—

You said, I started to say. *You* said she read out my words, my secrets, told everyone.

Girl, Starlene said. O girl. She looked up at the ceiling. For-give me, she said.

Kimberly laughed out loud. Crystal and those other bitches started laughing. They saw what had happened. They saw. Starlene was just as much of a liar as every one of them. And then I saw too. I saw what I had done. Look what I had done. Oh Lorilee. Girl.

A baby's cry broke the silence.

Crystal started to move toward the door.

The baby wailed and Starlene blocked Crystal.

Aw shit, Starlene said. She looked at Crystal and then around the room before she took off out the door she came in. She stopped. Don't make me come back, y'all. You'll see. She waved the knife at us. Crazy-like. You'll see.

They watched her run out.

And then they jumped Lorilee.

Somebody came down on the side of her head. Her ear may-be. One eye swelled up. Her other eye floated up to my face.

It was too much. All of it.

Stop. I know I yelled that. I tried. This time I tried to stop the end. The end that I caused. Tried to save Lorilee. Those bitches. Somebody—I don't know—two of them pulled me back. Held me away. I couldn't get to her.

Summer. Come on. Kimberly stood next to me. A smear of blood across her chin and neck. You know you want to. The girls holding me pushed me in toward Lorilee. She ain't no friend to you, she said.

This is for ruining everything, Crystal said. She drew her foot back and kicked Lorilee.

A stream of red started from the corner of Lorilee's mouth. I swear she had a little smile, looking just like that day we were all fooling around with Big Red, when we were letting the red pop pour out our mouths.

No.

Lorilee moved a little, like she wanted to pull herself up.

Oh look, she's getting up, somebody said. Fuck you, then.

The girls crashed down on Lorilee.

No. I started to swinging. Tried to pull somebody off, then somebody else. Stop it.

Go, I think she said. I couldn't hear but I think that is what Lorilee said. Words without voice. Go.

I couldn't get the words out. I couldn't get to Lorilee. My arms back again. I know they hit me because there were bruises. Shoulders and arms barely able to move. Later. Lorilee—

Her other eye closed. Her body jerked from the blows. Then it didn't anymore.

No. Not her too. Please.

Go.

Second Chance Girls

Of course we know who burned Second Chance Home for Girls to the ground. We know now. We probably should've killed *her* when we had the chance. When we look back, we wonder how we didn't know. But you know mortal minds: they see only what they want to see. Don't recognize mercy when it's right in front of their faces. Keep looking the wrong way, thinking it's the right way. We weren't looking the right way. We know that now too.

Nobody would've guessed it before, but of course it was her. She watched and waited. We guess she didn't see any other way. Somebody tossed a burning cigarette one day and it ignited the idea in her mind. The only way out. The only way to end this crazy life. The bearer of suffering, the conveyor of justice. She saw the smoldering cigarette and remembered the timber piled on the eastern side of the house. At the time, she exploded—calling us heifers who'd burn the house down with our stupidity. But now with a baby fussing in her arms, she knew that there was nobody else taking care of this child. Nobody else to deliver justice.

We are the witnesses.

We watch the cycle continue.

We are its guardians and protectors now.

The fire slapped up against the sides of the house, as if hell itself was pulling it to the ground.

The woman and the child will be safe to the end of their days. They will live because of us. The woman no longer needs to watch, bear the weight of suffering. She no longer has to pretend, switch allegiances when it suits her, when it protects her. She can just be. There is nothing to fear anymore. She has paid her debt and now she is free.

We are the multitudes. The girls who through fire became air.

We are its complicit witnesses. We will remember for eternity, and we will be the remembrance for all time to come.

Gratitude

I'm Justine and I'm an alcoholic and addict. I just want say that I am grateful today. I have a new life today. I am clean and sober, and I follow direction today. The Lord is my shepherd and He is good. I am his servant. I'm all about the Lord's work today. I have paid my dues and now I have a second chance. I see some heads nodding out there. Thank you. You know what I'm talking about: the Program gave me this second chance, like a new lease on life. I have a new trailer and a little girl named Grace. That's right. We have our own home planted firmly on this Earth.

I'm looking forward to getting to know y'all and Baton Rouge. Everyone's been so friendly. Love those gator sausages! I'm sure we'll be very happy here. It's a new start for my little girl and me. I have a home. I am the luckiest woman on Earth.

But for the Grace of God, there I go, that's what I say. That's right, Sugar. That's what I say.

Thank y'all for listening.

Queen of Swords

Salem, Oregon, July 3, 2016

The stream carried both of us, and we knew by then we were both its subjects and its objects, channels for its magic, agents for its work. She is gone, but she is always with me.

It was on the news and in the local papers, something that was easy to look up later, once the Internet came and connected us ordinary people to a tangible past, reframing it for us, we who had lost perspective, our memories warped with the passage of time. So I looked it up once. I don't remember the kerosene. That part I didn't know. The remains of one adult and eleven teenagers. Arson.

I'm not asking questions any more. I already know what I need to know.

I have you now, my girl. My beautiful, lovely girl. I have something to tell you. I have a story to tell you, Daughter. I lived it for you, so you will never have to. This is a love story, and it is for you.

I swim through the pain, the joy, equal currents in the river, shaping and reshaping the stones beneath the water.

We swim in the river of Time, our own currents touch and mingle and overlap and absorb other currents. We get caught in eddies only to be released suddenly, when we least expect it, thinking, that we were the ones who released ourselves. We can only surrender to the water, surrender to the currents that impel us to drift and rush and swirl, moving through this life as if it were the only one we might know.

But it isn't the only one, of course.

We will always survive because we always were.

We are here now. We will always be here.

Our eternal place, a pristine, shining lake, blessed by the soft pedal of heavenly rain.

Go.

About Heather Ostman

Heather Ostman, Ph.D., is Professor of English at SUNY Westchester Community College, where she also serves as Director of the Westchester Community College Humanities Institute.

She has published several short stories and scholarly articles, and she is the author of *The Fiction of Junot Díaz* (Rowman & Littlefield, 2017) and other nonfiction books. *The Second Chance Home for Girls* is her first novel. A version of its first chapter was published by *The Quint: An Interdisciplinary Journal from the North* in 2016.

Heather is President of the Kate Chopin International Society (www.katechopin.org).